Murder Between the Covers

A DEAD-END JOB MYSTERY

Elaine Viets

A SIGNET BOOK

SIGNET
Published by New American Library, a division of
Penguin Group (USA) Inc., 375 Hudson Street,
New York, New York 10014, USA
Penguin Group (Canada), 90 Eglinton Avenue East, Suite 700, Toronto,
Ontario M4P 2Y3, Canada (a division of Pearson Penguin Canada Inc.)
Penguin Books Ltd., 80 Strand, London WC2R 0RL, England
Penguin Ireland, 25 St. Stephen's Green, Dublin 2,
Ireland (a division of Penguin Books Ltd.)
Penguin Group (Australia), 250 Camberwell Road, Camberwell, Victoria 3124,
Australia (a division of Pearson Australia Group Pty. Ltd.)
Penguin Books India Pvt. Ltd., 11 Community Centre, Panchsheel Park,
New Delhi - 110 017, India
Penguin Group (NZ), 67 Apollo Drive, Mairangi Bay,
Auckland 1311, New Zealand (a division of Pearson New Zealand Ltd.)
Penguin Books (South Africa) (Pty.) Ltd., 24 Sturdee Avenue,
Rosebank, Johannesburg 2196, South Africa

Penguin Books Ltd., Registered Offices:
80 Strand, London WC2R 0RL, England

First published by Signet, an imprint of New American Library,
a division of Penguin Group (USA) Inc.

First Printing, December 2003
10   9

Copyright © Elaine Viets, 2003
All rights reserved

REGISTERED TRADEMARK—MARCA REGISTRADA

Printed in the United States of America

PUBLISHER'S NOTE
This is a work of fiction. Names, characters, places, and incidents either are
the product of the author's imagination or are used fictitiously, and any resemblance to actual persons, living or dead, business establishments, events, or
locales is entirely coincidental.

Praise for Elaine Viets's first Dead-End Job mystery, *Shop till You Drop*

"Elaine Viets has come up with all the ingredients for an irresistible mystery: a heroine with a sense of humor and a gift for snappy dialogue, an atmospheric South Florida backdrop, a cast of entertaining secondary characters, and some really nasty crimes. I'm looking forward to the next installment in her new Dead-End Job series."

—Jane Heller, national bestselling author
of *Lucky Stars*

"Elaine Viets's debut Dead-End Job mystery is a live wire. It's Janet Evanovich meets *The Fugitive* as Helen Hawthorne takes Florida by storm. Shop no further—this is the one."

—Tim Dorsey, author of *The Stingray Shuffle*

"I loved this book. With a stubborn and intelligent heroine, a wonderful South Florida setting, and a cast of more-or-less lethal bimbos, *Shop till You Drop* provides tons of fun. Six-toed cats, expensive clothes, sexy guys on motorcycles—this book has it all."

—Charlaine Harris, author of *Club Dead*
and *Poppy Done to Death*

"Fresh, funny, and fiendishly constructed, *Shop till You Drop* gleefully skewers cosmetic surgery, ultraexclusive clothing boutiques, cheating ex-husbands, and the Florida dating game, as attractive newcomer Helen Hawthorne takes on the first of her deliciously awful dead-end jobs and finds herself enmeshed in drugs, embezzlement, and murder. A bright start to an exciting new series. This one is hard to beat."

—Parnell Hall, author of The Puzzle Lady
crossword puzzle mysteries

For booksellers everywhere:
Your job is harder than it looks.
Your influence is greater than you'll ever know.

Chapter 1

"Helen, where the hell are you?" The creep used the intercom, so everyone heard.

"I'm in the back, stripping," she said. Now they all heard her reply.

"I don't care what you're doing, get out here," he said. "Now."

Helen Hawthorne quit stripping and wished she could start ripping. She wanted to rip out the black heart of Page Turner III with her bare hands.

He knew where she was. He also knew she couldn't complain when he played his little games. He was Page Turner, literary light and owner of Page Turners, the book chain with his name. Page was a multimillionaire, but not because of the three bookstores. The real family fortune came from mundane moneymakers such as pancake houses and muffler shops.

Page ran the bookstores because he had the same name as the founder. That was all Page had in common with his book-loving grandfather. The current Page Turner couldn't sell a book to a boatload of bibliophiles.

Helen flung open the stockroom door, expecting to see

Page. Instead she collided with Mr. Davies, the store's oldest inhabitant. Mr. Davies showed up every morning at nine, when the store opened, and stayed until it closed at midnight. He brought two peanut-butter sandwiches, one for lunch and one for dinner, and drank the free ice water in the café. All day long he read books. He bought one paperback a month, when his Social Security check arrived.

Helen liked him. He was as much a fixture as the shelves and chairs.

Mr. Davies was a small gray squirrel of a man, with big yellow teeth and inquisitive brown eyes. Now those eyes were bright with disappointment.

"You're dressed," the old man said.

"Of course I'm dressed," Helen said. "What did you think I was doing in there?"

"Stripping," he said hopefully.

"I was stripping the covers off paperbacks," she said.

Mr. Davies was more shocked than if she'd been stark naked. "That's terrible, a pretty girl like you mutilating books," he said.

"I agree, sir," Helen said.

Mr. Davies scurried off to his favorite reading chair, holding his book protectively, as if Helen might strip it, too.

Helen couldn't tell Mr. Davies why she'd been stripping. She'd been dealing with yet another of Page's mistakes. He'd bagged Jann Hickory Munn, the hot fiction writer, to sign at Page Turners on his national tour. But Page did no advertising, so six people had come to Munn's signing. Page was stuck with cases of books.

The unsold hardcovers were sent back. But most publishers didn't want paperbacks returned. The shipping would cost more than the books. Instead their covers were stripped and counted like scalps. The author paid for Page's miscalculation in lost royalties. Someone else always paid for Page's mistakes.

Page stood in the middle of the store, arms folded across his chest. He looked more like a boxer than a bookstore owner. A boxer gone to seed. Too many nights spent drinking with best-selling authors had transformed Page's barrel chest into a beer belly. His chiseled chin was buried in fat. His Roman nose was red and veined. But he still had wavy blond hair, and at six feet, he was a commanding figure.

"I need you to ring," Page said to Helen like a lord granting a boon to a peasant. The book buyers didn't know Page could not work his own cash registers. They were too complicated for him. Page retired to his quiet, comfortable office lined with his grandfather's priceless first editions.

Helen faced the horde of impatient customers. Another bookseller, Brad, was already ringing, but the line of customers was almost out the door.

"Next, please," Helen called as she opened her register.

The man who stepped forward was talking on his cell phone. He could have been a young Elvis with his thick black hair, heavy-lidded eyes, and sexy sneer. His black silk shirt showed a hint of tanned chest and no gold chains. Tight jeans. Narrow hips. Strong hands. Helen checked for a wedding ring. Nothing. How had this one stayed on the shelf?

The Hunk snapped his cell phone shut, another point in his favor. Some customers talked on the phone while Helen rang them up.

He threw two paperbacks on the counter. One had a cracked spine and curled cover. The other was crisp and new. "I'm exchanging this," he said, pointing to the sad specimen, "for this." Sexy voice, too. Soft, caressing, polite. He was a sweet talker, all right.

The Hunk plunked down the new Burt Plank thriller, and smiled like a man who always got his way. He would this time. Most stores would not take that battered book back, but Page Turners had a liberal return policy. The Hunk started to take the new Plank thriller and walk away. Helen grabbed it.

"I'm sorry, sir," she said. "I need to ring this up as an exchange and get a manager's approval."

"Why? They're both the same price."

Because Page Turner's pet computer nerd developed an overcomplicated system, Helen thought.

"Because we have a computerized inventory system," Helen said.

"This is ridiculous," the Hunk said, and suddenly his caress had claws.

He was right. It was ridiculous. Page Turners required more signatures for a simple book return than a bank loan.

"I can't believe this," he said. "What's taking you so long, lady?" He slapped his hand on the counter. Helen jumped. Her fingers slipped on the computer keys.

DENIED, the computer said.

Helen had typed in the wrong transaction number. She'd have to start all over again, retyping the ten-digit transaction number, five-digit store number, and six-digit date.

"Just give me my book," the Hunk said, reaching for the Burt Plank thriller.

"I can't do that, sir," she said, sliding it under the counter. Finally she typed in all the numbers.

"I hope you're done now," he sneered, and this time it didn't look sexy at all. He did not look like the young Elvis anymore. He was mean and arrogant.

"Not quite," she said. "I still need the manager's approval." She paged Gayle.

"For a freakin' paperback?" the Hunk said.

Helen looked nervously at the line. It was even longer. All those paying customers were kept waiting because of another half-witted Page Turner policy.

"*I want my book!*" the Hunk screamed.

Helen's face was hot with embarrassment. The other customers in line shifted uneasily. A few glared. She didn't blame them. She was new and slow. The store policy was old and stupid. It was a fatal combination.

Behind the Hunk, an elegant blonde in a blue sundress crossed her arms and said, "People like him should not be let out to ruin the day for the rest of us." The blonde was angry, but not at Helen.

A short woman with a majestic bosom and a New York accent said loudly, "Rude people stink."

"I am so tired of public rudeness," a pale gray-haired woman agreed. She had the soft voice of an NPR announcer, but the Hunk heard her and turned the color of raw liver. He didn't look nearly so pretty in that color. Helen understood now why he had that ringless hand.

By the time Gayle the manager ran up and typed in the approval code, every customer in line had condemned the Hunk. He took his book and left without another word. The bookstore customers had held their own antirude rebellion.

The elegant blonde handed Helen a *Paris Review* to ring up. "Don't let him upset you, dear. You're doing a good job," she said.

Helen had never felt so good about a dead-end job. Page Turner III was a jerk, and she wished she made more than six seventy an hour. But the customers could be surprisingly kind, the booksellers were fun, and she loved books. Work would be perfect, if someone would just murder Page.

For the next half hour Helen rang up stacks of computer manuals, romance novels, and mysteries until they blurred into one endless book. Then, suddenly, there were no more customers. They seemed to come in waves. By some silent agreement, everyone in the store would rush forward to buy books at the same time. Then they'd all leave together. The only sound now was the Muzak, sterilizing a Beatles song.

Helen looked at the clock on the computer. Four o'clock. She was off work in thirty minutes, not a moment too soon. She only hoped the rest of the customers were reasonably normal.

It looked like she was going to get her wish. The twenty-something woman at the counter looked like a tourist from Connecticut. She had a small sunburned nose, a short practical haircut, and baggy khaki shorts that showed knobby knees. She looked familiar, but Helen wasn't sure why.

"Excuse me, I'm looking for books on astrology," she said.

"They're in New Age, aisle twelve," Helen said.

"Where's that?"

"Between Religion and Self-Improvement," Helen said. Wasn't religion supposed to be self-improving? she wondered. Why did they need two categories?

"You can see it from here," Helen said, pointing. It was polite to point in a bookstore. Besides, she couldn't say, "It's the aisle with all the books on the floor." New Age attracted the biggest slobs in the store. Helen wondered why "free spirit" meant "inconsiderate."

The woman returned with a copy of *Astrology for Dummies*, which Helen thought was a wonderfully apt title. Something clicked, and Helen knew who the woman was. She'd just moved into Helen's apartment complex. Helen hadn't had a chance to introduce herself yet. The introduction would have to wait. Customers were lining up again.

The woman fixed her deep brown eyes on Helen and said, "I'm psychic. I know your past."

Helen paled. She'd buried her past after that terrible day in court. Even her own mother didn't know where she was now.

"I can tell you have come a great distance," the psychic said.

Helen felt the fear grip her stomach and pull it inside out.

She had run from St. Louis, crisscrossing the country to throw off her pursuers, before she had arrived in Fort Lauderdale.

"You are Russian," the psychic said.

Helen giggled in pure relief. She was as Russian as bratwurst and sauerkraut. Her family was St. Louis German. Helen had changed her name when she ran. This woman was no more psychic than a cement block.

"Not even close," Helen said cheerfully, shoving the book in a bag.

The woman handed Helen a card that said, MADAME MUFFY'S PSYCHIC SERVICE. HELPFUL ADVICE ON ALL AFFAIRS. TELL PAST, PRESENT, AND FUTURE. $20 PALM READING WITH AD. GET ONE FREE QUESTION IF YOU CALL NOW!!!!!

"Madame Muffy?" Helen said. "What kind of name is that? What sort of psychic wears a pink golf shirt?"

"Spirits on the astral plane do not care about frivolous earthly matters," Muffy said.

"True. But people here have certain expectations. You need some Birkenstocks and dangly earrings."

"Listen, sweetie, I have a lot of business clients. They want advice on the stock market," Madame Muffy said. "They don't want me traipsing into their office in some weird getup. There's a Lighthouse Point executive—I can't give you his name because my clients are confidential— who is a million dollars richer because of me."

"Right." Helen handed Muffy her book bag. Only South Florida would have a psychic called Muffy. Helen figured that was why Madame Muffy did such a rotten job predicting her past. She was too normal for the paranormal.

"May I help the next customer?" Helen said.

Two boys stepped up to the counter. The eight-year-old gave her a crumpled ten-dollar bill and a copy of *The Adventures of Captain Underpants*.

"Another Captain Underpants fan," Helen said. "Are you one, too?" she asked the older boy, a solemn twelve.

He looked offended. "That stuff's for kids."

"Who do you like?" Helen asked.

"Steinbeck," the boy said. "Ever read *The Grapes of Wrath*? Steinbeck rules."

Steinbeck rules. Helen's heart lifted when she heard those words. This was the future talking. There were still readers, despite what the cynics said. Helen couldn't stop thinking about the boy as she walked home on Las Olas.

Las Olas was the fashionable shopping street in Fort Lauderdale, but it had nothing for her. She passed trendy restaurants where the entrées cost more than she made in a day, and chic shops where hand-painted gifts cost more than she made in a week.

The Coronado Tropic Apartments were only four blocks from the bookstore. In the slanting late-afternoon light, the white two-story Art Deco building looked like a vision of old Florida. The building's exuberant S-curve seemed hopeful. The turquoise trim was jaunty. Purple bougainvillea spilled into the tiled pool in romantic extravagance. Helen ignored the fact that the nearly new air conditioners were starting to rattle and drip rust down the white paint.

Peggy, the woman in 2B, was on a chaise longue by the pool, with Pete the parrot on her shoulder. Peggy looked rather like an exotic bird herself, with her dark red hair and elegant beak of a nose. She was beautiful in an offbeat way, but Pete was the only male Peggy tolerated. She seemed to have given up on men. Instead, Peggy spent all her money on lottery tickets.

"Hey, Helen," she said, waving her over. "I've got a new system."

Peggy always had a new system for winning the lottery. Before Helen could find out what it was, a small woman in baggy khaki shorts interrupted. "Do you have the time?" she asked Helen.

It was Madame Muffy. Helen recognized the little psychic immediately, but Muffy did not remember her. People who wore name tags were often invisible away from their work.

"If you're really psychic, why do you need to know the time?"

"I use my powers for serious things." Madame Muffy stared at Helen until she said, "Oh, you're the bookstore lady. I just moved into 2C. I'm your new neighbor."

Helen hoped Madame Muffy could not read her mind. She was not happy about this charlatan living at the Coronado.

"Let me read your palm—both of you—as a gift for my new neighbors," Muffy said. "You can ask one question, no charge."

Helen started to refuse, but Peggy looked amused. "Come on, Helen, don't be a stick. It will be fun."

"Squawwwk!" Pete said. It sounded like a protest to Helen.

Three people and one parrot went upstairs to Muffy's apartment. Her living room was as plain as her preppy outfits. There was a desk with a computer, a small round table covered with a brown cloth, three white wicker chairs from Pier 1, and a large poster with prices for tarot, palm, and crystal-ball readings. There were no pictures on the wall. The speckled terrazzo floor was bare.

"You go first," Peggy said.

Helen sat down reluctantly and put her hand palm-up on the table. The table wobbled, and she realized it was plastic patio furniture. When Madame Muffy took her hand, Helen stiffened, although the psychic's touch was warm and gentle. "What is your question?" she said.

"What about my job?" Helen said.

"That's it?" Peggy said. "What about romance? What about your life?"

I can't risk any revelations about my life, Helen thought. "My love life is fine," she said. "I'm worried about work."

"You have a powerful aura," Muffy said. "As powerful as Martha Stewart's."

Helen saw her aura wrapped in white tulle and silk ribbons.

"You were meant to be a leader," Muffy said. "You were meant to make money and hold a powerful position. You almost had it, and then you lost it."

Helen could feel the blood draining from her face. In St. Louis she'd made six figures. She'd been director of pensions and benefits for a big corporation. Then she came home early one day and found her husband, Rob, who was supposed to be building a new deck, nailing their neighbor, Sandy. Helen had picked up a handy crowbar and ended her marriage with a couple of swift swings. She still remembered the satisfying crunching sound.

"I see you working with money. You like it. You understand it. But you are working below your capacity. Something in your past is blocking your success. Your life will not move forward unless you remove this block. For a thirty-five-dollar palm reading, I can find out the name of the person who is blocking you."

I can save myself thirty-five bucks, Helen thought. I already know the name. And I know what Muffy is: a fraud. Of course she saw me working with money. She saw me standing at a cash register. It doesn't take a genius to figure out I used to have money. I'm wearing four-year-old Escada. It's a little threadbare, but better than anything I can afford now.

That's what Helen hated most about bad psychics. They were good at messing with your mind. For a minute she'd almost believed the malignant Muffy could tell the future.

"You need me, sweetie, to straighten out your life," Muffy said. "Come see me when you're ready to talk."

"I will," Helen said, prying her hand from Madame Muffy's grasp. Right after I marry G. Gordon Liddy on Las Olas in rush hour, she thought.

"And you can get me a discount at that bookstore," Muffy said. "Next."

Peggy sat down at the undercover patio table and presented her palm. Pete the parrot patrolled her shoulder restlessly, letting out earsplitting squawks.

"Calm down, boy," Peggy said. She took back her palm to pet her parrot. Pete settled into a sulky silence.

"Now," Muffy said. "What's your question?"

Helen could predict that one. Sure enough, Peggy said, "When will I win the lottery?"

Madame Muffy took Peggy's palm and said, "I can give you some lucky numbers if you—"

She stopped suddenly, looked closely at Peggy's palm, and turned as white as the Pier 1 wicker. "I see death," she said. "I see death, destruction, and murder."

Then Madame Muffy fell face-forward on the table.

Chapter 2

Helen slapped Madame Muffy's face. The little psychic moaned, but did not open her eyes. Helen hit her again.

"Maybe I should get her a glass of water," Peggy said. Pete the parrot was silent, watching them with his beady, intelligent eyes.

"This is better," Helen said.

"I didn't know you knew first aid."

"I don't." Helen slapped Muffy again. "But I feel better slapping her. She pulled a rotten trick, scaring you like that."

"I'm not scared," Peggy said, but her voice was high and a little shrill. Peggy was not her usual cool self.

Madame Muffy opened her eyes. She was white as unbaked bread, except for the red slap marks on her face.

"Are you OK?" Helen said.

"I must have fainted. I have low blood sugar. Please leave."

"Can we get you some food?" Peggy said. "How about some orange juice? That's good for low blood sugar."

Madame Muffy turned even whiter when Peggy spoke. "Just go," she said, herding them toward the door. "Please. Leave me alone. I'll be fine as soon as you're out of here."

As they walked down the stairs, Peggy said shakily, "That was definitely weird. What do you think she means about seeing death, destruction, and murder?"

"She doesn't see anything but the next buck," Helen said. "At the store she told me I was Russian."

"She was trying to hit me up for money for lucky lottery numbers, but then she turned strange. What if she actually saw my future?"

Helen picked up Peggy's palm and said, "I see you winning the lottery and splitting six million dollars with your best friend, Helen."

Peggy laughed, although she still sounded shaky. "How about giving me twenty bucks for lottery tickets, as an investment in my future?"

"How about a glass of wine instead?"

Helen went to her apartment and fed her cat, Thumbs. Then she brought out a box of white wine, pretzels, a cracker for Pete, and insect repellent. Florida mosquitoes were ferocious in June. The two women sank into chaise longues by the pool and sprayed themselves into a cloud of protective poison. Helen poured two generous glasses of wine. They crunched on pretzels and talked about everything but what happened that afternoon.

"Look at the sweat running off me," Peggy said. "What's the temperature?"

"It was eighty when I was in the apartment," Helen said. "I know people complain about summer here, but the heat is worse in the Midwest. Those summers are like living in an oven. Florida heat feels soft, and there's always a breeze. It must be the ocean."

"Naw, it just means you're a real Floridian," Peggy said, crunching a pretzel. "Normal people can't stand summer in South Florida."

"I haven't lived here long enough to be a real Floridian."

"Nobody is *from* Florida," Peggy said. "But some of us

know we belong here. We can tell the moment we step off the plane or get out of the car. It feels right—the sun, the light, the humidity. June is the real test. That's when the tourists go home. The people who live here but aren't real Floridians go somewhere cool. The rest of us love it. No crowds at the beach, less traffic on the roads, and we can get a decent table at our favorite restaurant. Florida is ours again until winter."

Helen reached for another pretzel and started to hand one to Pete.

"No, don't. He's on a diet. He gained two ounces," Peggy said. Pete gave an indignant squawk.

Helen took a serious sip of wine before she asked her next question. "How long do you think Madame Muffy has been in Florida?"

"She's got to be a new arrival," Peggy said. "She's still pukey pale with a sunburned nose. Anyway, she wears shoes."

"Deck shoes."

"Still, if she spent any time here at all, she'd switch to sandals."

"Why did Margery rent to her?" Helen said.

"I think our landlady needed the money," Peggy said. "That apartment was vacant for months."

"I don't understand that," Helen said.

"Nobody wants to live in these old places anymore, except nuts like us who think they have character. The window air conditioners are noisy and there are always heat pockets. The rooms are small and the terrazzo floors are ugly. The jalousie doors leak. The bathrooms are old-fashioned and the kitchens are cramped. Most people would rather rent the new condos. The walls are made of cardboard, but they have all the modern conveniences."

"That explains why we're here. But what about Madame Muffy? She strikes me as a modern-convenience type."

Peggy intoned, "Only she knows. Only she can tell," and laughed. This time it sounded genuine.

By the second glass of wine, Madame Muffy's dramatic scene seemed funny. The two women talked until ten, when the mosquitoes began dive-bombing their arms and ankles. "It's time to go in before I'm eaten alive," Peggy said. She swatted another mosquito. It left blood on her arm.

"Yuck. Good night," Peggy said. Pete squawked good-bye. Helen packed up the wine, the pretzels, and the useless insect repellent, and walked across the lawn to her home.

The Coronado looked romantic under the subtropic stars. Palms whispered in the soft air. The bougainvillea shook more blossoms into the turquoise pool.

Helen inhaled the sweet, sticky scent of burning marijuana from her next-door neighbor. She'd never seen Phil the invisible pothead, but she always knew when he was home.

Helen opened her front door and was hit with a wave of trapped heat. She flipped on her air conditioner so it would be cool enough to sleep. It sounded like it was about to take off. Water dripped steadily down one side.

She loved her furnished apartment, but she had to admit the fifties decor was not everyone's taste. She could imagine what her suburban St. Louis neighbors would think of the boomerang coffee table, the lamps that looked like nuclear reactors, and the turquoise Barcalounger.

She knew exactly what they'd say about Helen living in two rooms with a drippy window air conditioner. But she was happier here than she'd ever been in her twelve-room St. Louis house, with her perfect Ralph Lauren fabrics and her imperfect husband. She liked the people at the bookstore better than the ones at her high-powered job. All she missed was her six-figure salary.

Now Helen could barely make ends meet. She paid her rent in cash, a deal she made with her landlady, Margery.

Helen explained that her ex-husband was looking for her and she didn't want to give him any way to trace her, which was mostly true. She left out the part about the court.

Helen did not want her name in any computers. She had no phone, no credit cards, no bank account, and no paycheck. Page Turner paid her in cash, too, another reason why she put up with him. The big chain bookstores wouldn't do that. Lucky for her, Page had a slightly crooked streak.

Now that she was alone, the scene with Madame Muffy gave her the shivers. She wondered if the little fraud got a real look at the future and it was too much for her. Helen decided that was ridiculous, but she double-locked the front door and put the security bar in the sliding glass doors.

Then she settled into her turquoise Barcalounger with a new hardback mystery. That was the best perk of her job. She could borrow books from the store, as long as she returned them in salable condition.

Thumbs, her six-toed cat, curled up beside her. Helen scratched his ears and he purred and kneaded her thigh with his giant paws. The big gray-and-white cat looked so much like a stuffed animal, Helen expected to find a tag on him. Only his enormous feet spoiled the illusion. They were the size of catchers' mitts.

Thumbs was supposed to be a descendant of Ernest Hemingway's famously inbred six-toed cats. At least that's what the guy who bought him in a Key West bar said. But the man lied a lot. Still, Thumbs did love to curl up with a good book.

The next thing Helen knew it was midnight, and she was awakened out of a sound sleep in the Barcalounger. The book was resting on her lap. Thumbs was in the bedroom, howling, loud, insistent howls. Something was wrong.

Helen threw down her book and ran into the bedroom. Thumbs was pawing frantically at the sliding glass doors. There were flying bugs, pale beige things with wings, outside the doors. No, wait, they were inside, crawling up the glass, and Thumbs was trying to stop them.

They were everywhere, coming through the crack in the sliding doors and crawling through the vents. They were squirming on the floor, squeezing through the jalousie glass, frying on the lightbulbs, flying at the pictures. They were crawling up the walls and across the ceiling.

Oh my god, they were in her bed. Hundreds, no, thousands of them. Helen wrapped her hand in a towel and tried to wipe the bugs off her spread, but there were more on her pillow. They were creeping through the fur of her teddy bear, blind, wormlike things. A chain of them dripped off the bear's ear.

Helen ran to the closet and pulled out her vacuum cleaner. Shoeboxes and purses fell out with it, and were soon writhing with the awful insects.

She began vacuuming up the bugs. She sucked them off the ceiling and pulled them off the light. She vacuumed them off the floor and swept them off her bedspread. And still they kept coming, waves of blind, beige, winged worms, like something that crawled on corpses.

Now they were in her hair and down her blouse and crawling over her feet. Their wings came off and fluttered through the air. Their bodies squished and crackled under her sandals. They crawled blindly over her naked toes and up her legs. Helen brushed them off and kept vacuuming.

Thumbs was howling so loud he drowned out the vacuum's scream. Then suddenly there was silence. The vacuum had stopped, clogged with insects. But still the blind beige things invaded her home, her bedroom, her bed, her body.

Helen could stand it no longer. She grabbed Thumbs, ran across the lawn, and pounded on her landlady's door.

"What the hell is going on?" Margery Flax said, yanking open the jalousie door so hard the glass rattled. In one hand she had a screwdriver—the drink, not the tool. In the other she had a Marlboro. Both had contributed to her lived-in face. Margery was an interesting seventy-six.

"What are you doing on my doorstep with that cat?" Margery bellowed. She was not a cat person, possibly because they did not come in the color she cared for. Margery loved purple. She was wearing a purple chenille robe, violet feathered mules with lavender sequins, and poppy-red toenail polish, which matched the bright red curlers in her gray hair.

"Bugs," Helen said. "Hundreds of them. No, thousands. Maybe millions. They're flying and crawling all over my apartment. I tried to stop them, but they keep coming. They're on my walls. They're in my bed and down my blouse. They're horrible."

Margery stubbed out the cigarette and took a deep gulp of her screwdriver. "What do they look like?" she said.

"They're kind of wormlike. Beige with wings, except the wings fall off and they start crawling."

Even now Helen felt them crawling on her. She looked down and saw one inside her shirt, on her bra.

"Here," she said, and handed an indignant Thumbs to Margery. He extended his claws.

"That cat scratches me and you're out of here," Margery said.

Helen shook out her blouse and gingerly picked up the ugly beige insect.

Margery looked at it and took another drink. "Shit," she said. "We've got termites." She handed the cat back to Helen.

"But you can exterminate them, can't you?"

"Depends. They can exterminate this building if there are too many. It could be the end of the Coronado. When they swarm like that, it means there are so many already, they're moving on to find more food. I've seen it happen before, old buildings like this. They get so riddled with termites it would be cheaper to tear down the place than fix it. That's what did in the Sunnystreet Motel."

"Where's that?" Helen said. She still felt itchy and crawly, but she couldn't see any more bugs on her.

"Where that vacant lot is now."

"The one with the sign 'Luxury Condos Coming Soon'?" Helen said.

"That's it. The termite inspector's foot went right through the roof. That was the end of the place. Betty sold out to a developer and moved to Sarasota."

The old buildings on the streets near the Coronado were disappearing to expensive high-rises. Soon the people who worked in the shops along Las Olas would not be able to live near their jobs. Helen felt a terrible pang of fear. She loved the Coronado. She didn't want anything to happen to it. She'd never find a place like this again. She'd have to live in a hot shoebox along the highway.

"But what if we're lucky?"

"Some luck," Margery said with a snort that should have blown out her sinuses. "We'll have to move out while they kill the termites."

"You mean I'll have to leave my apartment?" Thumbs let out an indignant yowl. Helen had been clutching him too tightly, hanging on to her cat to help her through the bad news.

"I mean we'll all have to leave. Every last one of us. They pump the whole place full of poison gas. It's the only way to kill the little bastards."

Madame Muffy was right, Helen thought. Here was death and destruction. Now all they needed was murder.

Chapter 3

Helen woke up. She did not know where she was. She could not move her arm.

Her cat, Thumbs, gave an indignant yowl and hit her in the face with his tail. The ten-pound tom had been snoozing on her elbow, and he did not appreciate this abrupt awakening. Helen realized where she was now. She'd been sleeping on Margery's sofa. After the termite attack last night, she had not wanted to go back to her apartment.

She looked at her watch. It was six a.m. She'd slept in her clothes. Her mouth felt stuffed with cat fur. She pulled on her shoes, folded the sheets and blanket, and picked up Thumbs. She should get out of Margery's before her landlady woke up. Officially the Coronado had a no-pets policy. That meant everyone had to pretend Pete the parrot and Thumbs did not exist, except in emergencies like last night. No point in waving the illegal cat in Margery's face.

As she tiptoed through the living room she heard Margery say, "You want coffee?"

"I'll be right back," Helen said. She slipped out the kitchen door into the sparkling, dew-covered dawn and walked across the courtyard. She opened her door and dumped Thumbs inside to face the bugs alone. "Sorry, boy," she said. "I can't do this without coffee."

It took two cups and a chocolate doughnut before Helen could face her apartment. A tail-twitching Thumbs met her at the door and led her straight to his water bowl. Hordes of dead insects floated on the surface.

"I'm sorry, buddy," she said. Her stomach flopped over when she saw his food dish. It was covered with a mound of dead beige bugs, like nuts on a sundae. She gingerly pushed the mess down the disposal.

The rest of the house was not as bad as she thought it would be. The floor had drifts and piles of insects, almost all dead, thank goodness. Wings, like fluttery bits of cellophane, littered the sills and tables. Helen got her clogged vacuum working again, then spent the next two hours cleaning.

Occasionally Thumbs would find a live bug blindly creeping up a wall or across a counter, and howl for Helen. She'd suck it up with the vacuum. By nine that morning, her home had been swept and polished and dusted until not a trace of the insect invasion remained. Thumbs prowled the perimeter as if he expected the enemy to return any moment.

Even after a shower, Helen still felt crawly. She pulled a blouse out of her closet to wear for work. There was a single wingless termite on the collar, like a decoration. She brushed it off with a shudder.

What if those horrible blind bugs had killed the Coronado? As she walked to work, all Helen could think about was her pretty little apartment complex, menaced by unseen invaders inside its walls.

There were no customers in the bookstore at ten that morning. The staff was at the front cash register, listening to Matt, the youngest bookseller. Whatever he was telling them, they weren't happy.

That was unusual. Around Matt, most people looked dazzled. His tight white T-shirt accented a body that set male and female hearts fluttering on Las Olas. Matt had dramatic shoulder-length dreads and a long dark face with a knife-blade nose. It was an unusual combination: the rebellious dreads and the sensitive face.

Helen walked in to hear him say, "The whole Page Turners chain will be closed by the end of the month. The Palm Beach store is just the start."

"They're closing Palm Beach?" Helen said. "That's their new showcase. It can't be closing."

"They're announcing it tomorrow," Matt said. "That's what I heard, anyway. The store quit getting in new books three weeks ago. That was the first tipoff something was wrong."

"Ridiculous," said Albert, the day manager. Albert was fifty-six, a dried-up, fussy man who walked as if he had a broomstick shoved alongside his backbone. He wore starched white shirts that he ironed himself, and, even more unusual for South Florida, a necktie.

"I know the Turner family personally," Albert said. Once a year he went to a cocktail party at the Turner mansion and never stopped talking about it for the next twelve months. "I've worked here thirty years. I knew the first Page Turner."

"He's dead," Matt said. His dreads and T-shirt were a sharp contrast to Albert's buttoned-up starch. "If I were you, I'd start cranking on my résumé."

"The Turner family would never abandon us. People as rich as they are have a sense of duty," Albert said. "If they are closing the Palm Beach store, it's just temporary. You'll see."

"People as rich as they are love money," said a third bookseller, Brad. "If the stores threaten their income, they'll close them in a heartbeat. We'll all be out of work."

At forty, Brad was skinny as a boy. He had two hopeless loves: Jennifer Lopez and young blond men with pouty lips.

He read every word written on J.Lo, and sighed over her love life. Alas, Brad's choice in men was not much better than J.Lo's. Everyone but Brad could see his romances with the blond pretty boys were doomed. Yet he stayed cheerful despite constant rejection. Except now.

"I hate looking for new jobs," he said.

Helen wondered who to believe: Albert, who had known the Turner family for years, or young, cynical Matt? She wanted to believe Albert. But she'd spent too much time in corporations. Matt was probably right. She felt the panic scratching in her insides like a small sharp-toothed animal.

It had taken months to find this job. She was barely getting by with the weekly paychecks. If Page Turners went out of business, how would she pay the rent? She was still paying off Thumbs' three-hundred-dollar vet bill at ten dollars a week. It didn't matter that she was dating Dr. Rich. Helen did not want charity.

June was the wrong time to look for a job in South Florida. The tourist season was over. Businesses were cutting back on staff or closing for the summer. The animal panic started gnawing at her guts.

Helen's cheerless thoughts were interrupted by an impossible vision. A young coast guardsman marched up to the counter and practically saluted. The rosy-faced blond looked like he'd stepped out of a recruiting poster. His uniform was white and crisp. His eyes were ocean blue. His manner was respectful.

"I'm here to pick up a special order of twenty-four sea-rescue manuals, ma'am," he said, making Helen feel a hundred years old. The two-inch-thick manuals were on a shelf behind the register.

"I'll get them," Brad said. The skinny bookseller suddenly morphed into Arnold Schwarzenegger. He staggered to the counter with the mighty manuals.

Helen rang up the order. "Thank you, ma'am," the guardsman said.

He did not see Brad. "Could I help you carry your books?" Brad asked, hopeful as a schoolboy.

"No, thank you, sir," the strapping coast guardsman said. He scooped up the twenty-four manuals in his massive arms and broke Brad's heart. Brad stared at the young man's tightly tailored pants all the way down Las Olas.

"How's J.Lo?" Helen said, hoping to distract him.

"She's on the cover of *National Scandal* again, and they picked the worst possible picture. They do that on purpose, you know."

He held up the offending magazine. A white card fluttered to the floor.

"Look at that floor," Brad said. "I picked up cards all morning and now there are another fifty. I'm so frustrated."

Helen did not think the cards caused his frustration. But the bookstore's magazine section did have a perpetual snowfall of postage-paid subscription cards. Blow-in cards, they were called. Mostly, they blew out. The white cards fell out of the magazines like square dandruff. Booksellers spent hours picking up the blasted things.

Brad kicked at the cards, then tore off his name tag. "I'm going to lunch."

Poor Brad, Helen thought, with the smug generosity of someone who was currently lucky in love. She was seeing Dr. Rich Petton, the vet who looked like a shaggy Mel Gibson. Her job worries disappeared in the pink haze that surrounded Dr. Rich.

She wished Brad could be as happy as she was. At least he came back from lunch smiling. "I've got it. I've been driven half-crazy by those magazine cards. Now I'll have my revenge."

Brad picked up all the postage-paid cards on the floor—an inch-thick stack. "I'm mailing them. I won't fill them in. I'll just drop them in the mail. The magazines want to hear from me, well, they will. But they'll pay."

His revenge was so perfect Helen couldn't stop laughing. Not even when a pale young woman asked her to find a book about "the last Russian princess, Anesthesia."

A worried Albert and a defiant Matt went home at four-thirty, and Gayle, the night-shift manager, came on. Helen kept ringing up sales. At five o'clock, a short, plump, white-haired man of about sixty-five walked importantly up to the counter. He seemed to have an entourage with him, even when he was alone.

"Is Mr. Turner here?" he asked.

"Yes, he's in his office."

"Could you tell him Burt Plank is here?"

"Burt Plank the author?" Helen said.

"That's me," said the little man, basking in her recognition. Helen couldn't believe it. Burt Plank wrote the Dirk Rockingham mystery series. He was a *New York Times* best-selling author. His character, Dirk, a millionaire cop, always got his man. He also got his woman. Fabulously beautiful females were always sliding under restaurant tables to give Dirk oral sex.

"Do you live in Fort Lauderdale?" Helen said.

Burt looked slightly offended. "Palm Beach," he said. "I have a private plane. I fly down to see my old friend Page Turner. Then I have dinner and return home. When do you get off work?"

"Seven o'clock," Helen said.

"Would you like to dine with me at the Riverside Hotel?"

"I'd love to," Helen said. "But I'd have to go home and change first."

"Absolutely not," he said. "You're fine just the way you are."

Burt Plank, best-selling author, thought Helen looked fine. Even the appearance of Page Turner couldn't spoil that moment.

"Burt!" Page Turner said expansively. "I hope you'll autograph some more stock for us. Those books of yours just keep on selling. Come on up to my office for a drink."

"See you at seven," Burt said.

Gayle the manager had been watching with disapproval. "Be careful. He's a real hound, just like Page. I'll bet he asked you out to dinner."

"He did. The Riverside Hotel."

"That's so he can sit outside and everyone going past can say, 'Is that Burt Plank?'"

"I thought it was because the place has good food," Helen said coolly. She liked Gayle, but the manager was overprotective. Gayle was gay, but she never hit on Helen. Rumor said that Gayle had a married lover who wasn't out of the closet. Of course, rumor also said the store was closing.

"Besides, aren't you seeing someone?" Gayle said.

"I am, but Burt"—Helen got a little thrill at dropping a celebrity name—"and I are only having dinner. There's nothing romantic about him. He's short, pudgy, and old enough to be my father. He certainly doesn't look like his character Dirk Rockingham."

"He does in his own mind. There he's a foot taller, thirty years younger, and a lot more muscular."

"Gayle, relax. It's only dinner. I thought it would be fun to have some literary conversation."

"The closest you'll get to literary conversation is when he talks about all the money he makes from those books."

Gayle was waiting at the bookstore counter like a stern mother when Burt Plank came out of Page Turner's office. That is, if moms wore black jeans, metal-studded leather belts, and Doc Martens. Her arms were folded across her chest. "Take good care of my best saleswoman," she told Burt.

"I plan to wine her and dine her." Helen could smell bourbon on his breath. Burt guided her out of the store with his small damp hand on her back. His hand slid a little down past her waist and rested almost on her buttock. Helen thought of removing it, but decided not to make a scene. Instead she moved briskly ahead until his hand slid off naturally.

Burt was dressed for Palm Beach, which meant he looked silly in Fort Lauderdale. The British yachting jacket and white linen pants seemed pretentious. The gold chains at his neck and wrist were overdone. He's supposed to be overdone, Helen thought. He's a celebrity.

She wished he didn't look quite so much like a sugar daddy. At least no one will confuse me with a bimbo, she thought. Not in a six-year-old pantsuit and flat shoes.

When they walked between the golden lions at the entrance to Indigo, the hotel restaurant, the staff started fussing over them. Helen enjoyed it. Burt was offered the best table in the house, but he did not want to sit inside. He insisted on a table outside on Las Olas, practically on the sidewalk. They ate their appetizers to a whispered chorus of "Isn't that Burt Plank?" Burt puffed out his chest every time he heard those words.

The food was sculpted into artistic shapes and placed into pools of colored sauce. It sure beat her usual dining experience—a can of water-packed tuna over the kitchen sink.

"You are the most interesting woman at the store," Burt said, ordering more wine. It was a rather thin compliment. The only other woman was Gayle, and she had no interest in Burt or any other man. It was also the last time he devoted any conversation to Helen.

"Tell me about your next book," Helen said. She wanted

to know how he worked out his exciting plots. Maybe he'd drop the names of New York editors and agents.

"Like Dirk, I enjoy flying my own plane," he said. "But I'm thinking of trading in my Cessna for a single-pilot jet. A Raytheon Premier One. I made more than a million dollars on my last book, including the movie rights, and it's time Dirk and I had an upgrade. It's not an extravagance. With my own jet, I don't waste time hanging around airports, waiting for a flight. Do you like to fly?"

"Hate it," Helen said, wondering when Burt would talk about how he wrote those books. "Do you use a word processor?"

"Yes. I've just bought a new laptop. It's the lightest one available. Cost me . . ."

Helen concentrated on her duck, oven-roasted with jasmine-scented charcoal. Burt had ordered for both of them. It sure beat canned tuna.

"And then I thought I'd get a Ferrari."

"A Barchetta?" said Helen, who knew a little about Ferraris.

Burt looked startled. "No, a Testarossa."

"Nice car. And about two hundred thousand dollars cheaper than the Barchetta," Helen said. Burt looked like he'd been punched in the stomach by Dirk Rockingham.

The waiter removed their empty plates. Burt ordered cappuccino for two, without consulting Helen, and began talking about his "seaside mansion" in Palm Beach. He actually used those words. Helen stifled a yawn.

"Are you sleepy?" he said.

"It's been a long day." And this dinner was as literary as a stock-market report.

Helen felt a tickling sensation on her thigh. Oh, god, not another bug. Not after last night. If it was a palmetto bug she'd scream, even if she was in one of the best restaurants on Las Olas.

"You need to relax," Burt said. "I've had a vasectomy. I'm safe." That's when she realized the small creature creeping along her thigh was Burt Plank's hand.

Helen removed it like a cockroach. Burt looked surprised.

"You'd better get your dessert from the menu." Helen stood up and left the restaurant, passing the waiter holding two cappuccinos. The last thing she heard was, "Is that the woman with Burt Plank?"

What a fool she was. A literary dinner indeed. She was just another cheap date. For the price of a meal, she was supposed to warm the great Burt Plank's bed while he talked about the one he loved—himself. She had a perfectly good man, but no, she had to dine with a literary light.

Nothing had gone right today. First the rumors about the store closings, then the long, dull dinner with Burt. It was nine o'clock, and she suspected Margery would have more bad news when she got home.

Her landlady was sitting by the pool, smoking Marlboros and staring sadly into the night. Her deep purple shorts set looked like mourning clothes.

"I was right, but I sure as hell didn't want to be. We got termites," Margery said. "The inspector came out today. They can save the place, but they're going to have to tent it."

"What's that mean?" Helen said.

"I forgot. You're not from around here. They wrap the whole building in giant tarps, and then pump in poison gas. Everyone has to be evacuated for three days."

"Three days! Do I have to move out now?"

"No, it takes awhile to set it up."

"Will the termites come back tonight?" Helen said. "Is it safe to sleep in my place?" She couldn't stand to fight another insect horde.

"Keep your front lights off after dark. That's probably what attracted the swarm."

"Where will we live during the tenting?"

"I've got a friend who has a beach motel in Hollywood. I'll put you up at my expense. How's that? Three days on the beach. It's my present for the inconvenience."

Helen no longer saw the sadness in Margery's face. All she heard were those three words: a beach vacation. Helen hadn't had a vacation in years. Even in St. Louis, she'd either worked through most of her vacations or spent the time calling her office to learn the latest disaster. Now she'd have three days on the beach. Her life was definitely taking a turn for the better.

Maybe she should have picked up that crowbar sooner.

Chapter 4

"Death, destruction, and murder." That's what Madame Muffy predicted, and now Helen saw it all around her. There was death and destruction at the Coronado.

As for murder, the whole staff wanted to kill Page Turner III.

The next day, Page announced that the Palm Beach store was closing, effective immediately. Matt had warned them. But the booksellers couldn't have been more shocked if terrorists had blown up the place.

Brad kept wandering around saying, "I don't believe it."

"Believe it," Matt said. He was Cassandra in a white T-shirt.

"It's only temporary," Albert insisted.

Helen said nothing. The Palm Beach store had opened with great fanfare less than a year ago. Why was Page closing it so quickly? It didn't make sense.

Brad called a friend who worked there. "The Palm Beach staff is shell-shocked," he reported. "They didn't get any notice. They're not getting any severance pay. They're all out on the street."

"What about the books?" Helen said.

"Our store will sell them. The Wilton Manors store won't get any."

"Then it will close, too," Matt said. He was relentless.

"Do you know that or are you just talking?" Albert said.

"I believe," Matt said firmly, "that Wilton Manors will close very soon."

But we're safe, Helen thought, and felt guilty for entertaining that hope.

Brad said it out loud. "We'll survive because we have the Palm Beach books."

"We'll close before the last Palm Beach book is sold," Matt predicted.

The other booksellers, except for loyal Albert, must have agreed. Within an hour, newspapers began missing their help-wanted sections. The copy machine ran constantly. There were whispered phone conversations for suspected job interviews.

When Helen stopped in the café for her midmorning coffee, she saw the dreadlocked Matt studying the paper. He looked up guiltily. He'd been reading the employment section. "It's hopeless. Nothing here but jobs for telemarketers and debt collectors."

"I'm not that desperate," Helen said. "Most employers want too much work for too little money. Look at this ad: 'Nanny, excellent English required, two lively boys, must love dogs.' Eight lousy bucks an hour."

"It says that in the ad?" Matt grinned.

"I added the last part. But you know what that means. The dogs and the kids run wild. No, thanks. I'm going to keep looking."

"Me, too," Matt said.

"Why don't you go back to school, Matt? You're young and smart."

"And broke," he said. "I'm trying. But scholarships are getting cut back, too. Page Turner is cruel. He could have

given the Palm Beach staff a few thousand dollars in severance. That's pocket change for him. Instead, he strung them
along, then dumped them. He'll pay for that."

"People like him never pay for anything," Helen said.

The one bright spot was Helen's beach vacation, but she
bought it at a high price. She had to work three nights.
Helen was used to irregular hours at the bookstore, but she
hated nights. The customers were bizarre. The store was
dirty and disorganized after a busy day. And Page Turner
was so cheap, he made the night booksellers clean the rest
rooms.

Still, if it got her beach time, Helen would clean toilets at
midnight.

She had to work two of the dreaded nights before her vacation.

Wednesday, there was Melanie.

Helen knew it would be a bad night when Page Turner
III showed up at seven. He had the flushed face and hearty
manner of a drunk about to turn mean. He was carrying a
Bawls, bent straw dangling from the bottle.

Bawls was a high-caffeine drink with guarana, which
was something exotic from the Amazon. He added a hefty
jolt of something less exotic from the liquor store. Vodka,
probably. Caffeine drinks laced with vodka were the current
club scene rage.

He held up the bumpy blue glass bottle and yelled,
"Who's got Bawls?" The staff didn't laugh. He didn't notice.

An hour later, a slender young woman with masses of
blond hair came up to Helen's cash register. She gave the
impression of being small and fragile, but she was almost
as tall as Helen and well muscled. Maybe it was her girlish
clothes. She wore a short, pale blue wraparound skirt, a
low-cut ruffled top, and clear plastic high-heeled sandals

that showed her toes. They made her look vulnerable and naive.

"I'm an author," she said proudly. "Melanie Devereaux DuShayne. I have an appointment with Page Turner."

"Another one for the harem," Brad said, too loudly, and rolled his eyes. Helen glared at him. Most of the time Brad was funny. Tonight he was not.

"I'll take you to his office," Helen said. She felt like she was leading a lamb to the slaughter. Or a lamb to the wolf.

"Is your book published?" Helen asked Melanie as they passed the velvet rope barrier and walked up the stairs to Page's office. Ninety-nine percent of the women who went into Page's office were not published authors, and never would be, despite the promises made on his couch. Page said he knew New York agents and editors, which was true. But he wouldn't waste his precious contacts on a passing fling.

"Oh, yes, with UBookIt." She opened a blue flowered purse and pulled out a trade paperback called *Love and Murder—Forever: A Romantic Mystery or Mysterious Romance.*

It was a print-on-demand book. Helen tried not to sigh. Another gullible author.

Print-on-demand, or POD, meant the books were printed as ordered. There were no large advance press runs, as with conventional books. Some POD publishers, including Melanie's, used this new technology for an old scam. They ran a vanity press. Poor Melanie paid a hundred and fifty dollars to get her book published, bypassing the usual process with an agent, an editor, and a publisher. UBookIt sold her paperback novels for an outrageous twenty-nine ninety-five. UBookIt's advertising implied their authors became best-sellers reviewed in the *New York Times.*

Publishing virgins like Melanie fell for that line. Actually, she had a better chance of being crowned Miss Black America.

Helen felt sorry for POD authors like Melanie. They were so eager. So hopeful. So duped.

Most newspapers would not review POD books. Most bookstores would not sell them or give signings for them. Certainly not snooty Page Turners.

Helen knocked on the door and Page opened it, wearing a smoking jacket like a roué from a forties movie. He put his massive arm around Melanie's shoulders, and Helen saw his hand was slyly heading for her breast. Melanie was staring at his office, which took up the whole floor. The spectacular view of Fort Lauderdale was almost overpowered by his five thousand first editions.

"Look at all these books," she said, wide-eyed. "Is that really Ray Bradbury's *Dark Carnival*?"

"Signed," Page said. "That's an autographed Dorothy Sayers. There's a signed first edition of John Steinbeck's *Grapes of Wrath*. On this shelf is a Faulkner first edition. My family knew him, naturally. I have Dashiell Hammett and . . ."

They were all collected by his grandfather, Page Turner I, a man who knew and cultivated the greatest names in fiction. Page Turner III's only additions to the collection were a signed set of Burt Plank novels. Helen wondered how Dorothy Sayers felt sitting next to him.

Page didn't point out that the locked cabinet behind him contained nude videos of the women he dated—videos they must now regret. Brad said Page and Burt Plank watched them like stag films. He'd come in once to get the staff schedule and seen the two of them laughing like drunken frat boys.

The enormous leather couch seemed to squat there like a malevolent beast. Staff gossip said there was a hidden camera over it. Helen did not want to see any more. She quietly shut the door.

An hour later, Melanie the POD author came down the stairs, flushed and pretty, blond hair gleaming.

"Mr. Turner is going to give me a signing," she said, dancing in the aisle. "Imagine me at Page Turners! And he said he could get his good friend Mr. Burt Plank to give me a blurb. I'm so excited."

Helen shuddered. She knew what Melanie would have to give the plump Plank for that blurb. I have a nasty mind, she thought. But then she noticed Melanie's blue wrap-around skirt was on inside out.

So did Gayle, the night manager. "I'm not letting him take advantage of another woman," she said. "He lies. He lies to them all and gets away with it because he's the great Page Turner."

Melanie came tripping up to the cash register in her clear plastic heels. "I want to order two more copies of my book."

"It will take two to five weeks," Helen said. If she was lucky. UBookIt was as slow as it was crooked.

"My baby is worth waiting for," Melanie said. "Where's the ladies' room?" Helen pointed over by the exit sign. Melanie headed in that direction, fluffing her hair.

"I'm going to have a chat with her," Gayle said. "Wait two minutes and follow me in."

Helen did. The white-tiled bathroom stank of peppermint disinfectant and old diapers. Someone had left a half-empty latte on the sink and a *Bride's* magazine by the toilet.

She heard Gayle saying, "Yes, he did. He was dating this woman while he was engaged to his current wife. She read about his engagement in the newspaper, came running in here, and threatened to kill him. He humiliated her. Ask anyone who's worked here awhile. They'll tell you. She wasn't the first—or the last. You're just one in a long line."

"No!" Melanie said. "Mr. Turner said I had talent. He said he would give me a signing."

"No, he said he would *try*. Next he'll say he tried, but your books weren't available from the distributor. And they won't be, because they're print-on-demand. Page Turners never has signings for POD authors."

"But he said he'd get Mr. Plank to endorse my book," Melanie said, and Helen heard her awful desperation.

"Yeah, you'll get a blurb," Gayle said. "If you get out your knee pads. You know what Burt Plank's last blurb said? 'Good is not the word for this book.' You want that on your cover?"

"It's not true. You're just a jealous old dyke."

Helen spoke up then. "It is true," she said. "Ask Mr. Turner to set a date for your signing. I'll bet my next paycheck that's when he says your books are not available."

"You're lying. Both of you." Melanie was almost sobbing now. "Mr. Turner is an honorable man. I'll prove you wrong. I'm going up there right now and ask him."

"While you're in there, ask to see his videos," Gayle said. "He keeps them in a locked cabinet by the couch. I bet you've already starred in one. He watches them with his buddy Burt Plank. That way Burt can preview the coming attraction."

"Mr. Turner would never do that."

"There's a camera hidden in the vent over the couch," Gayle said. "Check it out next time you're on your back."

That was nasty. Helen thought it was Gayle's payback for the "jealous old dyke" remark.

Melanie flounced up the stairs to Page's office. She was back down in ten minutes, cheeks flaming, blond hair flying every which way. She didn't say anything to Helen or Gayle as she walked through the store, head high.

"There goes another fool," Brad said when she passed

his register. Melanie's head snapped back as though she'd been lashed, and her cheeks grew redder. She'd heard him.

Helen wished Brad had not said that. But even more, she wished Page Turner had not taken advantage of Melanie.

"That son of a bitch," Helen said.

"I wish Page Turner was dead," Gayle said. Helen looked at Gayle, her face white with rage, and wondered how Page had hurt her.

At midnight the store closed and the staff chased out the last customers. Page Turners was a mess. Helen opened the women's rest room and groaned. The stalls, mirror, and sink were draped in toilet paper. Even the waste can was decorated. More paper crisscrossed the floor. Worse, it was wet.

"What's wrong?" Gayle said.

"We've been TP'd. Wet TP. I just hope they used water."

"Oh, gross."

It took the two women an hour to clean it up, and they still had to put the store in order. Stray books were piled everywhere. Sticky café cups and napkins were abandoned on shelves and floors.

"Screw it," Gayle said. "Let's leave. This store is going to close anyway."

That's when Helen knew Page Turners was dead.

Thursday brought more rumors that the entire bookstore chain was closing, and more whistling-in-the-dark denials.

"The Turner family can't close our store," Albert said, all starch and sanity. "We're the flagship, started by Page's grandfather."

"They can do anything they want," Matt said, the dread-locked rebel. "And they will."

"How do you know?" Albert said, looking every day of his fifty-six years. "You're what—twenty-two?"

"Twenty-four," Matt said. "But I don't have your handicap."

"What's that?" said Albert.

"I don't believe white men. Especially rich ones."

Albert flushed, but said nothing.

The strain showed in the store. Lively little Brad nearly burst into tears when a customer berated him. He argued that his beloved J.Lo should have stayed with Puff Daddy. Helen took that as a sure sign he'd snapped.

Stuffy Albert was rude and peremptory. Matt disappeared for two hours at lunch, which made more work for everyone.

Only gentle Mr. Davies remained unchanged, sitting in his nook in the back, reading his beloved books. He presided over the store like some literary spirit. Thursday night, Helen found Mr. Davies asleep over his paperback when the store closed. She woke him up.

"Oh, dear, dear, I'm so sorry. Did I hold you up? I know you want to go home." He gathered his book and sandwich wrappings and headed for the exit.

Helen was back at the store at nine the next morning. She didn't care that she'd had six hours of sleep. Today was Friday. Her beach vacation started this evening. She couldn't take another weird late night.

Instead, she had a bizarre day. The first man at her register had coal-black hair, eyes like twin pools of tar, and a copy of *How to Cast Out Devils.*

"I want to return this book," he said.

Helen was afraid to ask why. She didn't know which scared her more: if the book worked—or if it didn't.

She gave him his money back without comment.

"Is this a full moon?" Helen asked Brad. Like most people in retail, she believed the full moon brought out the crazies. "We're going to have fun today at the registers."

"Not me," Brad said. "I've got slush duty."

"Poor you," Helen said. She meant it. "Slush" was the staff word for the books people left all over the store. Art books heavy as paving stones were abandoned in the Children's section. Mutilated children's books were dumped like slashed corpses in Mysteries. Bodice-ripping romances turned up in Sports. Copies of the *Kama Sutra* wound up in the Pregnancy section.

The living room attracted the most slush. Old Mr. Turner had created "book nooks" for his customers. Brown leather wing chairs with comfortable reading lamps were scattered all over the store. In the center, sheltered by mahogany bookcases, he designed a living room with a beautifully worn Persian carpet, comfortable leather couches, and armchairs. Here, the slush gathered in three-foot heaps, until it was retrieved and reshelved by tired, footsore booksellers.

Brad, skinny and agile as a monkey, could carry an amazing number of books. He returned from the slush run with tomes stacked to his chin, and a wild look in his eyes. He dropped the books on the shelving cart and said, "Do you have anything I can use to clean the coffee table? Someone knocked over a caramel latte and covered it with a stack of Harry Potter books."

"Are they ruined?"

"Four totaled, and the finish is coming off the coffee table."

Helen rummaged under the register for paper towels, spray cleaner, and furniture polish and put them on the counter. She heard Brad say, "Thanks," and stood up to face the sublime smells of hot grease and pepperoni. A delivery man was at the counter with a fragrant pizza box.

"Pizza delivery for Clemmons," he said.

"We don't have a Clemmons on the staff," Helen said.

"It's not for the staff. It's for a customer. Large pepperoni and mushroom. He called on his cell phone. Said he'd be in the living room."

Helen paged him. Clemmons turned out to be a much-pierced young man in a black T-shirt. Helen was used to people treating Page Turners like their home. They put their feet on the sofas, spilled coffee on the carpet, and left books everywhere. But ordering a pizza went too far.

"Sir, we have a café where you can buy food," she said.

"Too expensive," Clemmons said, taking his pizza to the living room.

Helen tried to keep above the chaos by thinking of her beach vacation. Rich was meeting her tonight at the motel. They had three days together on the romantic ocean, their first long weekend together.

These rosy dreams departed when Page Turner lurched in carrying a Bawls-and-vodka. He was not flushed and jolly this afternoon. He was plain drunk. He walked around the bookstore, annoying customers with his vulgar question. He even went back to Mr. Davies' nook, held up his blue bottle, and said, "You got Bawls, buddy?" The old gentleman seemed embarrassed for Page. Helen was relieved when he finally stumbled off to his office.

Page's wife, Astrid, called and said, "Can I speak with the son of a bitch?"

"Which one?" Helen said.

"The one who owns the store."

Helen paged him, but he did not reply. Rather than keep the owner's wife on hold, she went to his office. There she heard an angry woman insisting, "You are. I know you are. My mother said so."

"Your mother's crazy. And so are you. Get out."

Helen knocked on the door.

"What?" Page said.

"Your wife is on the phone," she said.

"Just what I need. Another crazy woman," he said.

The door opened. The little psychic Madame Muffy stumbled out, clutching a bottle of Bawls with a bent straw.

Where did she come from? Was she Page's newest girl-friend? Muffy didn't seem his type.

At four-thirty, Page called the staff together for an announcement. "The Wilton Manors store will close this weekend," he said.

There was a shocked silence. Matt radiated "I told you so" vibes. Helen could almost see them flashing in neon over his dreads.

Why close that store so soon after Palm Beach? This was crazy. This was something a drunk would do, Helen thought.

"This store will receive no new books until further notice," Page said, and hiccuped loudly. "That should make your job easier. Less to shelve. Because there will be less work, all hours will be cut. Full-time workers will be cut from forty to thirty hours a week, part-time from twenty to ten."

Helen had just been whacked with a sixty-seven-dollar pay cut. Maybe if she didn't eat, she could pay her bills. If the store closed, she would not get unemployment. She was paid in cash under the table.

She looked over and saw that Albert had gone lard white. He was clutching his chest. Helen was afraid he was having a heart attack.

"Does that mean we're closing?" Matt asked.

"It means we're not getting more books until I say so," Page said. "That's all it means." He walked up the stairs to his office.

Albert began talking to himself. "What am I going to do? I'm fifty-six years old. Who will hire me? Where will I get health insurance?"

"I told you," Matt said. "Never believe a rich white guy."

The phone rang. It was Page's private line. The ringing stopped and the light for that line went on.

Five minutes later Page Turner staggered out of the

bookstore, holding a bottle of Bawls and whistling a happy tune. The staff watched silently until he disappeared from view. Then everyone talked at once.

"I'm going to be out of work again," Helen said to Matt. She was almost in tears. "I'm going to have to look for another job. I hate it. I hate it."

She remembered the petty humiliations, the endless forms to fill out, the interviewers who said she was overqualified, the worries about making the rent. A surge of self-pity washed over her. "I hate him," she burst out.

"We all hate him," Matt said. "Man doesn't care what he does to people."

Loyal Albert said nothing.

"I've got to cash my paycheck before the bank closes at five," Matt said. "I'll be back in fifteen." It wasn't his break, but no one cared anymore. They stood in a small, shocked group, trying to absorb Page Turner's announcement.

Matt returned ten minutes later, his eyes black with rage. "My paycheck bounced."

"There must be some mistake," Albert said.

"There's no mistake," Matt said. "The bank said there was not enough money in the account to meet the week's payroll. The man's closing these stores for a reason. They're losing too much money."

This didn't sound right to Helen. She was ringing up plenty of book sales. The Las Olas store had to make money. Where did it go?

"Page Turner and his family are worth millions," Albert said.

"You don't think the payroll comes out of his personal checking account, do you? It's the store that's broke, and he doesn't give a rat's rump." Matt took off his bookseller badge.

"Where are you going? You have another two hours," Albert said.

"Good-bye. This rat is leaving the sinking ship," Matt said.

"You can't just go."

"I'm already gone. So long, sucker. I'll get my things out of my locker."

Albert looked stunned. "What will I do if my paycheck bounces? My health insurance is due this week. I have to pay Mother's and mine."

Albert never understood the careless cruelties of the rich. Helen, who had once made six figures, did. If you'd always had money, you didn't know what people like Albert suffered for three hundred dollars. Page would order a three-hundred-dollar bottle of wine to impress his author friends. But he wouldn't bother to cover a three-hundred-dollar paycheck for a faithful employee.

Helen saw tears on Albert's face. "Are you OK?" she said.

"If I can't take care of Mother, I'll kill myself," he said.

"You'd be better off killing the man who did this to you," Matt said as he headed out the door.

Chapter 5

Helen found a solitary bagel in her fridge. It was speckled with green-black mold. She tried to scrape off the mold, then decided the bagel wasn't worth packing and tossed it.

The low-fat mozzarella, which was supposed to go on the speckled bagel, was worth saving. It went into the bag of groceries, along with a jar of pasta sauce, half a stick of butter with toast crumbs, and the other discouraging contents of a single woman's kitchen. Helen had to pack up everything edible in her apartment, even Thumbs' catnip toys. Margery had warned her not to leave any food behind when the Coronado was tented for termites.

"All the food has to go, or it will be contaminated," her landlady said. "Remove all your medicines, cosmetics, body scrubs, spices and herbs. The gas kills everything that breathes oxygen, so all the plants have to be out of there or they'll die."

Helen's illegal cat and Peggy's forbidden parrot also had to go. Helen understood now why Margery was giving the Coronado residents three days at the beach. The tenting preparations were time-consuming and tedious.

Helen checked the last cabinet. She threw out some stale

graham crackers and stuck a jar of crunchy peanut butter in the bag. That was it. Her clothes were packed. Thumbs was meowing in his carrier. She lugged her suitcase, food bag, and cat carrier out to Margery's big white Cadillac. Her own car needed eight hundred dollars in repairs. It could rust in the Coronado parking lot until she won the lottery—and Helen didn't buy tickets.

Margery and Helen were the last to leave the Coronado. Her landlady was about to drive off when Helen said, "Wait! I forgot a suitcase."

"And there goes the damn phone," Margery said. "We'll never get out of here."

Helen hastily opened her closet and pulled out the old Samsonite suitcase wedged between the wall and the water heater. Inside was a discouraging bundle of old-lady underwear. At least, Helen hoped it would discourage any thief. Under that stretched elastic and snagged nylon was all the money she had in the world: $7,108 in cash. This was also where she hid the untraceable cell phone she used to call her mother and sister.

She was almost ready to leave when she remembered Chocolate, her teddy bear. She picked him off the bed, felt around inside, and pulled out eleven bucks. Chocolate was indeed a stuffed bear.

Helen threw the Samsonite in the backseat just as Margery came out. "Your boyfriend called. He couldn't stay on the phone. He's got emergency surgery on a Lab. The dog was hit by a car and it's in bad shape. He'll be with it all night."

Instead of me, Helen thought. Whoa. What is the matter with me? I'm jealous of an injured dog.

The lights were just coming on at the Coronado. White lights twinkled in the palm trees. The pool shone like a sapphire. Floodlights showed the old building's swooping curves.

"This is the first time the Coronado has been empty since Zach and I built it in 1949," Margery said. "It was right after the war, when we were first married. We had such plans."

That was about fifty-five years ago, Helen calculated. Margery would have been twenty-one years old. She tried to imagine Margery as a young bride.

"It's a beautiful place," Helen said, hoping Margery would talk about her plans and her long-dead husband, Zachary. But Helen could almost hear the door slam on those memories. Margery said nothing on the drive to Hollywood beach. The farther they got from the Coronado, the more she seemed to shrink and fade. The purple outfit she was wearing was so old and washed-out, it was almost gray. She didn't light up a cigarette, either. That should have made Helen happy, since she hated cigarette smoke. But Margery didn't seem the same without her dragon wreath of smoke. She didn't even seem to notice Thumbs' racket. The unhappy cat howled nonstop in his carrier.

When they turned off A1A, Helen saw the moonlit ocean. "It's gorgeous," she said.

Margery still said nothing. She pulled in at the Beach Time Motel, a 1950s two-story L painted pink and green. Plain, clean, and cute, it reminded Helen of the places she stayed on family vacations.

"We're here," Margery said. "If that cat carries on like that all weekend, you'll be sleeping on the beach."

Helen's room had a sagging bed with a harvest-gold spread and a kitchenette barely big enough for a coffeepot. But the ocean view was spectacular and the sound of the surf was soothing. Thumbs calmed down once he was liberated from his carrier. He gave himself a bath on her bed, sending fluffs of cat hair into the air.

By the time Thumbs was settled with his food, water, and litter box, it was six-thirty. The termite tenting party had started. Cal the Canadian was barbecuing in the motel courtyard, flipping burgers and turning hot dogs. Peggy arrived with a salad of sliced celery, chicken, and sesame seeds.

"Birdbrain here kept going after the sesame seeds," she said. She put the salad on a picnic table and went over to give Cal a hand at the barbecue. Pete sat solemnly on Peggy's shoulder, so unsure of his surroundings he hardly squawked, although he eyed the sesame-seed salad.

Sarah, a friend of Helen's who used to live at the Coronado, brought baked beans swimming in molasses and bacon and a platter of fried calamari. As Sarah's generous figure attested, the woman had no fear of food. Cal immediately abandoned Peggy and the barbecue grill to cozy up to Sarah. He laughed loudly at her jokes and tried to entertain her with stories of his own.

"I think you have a conquest," Helen whispered when Cal went for another Molson.

"I'm not that desperate," Sarah said. "That cheap Canadian is looking for free room and board."

"Sarah! How can you say that?"

"Because his idea of a covered dish was two tomatoes on a plate, unsliced."

"I mean, how can you say he's only interested in your money? You're an attractive woman."

Sarah had curly dark hair, bright brown eyes, and pretty hands that she showed off with good jewelry. Tonight she wore a hot-pink muumuu and flowered sandals. "I'm a fat woman with a fatter bank account. Cal hates to work. Besides, would you date him?"

"I did. You know what happened. He stiffed me for dinner."

"See? How's your vet friend?"

"He's spending the night with a sick Labrador," Helen said, unable to keep the disappointment out of her voice.

"He'll be here tomorrow, don't you worry," Sarah said. "Cal's coming back. Don't leave me. He won't come over when you're here."

"That's because he still owes me money," Helen said. Cal saw Helen, made an abrupt U-turn, and went back to helping Peggy. Helen stayed with Sarah, acting as an effective anti-Cal device.

Everyone seemed to be avoiding someone tonight. Madame Muffy the preppie psychic stayed away from Peggy and Helen. Cal steered clear of Helen and Margery. Phil the invisible pothead avoided everyone. He never came out of his room, but a persistent cloud of pot smoke proved he was having his own party.

Despite Cal's stingy contribution, there was plenty of food. Margery had brought hot dogs and hamburgers, buns, and chips. Helen made deviled eggs. Madame Muffy baked a luscious chocolate cake. Beer, wine, and soda were chilling in a cooler.

"What's the wine?" Peggy called, busy at the barbecue grill.

"The box says it's 'chilled red.' Has an expiration date of September 2005," Helen said.

"Sounds like a good year. Pour me a glass."

"Will do," Helen said. Sarah took a glass, too. So did Margery.

"What about you, Muffy?" Helen said, holding up the wine box and hoping to establish normal neighborly relations.

"No, thank you," Muffy said primly. She was a study in baggy khaki. Helen wondered why a young woman was so defiantly drab.

"You want a Coke instead? Or a Sprite?"

"I don't drink alcohol or soda," Muffy said. "They're all poison, filled with caffeine and chemicals. I brought my own natural fruit juice." She poured herself a glass of something brown. She did not offer it to anyone else.

Helen felt like she'd offered Carry Nation a shot and a beer. So much for mending fences with Madame Muffy.

The conversation fell flat. Worse than flat. It seemed to lie there like something dead. Peggy picked at her salad, eating less than Pete. Madame Muffy cut her burger in two, then in quarters. Margery rolled a hot dog around on her plate.

Only Sarah and Cal had any appetite. Cal ate as if food was about to be outlawed. He wolfed down three burgers, two hot dogs, most of Peggy's salad, a half dozen deviled eggs, and hefty helpings of calamari and baked beans.

Helen tried to eat, but she wasn't hungry. She put a bunless burger on her plate and stared at it. It was all alone. Like her. Rich had canceled their romantic night for a sick dog.

When Helen looked up, Peggy and Pete had disappeared. Madame Muffy and her juice went missing soon after that. Helen wished Cal would disappear. Instead, he droned on about how Canada was superior to America. Margery didn't bother debating him, another sign she was not herself. Normally, she was the purple-clad defender of the USA. Helen and Sarah struggled to carry on a conversation.

The evening broke up about nine with polite thank-yous. Sarah gathered up her dishes and left. Margery packed up the extra buns and chips and put away Peggy's salad. Helen ate the last deviled egg. Cal took back his two unsliced, untouched tomatoes.

Helen had a restless night, but she could not sleep in Saturday morning. She'd promised to go with Margery for the final walk-through at the Coronado before the crew put the termite tent on. Helen felt like she was visiting a sick friend in the hospital.

Truly Nolen was doing the job. In South Florida, their bright yellow Volkswagen bugs with the mouse ears, whiskers, and tails were as common as the pests they killed. When Helen and Margery arrived at the apartments at nine, a flatbed truck was already there. George and Terrell would put the monster yellow-and-black-striped tarps on the building.

George, thin and whiplike, threw the tarps off the truck and manhandled the long ladders. The tarps were rolled up like tacos. Also on the trucks were long strings of metal clamshell clamps, which looked like big spring clothespins. The tarp ends would be rolled together and clamped shut, forming a seal. George did most of the roof work. Terrell, big and muscular, clamped down the building's sides.

Signs were posted all over the Coronado: DANGER: DEADLY POISON—PELIGRO VENENO MORTAL. For those who could not read, there were skulls and crossbones.

Trevor, the fumigator, was nailing the last sign on the gate. He was about five-eight, with powerful shoulders and a strong, square jaw. He'd dressed up his drab uniform with gold chains that gleamed against his dark skin.

"Ah, good," he said. "Let's do the final inspection."

As they went through each apartment, Helen had a voyeur's view of how everyone lived. All the cabinets were open. Helen saw the same things in each apartment: miscellaneous mugs, stacks of Tupperware, ugly glass vases from florists. They had a pathetic garage-sale look.

Trevor checked the refrigerators, cabinets, and stoves for food. He looked carefully in each room, making sure no one was left behind. He was obsessive about it.

"An old woman hid in her home once because she didn't want to leave. Poor thing died. Happened to another company, but it's every fumigator's nightmare. I don't want it to happen to me."

Trevor moved with assurance through other people's

homes. Helen and Margery trailed behind him. Helen felt guilty about snooping, but she also enjoyed it.

Cal the Canadian had furniture for a colder clime: heavy velvet sofas and chairs, thick carpets, and a coffee table big as an aircraft carrier. Clothes were dumped on chairs. Books and newspapers were scattered on the floor. His rooms seemed small and crowded. Even his fridge door was cluttered with photos of his daughter and grandchild. His cupboards and refrigerator were bare of food, and there were no medicines in the bathroom. Cal's place was safe.

Peggy's home looked light and airy. Bright colors and white wicker, painted wooden fish, and pretty seashells made it a pleasant place to live. Her huge four-poster bed looked like something in a magazine. Helen noticed there were no photos except for ones of Pete. In the kitchen, Peggy had left behind a box of birdseed, bananas, and a bag of rice. Helen packed them up for her friend.

"Some people can't follow simple instructions," Margery grumped.

"Peggy must have been distracted," Helen said.

After each apartment was inspected, the door was locked with the owner's keys. Then the doorknob was fitted with a metal shield that had a second lock.

"Only the company has these keys," Trevor said as he secured the doorknob shield. "The doors are double-locked to make sure the owners don't come back and do something stupid. Before we put in the poisonous Vikane gas, which has no odor, we have to put in Chloropicrin, which is essentially tear gas. That's to keep people out. The tear gas makes their eyes stream. Sometimes, even that isn't enough. People will break into their own homes because they forgot a shirt for work or left their purse behind. They think they can hold their breath long enough to get in and out, but they can't. They're overcome by the gas."

"What happens then?"

"Some live. Some die." He shrugged. "There's no known antidote and the symptoms are different for every person. You might have a heart attack. I might have convulsions. Vikane affects different people in different ways. It's not a good way to die.

"One man went back into his place during a tenting, sat down in his favorite chair, and turned on the TV. He'd lost his business and wanted to commit suicide. They found him with his finger still on the remote, flipping through the channels for all eternity.

"A pair of cheating lovers sneaked back in because they knew his partner would never think of looking in the tented bedroom. They were found dead together."

The canvas tarps were shrouding the windows now, and the rooms were dark as caves. The canvas flapped in the breeze and created an odd snapping sound. As Helen walked through the dark, hot rooms, she seemed to see death everywhere. She wondered why Trevor bothered with the locks, when the windows were left open.

Margery must have been thinking the same thing. "What about burglars?" she said.

"They die, too," Trevor said. "If a thief gets in there, well, he's not going to tell the hospital he inhaled Vikane in a termite tent. By the time the hospital figures it out, he's dead."

"So how do you survive inside when the tents come off?" she said.

"I use a SCBA respirator," Trevor said. "George has one, too, in case I get overcome. I'll go in and open everything up. It will be safe for you to come back late Monday."

"What's a SCBA respirator?" Margery said.

"It looks like a diving tank, but it has a full face mask connected to the breathing hose. It's not to be confused with a scuba tank. Diving gear doesn't really work for this."

"What about those charcoal gas masks, the kind used in Desert Storm?"

"We tried them," Trevor said. "They don't work as well. You need a self-contained breathing apparatus. You can buy it at a fire-equipment place or on the Internet."

"So why don't burglars use them?" Margery asked.

"Too expensive," Trevor said. "A SCBA unit costs about two thousand dollars a tank. If a burglar had two thousand dollars, he wouldn't need to be a burglar."

"Breaking into this place wouldn't pay for the tank. Nobody here has the Star of India on her dresser," Margery said. "All a burglar would get was some old TV sets, a video camera or two, and Grandma's engagement ring." Helen thought her landlady had a real talent for crime.

"It's not worth the risk," Trevor agreed.

Still, Helen was glad she'd taken her suitcase full of cash to the beach.

Madame Muffy's place was as dull as its owner. The living room was still a palm-reading parlor. The bed had a beige comforter. Three unpacked boxes served as a nightstand. There were no photos, pictures, or anything personal. Helen had seen hotel rooms with more personality.

Finally, they entered the home of Phil the invisible pothead. This was the apartment Helen had been waiting to see. Naturally, it reeked of pot. The sagging couch was covered with a madras throw and *High Times* magazines. Three coffee-ringed pine boards on cinder blocks served as a coffee table. It held a bong, a roach clip, a Clapton mug with black coffee, and a barrette in the shape of a guitar.

"What's he doing with a hair barrette?" Helen said.

"It holds his ponytail. That's no ordinary guitar," Margery said respectfully. "It's a Fender Strat, same as Clapton plays, in solid silver."

"You'd think he'd use pot metal," Helen said. Once again, she wondered how her landlady knew these things.

She examined the plastic milk crates full of albums. "I'd love to help myself to these." There were original LPs from Clapton's days with Cream, the Yardbirds, and John Mayall and the BluesBreakers. Helen slid out one record. Oddly, it was beautifully cared for, without the dirt and scratches druggies inflicted on their albums.

The walls were covered with vintage posters, including one for Cream's *Goodbye* album. The room's centerpiece was on a stand: A Clapton-model Fender Strat guitar. It was 7-UP-can green, better known as stoner green.

There were no medicines in the bathroom. In the kitchen, Trevor opened the freezer. Inside was a glass vial of clear yellow liquid and a fat bag of pot.

"Got to get rid of that, ma'am," the fumigator said. "The herb will get contaminated."

Helen started to pack the pot with the bananas, but Margery said, "Throw that out. I'm not driving around with an illegal substance in my car. What if I got stopped?"

Helen couldn't imagine the cops stopping Margery for a drug bust, but she did not argue.

"And what's this?" her landlady asked, pointing to the vial.

"Urine sample, ma'am," Trevor said. "For drug tests. If you smoke the herb, you can't pass the test. Some people buy clean samples on the Internet. If their job requires mandatory drug testing, they palm the sample and use it instead of their own fluid. But the gas will ruin it. It should be thrown out, too."

"Why don't you throw that out while the inspector and I walk through my place?" Margery said, and Helen knew she was not invited to look in her landlady's closets and cabinets. Helen owed Margery a few favors, but she thought handling a frozen urine sample canceled them all. She found a plastic grocery bag, picked up the vial with it, and dropped it in the Dumpster.

The Coronado was nearly covered with tarps. Clear plastic hoses for the poison gas snaked along the sidewalks and across the pool. The ends of the hoses were taped to floor fans in the hallways. The fans were whirring softly. They would dissipate the poison gas through the apartments.

The Coronado looked like a disaster scene, as if a tornado or hurricane had hit. The chaise longues by the pool no longer seemed inviting. Helen saw an abandoned pair of flip-flops. They looked sad.

In the harsh sunlight, Helen could see the cracks that had been cheaply patched and painted over. The Coronado was showing its age. So was Margery. She came out of her own apartment and suddenly looked every day of her seventy-six years.

Helen and Margery left Trevor as he was pumping poison gas into the apartments. The Coronado was wrapped like a present.

Helen felt tired and sad. This should be a hopeful occasion, she thought. The Coronado could be saved. But it looked like death in a pretty package.

Chapter 6

Dr. Rich was waiting for Helen when she returned from the Coronado. She stopped at the entrance to the motel courtyard to admire her man. She liked his slightly shaggy blond hair and beard, his subtle brown Tommy Bahama shirt and khaki shorts. He looked cool and relaxed, sitting under a striped umbrella.

"How's the Lab?" she asked, kissing him hello. Rich smelled of spicy aftershave, coffee, and lime.

"He lost a leg, but he'll make it. How's my buddy Thumbs?"

"He's fat and happy. Want to see him?" They went inside to Helen's room. Rich sat on the sagging bed and scratched the cat's belly until he purred. Helen began to get restless. Was he ever going to forget his animals and remember her?

When the cat was drooling in stupefied delight, Rich looked up and said, "What do you want to do today? Sit out on the beach?"

"Not really," Helen said. "I burn easily."

"So what do you want to do?"

"I could think of a few things," she said. How dense was this man?

"Like what?" he said, scratching the cat again.

Like leaving that damn cat alone, Helen almost said. Then she saw he was grinning. He reached out and pulled her onto the bed and kissed her. His lips were soft and his beard was nicely scratchy and his weight on her was just right, not too heavy, but solid and muscular. He kissed her so hard, she forgot about the bookstore, her money worries, and where she would find another job.

"Why, Rich, you animal," she purred.

"You didn't get much of a tan for someone who spent three days on the beach," grumped Margery on Monday afternoon.

"I burn easily," Helen said. Boy, do I, she thought. I've had one hot weekend.

"Humph," Margery said. "I can't see the point of an ocean-view room if you keep the curtains shut the whole weekend."

"We took lovely moonlit walks on the beach," Helen said. Because we didn't get out of bed until after dark, she thought. If Thumbs hadn't woken us demanding dinner, we might have slept all night in each other's arms. Sunday was more of the same. When Rich left at five Monday morning, she'd stretched luxuriantly, then drifted off again on sleep-warm pillows that smelled of his spicy aftershave. She woke up at noon and treated herself to lunch at a beach restaurant with the eleven dollars she found in Chocolate the stuffed bear.

Now it was two-thirty. Time to return to reality. Margery would drive her back to the Coronado. She had just enough time to unpack and get Thumbs settled. She had to be at the bookstore at five. Helen had to work one more night, but she didn't even mind that.

She sighed happily and put the cat carrier in Margery's big white car. Her body ached in all the right places.

"Think Rich is a keeper?" Margery said.

"That would be nice," Helen said. But complicated. How would she explain her ex-husband and that awful scene in court? How could she tell Rich that she was on the run?

What had he said as he left this morning? "Now that I've found you, I won't ever let you go." His words sent shivers through Helen, but they weren't entirely of delight. Was Rich romantic or possessive? I'll worry about it later, she thought, loading her last suitcase into the trunk.

"That's it," she said.

"Let's see what they've done to the Coronado," Margery said. Now that she was going back home, Margery sounded like herself again. She looked like herself, too, in an outrageous shorts set abloom with magenta roses. She wore cherry-red nail polish and flirtatious dark purple kitten-heeled slides that showed off her good legs and slender ankles.

The giant tarps were gone from the Coronado. The DANGER signs had disappeared. Purple bougainvillea blossoms floated in the pool once more. Parrots screeched in the palms. Newspapers waited at the front doors. The Coronado was its old romantic self, except for the termite company's locked shields on the doorknobs.

All the Coronado residents were gathered by the pool, minus Phil the invisible pothead. Helen had never seen him, but she figured she'd recognize him by his smell.

Trevor removed a doorknob shield with ceremony and opened Cal's apartment. The Canadian looked inside and said, "Nothing's changed. I thought you might exterminate the dirt."

There was polite laughter. Madame Muffy was next. The preppie psychic went into her place without a word. The shields were taken off Margery's, Phil's, and Helen's doors. Peggy's apartment was last, but Helen did not stick around for the final opening. Thumbs was howling to go home.

She set his carrier down in her kitchen. He was climbing out with ruffled dignity when the screaming started.

She heard Trevor say, "Oh, Lord, no." Helen opened her door and saw him run inside Peggy's apartment.

Peggy ran after him, then screamed. Pete the parrot, confined to a cage in her car, began making a racket.

Margery pushed her way into Peggy's apartment, then said, "What the hell?" in a stunned voice.

Helen followed them, slightly dazed. She could smell something powerfully bad. Poison gas? Then why had Trevor run in without his breathing gear?

Peggy, Margery, and Trevor were standing in the bedroom. The room was dominated by an enormous four-poster bed. It seemed bigger than ordinary king-size. Emperor, maybe, or potentate. The bed was covered with pale sensual linens, soft piles of pillows, and gauzy hangings. No woman should sleep alone in a bed like that, Helen thought.

There was a man in Peggy's bed. A rich man. He wore a suit that Helen could see was expensive, even from across the room. Sticking out of his well-tailored back was a cheap butcher knife.

"Is he alive?" Margery said. Helen knew he wasn't. That wasn't poison gas she'd smelled, but death and decay.

"Let's turn him over to make sure," Trevor said. He moved the body enough so they could see the face. It was obvious the man was dead.

It was also obvious he was Page Turner III.

What was a dead Page Turner doing in Peggy's bed?

He sure wasn't there when the place was tented on Saturday. Helen could testify to that. She'd seen Peggy's empty bed. She'd watched Trevor lock the door.

Did Peggy know Page? Helen had never heard her mention his name. She'd never seen the man at the Coronado.

So how did Page get in that apartment? Who knifed him in the back? It had to have happened this weekend, when the place was tented and pumped full of poison gas.

Peggy's door was double-locked. She didn't have the key to open her own home. The only one who could get in the tented building alive was Trevor.

Helen thought Trevor had acted oddly from the moment Page Turner's body was found. While Margery called 911, Trevor whipped out his cell phone and called an attorney.

"Now, that looks suspicious," Helen whispered to her landlady as they waited for the police. "An innocent man wouldn't need a lawyer."

"An innocent African-American man would," Margery said. "This state has an impressive record of railroading black people."

"I can see him getting a lawyer if the police questioned him," Helen said. "But I can't understand Trevor having a lawyer ready unless he was guilty."

"You'd make a good cop," Margery said. It was not a compliment.

Helen counted six police cars, sirens blaring and lights flashing. "We're going to have a swarm of police," Margery said. "Page Turner was a big political donor. His pals are going to put pressure on the police to solve his death. They'll turn this place inside out."

Helen was suddenly aware of the afternoon sun beating down on them. She felt dizzy. Peggy looked ready to pass out. Cal was sweating in a most un-Canadian way. Even Margery was wilted.

Two grim-looking homicide detectives arrived and asked everyone to wait in their apartments, after their places had been searched. Search warrants materialized.

"Do they suspect us?" Helen said, horrified.

"They suspect everybody," Margery said. "This will be quick. They're making sure we don't flush away any evidence, or pull a gun on them, before they send us to our rooms."

The Coronado was armed to the rooftop. Floridians liked their firepower. Margery had a .38 police special and a permit for it. Madame Muffy had a neat little .22. The big surprise was Cal. He had a whopping Smith & Wesson .44 Magnum. "For protection," he said. "America has more crime than Canada."

Helen didn't have any weapons. She wondered if that made her look suspicious. When Margery got the OK to return to her apartment, Helen started to follow her, but the two detectives would not let the women stay together.

"I need to use Margery's phone," Helen said. "I'm working at Page Turner's bookstore tonight. I have to call the manager and tell her I'll be late." She also wanted to tell the booksellers their boss was dead in Peggy's bed.

"Sorry, ma'am," the detective said. "We'll notify the bookstore that you won't be in to work."

"I'm going to miss a whole night?" Should she sound more distraught over Page's death? She couldn't. Damn that man. She would not be paid for this lost time. Page Turner cost her another forty-six dollars and ninety cents.

The cops meant business. Uniformed officers were posted at the Coronado entrances.

Helen went to her apartment and paced. Thumbs paced with her. The sirens hurt his ears and the unexpected activity unsettled him. Helen was equally jumpy. Police made her nervous. What if they found out she was on the run? They'd ship her back to St. Louis. She tried to imagine life without the Coronado. She needed the sunset wine sessions with Peggy by the flower-draped pool. The jibes of her purple-clad landlady. The taffeta rustle of palm trees and the perpetual burning-leaf smell of Phil's weed.

Oh, my Lord, she thought. Phil! He must have slipped back in during the excitement. If he was in a marijuana daze, he'd be busted for sure. She had to warn him. She'd never seen him, but he'd saved her life once. She owed him. She opened her door and saw the uniformed police officer at his post. She was about to make a warning racket when she sniffed the air. It reeked of patchouli oil, the scent of the sixties. Phil must have set fire to a barrel of the stuff. He was safe.

For the rest of the evening, Helen stood at the window and stared out between the slits of her miniblinds. She watched the crime-scene unit arrive, two women. Then the Broward County medical examiner, a man. The police brass were next, all men, all self-important.

It was seven o'clock when the two homicide detectives, Tom Levinson and Clarence Jax, knocked on her door. Jax was short and burly, with abrupt, aggressive movements. He had red hair and freckles and, she suspected, the temper to go with them. Levinson was taller and slimmer, with a rugged face and dark hair. He had quick, light movements, and Helen wondered if he'd had martial-arts training. Even in their boxy suits, Helen could see the muscles bulging on their thighs, arms, and shoulders. Too bad they were cops.

Jax sat down on her turquoise couch with the black triangle pattern. Levinson was walking around, examining the 1950s furniture—the lamps like nuclear reactors, the boomerang coffee table. "Neat stuff you've got here," he said, but he wasn't admiring her secondhand furniture. That cop had eyes like a laser. What was he looking for? Drugs? Contraband? Evidence she'd killed Page Turner? Could he see the suitcase stuffed with seven thousand dollars stashed back in her closet?

She offered the men coffee or soda. Both said no. Jax wanted to get down to business. "Your name?"

"Helen Hawthorne," she said. The first words out of my mouth are a lie, she thought.

"How long have you lived at the Coronado?"

"About eight months," she said, glad she could tell the truth that time.

"And before that?"

I was crisscrossing the country, hoping to lose my pursuers. Before that, I was in St. Louis, living in a fool's paradise with an unfaithful husband.

"I was in the Midwest, like most Floridians. Nobody's from here." Helen tried to smile. Her lips were dry and awkward.

"Where in the Midwest?" Jax's question sounded casual, but she was sure it wasn't. His partner, Levinson, was still laser-searching her apartment, picking up knickknacks, examining flower vases. She wished she could hold Thumbs, but her cat had abandoned her. He was hiding under the bed. She wanted to join him.

Where indeed? She couldn't say St. Louis. Jax would find out about her past for sure. She knew Chicago well, but didn't have a Chicago accent. Helen picked a city she figured no one knew anything about.

"Cincinnati."

"Nice city on the river. Sort of like St. Louis, where I went to college, except Cincinnati makes better use of its river views. Where'd you live in Cincy?"

"Near the baseball stadium," she said. The only thing she knew about Cincinnati was that it had a stadium like St. Louis. Just her luck Jax knew St. Louis. Helen was sweating now. She could feel sweat popping out on her forehead, running down her arms. She looked Jax in the eye and wondered if all liars did that. A fat drop of sweat plopped into her lap.

She was relieved when he switched to questions about Page and the termite tenting. Yes, she and Margery had accompanied Trevor on the final walk-through. She saw nothing suspicious in Peggy's apartment. Certainly no bodies.

Yes, she knew Page Turner. She worked at his bookstore. What kind of person was he?

A rat, she thought. A cheat, a liar, a seducer. A rich man who stiffed his poor help.

"He wasn't real popular with the staff," Helen said. She figured Jax would find that out fast enough. "He closed two stores and let the booksellers go without any severance. He bounced our paychecks." Well, not mine, she thought. I was paid in cash. But she couldn't mention that, either.

"Was anyone mad enough to kill him?"

We all were, Helen thought. "What good would that do?" she said. "The stores would still be closed."

Did Page have any friends or visitors his last day at the store? What time did he leave? Did he seem concerned, worried, angry, or upset?

"I think he was drunk," Helen said.

Jax hit her with a hailstorm of questions, but she could answer them honestly. She began to relax. Did Page Turner drive away or did someone pick him up that last Friday? Did he have many visitors at the store? Who? Men? Women? Both? Did his guests stay after hours? What kind of cars did they drive? Did Helen know their names or what they did?

"One of his regular visitors was Burt Plank," she said. She did not mention the sex videos they supposedly watched.

Who would benefit if Page died?

No one, Helen thought, except maybe his wife. "I don't know," she said. "I don't know anything about his private life." But I've heard a lot of ugly rumors.

Jax's other questions were about Peggy, and how and why Page was in her apartment. Helen said she was a friend of Peggy's. They sat out by the pool after work and talked. No, Peggy was not dating Mr. Turner. Helen didn't think she even knew him. Peggy had never mentioned his name.

To her knowledge, Peggy was not dating anyone. She'd never seen a man at Peggy's apartment, or a woman, for that matter. Peggy lived alone, except for her parrot, Pete. She had a job. She was an office manager for some place in Cypress Creek, but she never discussed it. She talked mainly about her plans to win the lottery.

Funny, lively Peggy sounded so sad when Helen described her life. Peggy wasn't a sad person, was she? Helen asked herself that question. Jax continued to bombard her with others:

"Where was Peggy Friday night?"

"At the beach barbecue with everyone else," Helen said. "She brought a salad."

"When did she leave?"

Helen had no idea. She didn't see Peggy all weekend. She didn't see anyone but Rich.

Helen signed a statement saying all her lies were true and the detectives left. She still couldn't go anywhere. They were interviewing other Coronado residents.

Only one good thing happened that evening. At five o'clock, a florist arrived with a dozen red roses for Helen. The police checked out the vase, then let the flowers through. They were gorgeous, with extravagant bloodred petals and a heady hothouse perfume. They were the first flowers Helen had received since her tenth anniversary with the man who betrayed her. The card said simply, *Forever— Love, Rich.* Helen wasn't sure she was ready for forever, not after one weekend, no matter how good.

She was haunted by the scene in Peggy's bedroom: The rich man dead in the sumptuous bed. The bloated body on the sensuous sheets.

Death was forever, not love.

Chapter 7

That night, Helen's worst fears crawled out from where she'd buried them. She saw Page Turner dead. She saw herself in handcuffs. The police would figure out who she was and send her back to St. Louis and the court's cold justice.

Homicide detective Clarence Jax and his partner, Tom Levinson, were smart. She saw how Tom had laser-eyed her home. She heard Jax's questions. Jax had gone to school in her hometown. He could easily find out she was on the run, if he started checking. She'd changed her name, but not her appearance.

She could grab her suitcase full of cash and hit the road, but that would look even more suspicious. If she was lucky, she was a minor part of a major investigation. If she ran, she'd become the focus for all the wrong reasons. Reason said to sit tight. Panic told her to flee.

She wished she'd talked to Margery after the police left last night, but she fell asleep in the warm rose-scented evening and did not wake up until after midnight. Now Margery's lights were off.

She sat on her bed, holding her cat Thumbs and waiting for dawn. His soft warm fur and contented purr comforted her, and made her believe that everything would be better in daylight. Then she saw Page Turner again, gray-green with death. Suddenly, Helen remembered there was something odd about his body. He'd been knifed in the back, but there was no blood. Why? Was he already dead from the Vikane gas when he was stabbed? Or did the knife hold in the blood?

Helen wished she felt sorry that Page was dead, but she didn't like the man. His death created even more problems than his life. Would the new bookstore management honor Helen's cash-under-the-table deal? Would the store stay open? Or would it close, too, now that its namesake was dead? That was a death she would mourn. The old store with its book nooks and wing chairs was a lovely place.

At seven that morning, she saw the lights were on in Margery's kitchen and knocked on the door. She found Peggy wrapped in Margery's purple chenille bathrobe, pale and shaken, a cup of coffee growing cold in front of her.

"How long did the police talk with you?" Helen said.

"Hours," Peggy said.

"What did they ask you?"

"Everything."

It was all she could get out of her red-haired friend. Peggy took one bite out of a chocolate croissant and left it on her plate. When Margery brought in the newspaper, Peggy didn't even check the winning lottery numbers.

Margery, in shorts the color of an old bruise, was smoking like a pre-EPA chimney and talking to herself. Her muttering was interspersed with earsplitting shrieks from Pete. Peggy's apartment was still a crime scene, so she and Pete stayed the night with Margery. The landlady was not happy about living with a parrot. It was hard to pretend Pete didn't exist when he was squawking in the kitchen.

"Does he have to throw seed around like that?" she complained.

Peggy roused herself from her stupor. "He's upset. I'll clean it up."

"Do they make parrot Prozac?" Margery said.

Helen wondered if they made landlady Prozac. "I wish you could stay at my place," she told Peggy, "but I don't think Pete and Thumbs would get along in close quarters."

"It's only for a day or so," Peggy said. Then she went back to staring at her cooling cup of coffee.

"Let's see if anybody talked to the reporters last night," Margery said, and flipped on the local TV news.

Page's death was the lead story. She was not surprised that the police had taken Trevor the termite fumigator in for questioning. There was a shot of him going into police headquarters accompanied by an African-American man with a briefcase.

The bizarre death of Page Turner had attracted hordes of reporters. They'd hung around the Coronado parking lot last night, trying to interview the Coronado residents. Peggy had no comment. Phil the invisible pothead was nowhere to be seen. Margery's response to the TV reporters had to be bleeped.

But Cal the Canadian expounded on the violence of American society. And drab little Madame Muffy came to life in front of the cameras. She looked young and pretty on TV. Her dull clothes gave her a credibility that fringe and beads would not. She told the reporters she'd predicted Page's murder when she read Peggy's palm.

"I saw death, destruction, and murder," Madame Muffy said. "Her fatal future was written in her palm. Peggy had a dark aura."

Helen thought this was a violation of client confidentiality.

"I went to the bookstore to warn Page Turner of his impending death, but he did not want to be saved from his terrible fate. He laughed at me."

Helen remembered the scene at the bookstore, where Page called Muffy crazy and threw her out of his office. At least she was telling the truth about that.

Madame Muffy's sensational interview added to Helen's misery. Page Turner's murder could become a national story. Helen could not be seen on TV.

"I can't go to work if the reporters are still in the parking lot," she said. "If this gets on network TV, my ex might find me." Margery knew Helen's ex was looking for her but she didn't know why. Her landlady looked out her back window and said, "It's safe. They're gone."

Helen was relieved—until she got to Page Turners. This morning, the press pack was waiting outside the bookstore. Helen ducked around back and pounded on the loading-dock door until Albert opened it. The day manager was pale as a lost soul. His white shirt was wilted. The starch had gone out of him, too.

"What should I do? The store opens in fifteen minutes. Should I let in those reporters?"

"Call Gayle's cell phone and ask her," Helen said. Albert seemed relieved to yield his authority to the night manager.

She could hear Gayle shout her answer. "For God's sake, don't let them in the store."

"There are so many, how will I hold them off?" Albert said, desperate as General Custer at Little Bighorn.

"Keep the doors locked. I'm on my way."

Helen saw Brad elbowing his way through the reporters. Albert unlocked the door and the little bookseller slid inside. His shirt was twisted and his hair stuck out at odd angles. "Today, it's reporters," he said, straightening his clothes. "Yesterday, it was the police. You missed that, Helen. They found the sex videos. Dozens of them. Took them out by the boxload."

"So they really exist."

"Oh, yeah. I bet there's going to be cops begging for that assignment. I heard you saw the body. Was it horrible?"

"The worst. I won't ever forget."

"Did Page Turner suffer?"

"I don't think so," Helen said.

"Too bad," he spat. Helen did not know how Brad's skinny body could hold so much hate. She was afraid it would overflow and scald her.

Helen hid in the break room and made phone calls. She thanked Rich for the wonderful roses. He'd heard about the murder and wanted to take her away, but Helen insisted she was fine. She talked with her friend Sarah, who was equally worried. Helen assured her that she'd be all right.

At nine-fifteen, Gayle arrived, an avenging angel in Doc Martens and a black turtleneck. She read a prepared statement asking the press to respect the Turner family privacy and please stay out of the store. The reporters interviewed customers going in and out for a while, then drifted away.

Rich called again at eleven. And at noon. And at one and two. Albert, his composure regained, frowned with disapproval every time. "It's your boyfriend," he'd say, handing her the phone like it was a dead fish. When Rich called at four she said, "I appreciate your concern, but I can't keep taking personal calls at work."

"I'm worried about you," he said. "There's a killer loose."

"I'm fine. I'm in a bookstore. It's perfectly safe."

"That's what Page Turner thought. Be careful talking to strange men."

"It's South Florida. All the men are strange." A man walked up to her register, his feet making an odd *slap-slap* sound. He wore a Hawaiian shirt that clashed with his tattoos. Helen looked down and saw knobby knees and Day-Glo swim fins.

"Forgot my shoes," he said, and handed her a copy of *Guns & Ammo*.

Helen put Rich on hold while she rang up Swim Fins, and hoped he wouldn't be there when she came back.

But he was, giving advice and orders. "Don't speak to any men. Don't encourage them in any way. It could be a serial killer. They're attracted to unstable situations. It's where they hunt women."

"Rich, I'm forty-two. I can take care of myself. I really have to go. Please don't call again. I need this job."

This is Page Turner's fault, she thought. His death had unleashed some streak of protective paranoia in Rich. It was ruining her romance.

Page was not done causing problems for Helen. When she got off work at six that night, Helen called Margery and asked if the TV reporters were back at the Coronado.

"I ran them off my parking lot, but the damn satellite trucks are parked in the street, thanks to that blasted Madame Muffy," Margery said. "She's outside talking to them again. I ought to raise her rent. I can't even sit out by the pool with a glass of wine or I'll wind up on TV looking like a lush. Call me in another hour, and I'll let you know if they've left."

Helen sat in the café, eating free, slightly stale eggplant sandwiches and drinking coffee bought with her employee discount. She found a paper on the table and read the employment ads. Most were for people with special training: Welder . . . window installer . . . wood finisher. All skills Helen didn't have.

Wait! Here was something she could do. A "busy young company" wanted a word processor. They paid nine dollars and eighty cents an hour, good money in South Florida. *Must know spelling and grammar*, the ad said. *Fax résumé attn. Sally*. There was no address or phone, only the fax number.

Helen checked her watch. It was seven p.m. She slipped into the bookstore's deserted office and typed up a résumé with impressive speed. That alone should qualify me for the job, she thought. She checked it for errors. Perfect.

She tried to fax the résumé, but the line was busy. She kept trying in between calls to Margery. She still had not gotten through to the company by ten o'clock, when Margery told her it was safe to come home. Helen figured the busy young company must have taken the phone off the hook.

The next morning at Page Turners, she faxed the résumé once again. The line was busy. She tried fifteen minutes later. Still busy. She tried all morning whenever she could get into the office. The fax line stayed busy.

At noon, Helen called the phone company to see if something was wrong. The fax line was not out of order. By five o'clock, Helen knew she didn't have a chance for this dream job. The company must have had hundreds of faxes already. The phone line was jammed with job hopefuls.

But she tried the fax line one more time before she left. It was still busy.

That night, the TV news stories said Trevor the termite fumigator was cleared. Margery had the inside scoop when Helen got home. No reporters were lurking about, so Margery was smoking and sipping a screwdriver out by the pool. Peggy and Pete were nowhere to be seen.

"I called a friend on the force," Margery said. "I found out Trevor had an alibi for the time of the murder, but he'd been hiding something. They cut him loose because he had no connection to the murder."

"How come?"

"Can't find out any more. My source clammed up."

"I know who will tell us," Helen said. "I have my own inside source."

"You do?" Margery couldn't hide her surprise.

"Sure, Trevor. We got along great on the final walk-through. I think we bonded after I had to take that frozen urine sample out to the Dumpster. If he's innocent, he'll want to tell the world. We can talk to him tomorrow. I don't go in to work until eleven."

Helen called the termite company the next morning and said the crew had left some clamshell clamps behind and she would drop them off if Trevor was working in the area. The receptionist told her where Trevor was tenting on Hollywood Boulevard. Margery drove Helen there in her big white Cadillac. Helen thought it was like driving a living room. The seats were like sofas. There was room for a coffee table and a TV.

They found Trevor tenting a two-story motel. Trevor looked a little thinner after his ordeal, and he seemed a bit subdued. But he did not mind telling them what happened. They stood out by the motel pool and Trevor worked on a cylinder of Vikane gas. Helen was fascinated that the top of the gas cylinder was coated with dry-ice frost.

"Everything looked normal on Monday morning," he said. "I put on my SCBA gear and went into your tented building. Nothing was disturbed. No one had touched the clamps on the tent. Except when I opened Peggy's apartment, I found that man, Page Turner, on the bed. One look and I knew he was dead."

"It must have been horrible," Helen said. She remembered those hot, dark rooms, the canvas flapping ominously in the breeze.

"It was a shock," Trevor admitted, connecting the Vikane to a plastic hose. "I turned the dead man over enough to see the face. He was starting to smell like a meat freezer when the electricity went off. I'd never seen him before. I thought somehow this man died of Vikane. It was all my fault. I didn't check the room."

"But you did," Helen said. "Margery and I were with you. We would have said you did your job."

"I wasn't thinking," Trevor said. "I knew there would be trouble. I was a black man. This was a white neighborhood."

Maybe Trevor did not believe that two white women would stand up for him.

"I was the only one who could go into the tent when it was filled with tear gas and poison. I had the breathing apparatus. I was the first and easiest suspect. I panicked, shut the door, then relocked it. I did not tell George and Terrell, the guys working on the tent. I was sweating, but not from the heat. I completed my rounds, all the while asking myself, Should I move the body? Should I dump it in the Everglades? How am I gonna haul a body out of here? The neighbors are watching.

"For a long time, I sat in my truck, thinking about what to do. This was a fumigator's worst nightmare. The only people who would understand how I felt were other fumigators. So I called two friends in the business. They gave good advice. They told me moving the body was only going to make me look guilty. 'Stay cool,' they said. 'Get a lawyer.' They knew a good one who would work cheap for a brother."

"So what did you do?"

"I saw the lawyer," he said. "When it came time to open the doors Monday afternoon, I unlocked Peggy's apartment and looked surprised. I pretended I'd never seen that dead man before.

"When the cops showed up, I was the number one suspect, just like I expected. The fact that I had a lawyer made the cops more suspicious. I went downtown for a talk with them. The company had their lawyer. I had mine. Next, the state inspector weighed in, looking for violations. I sat tight and kept my mouth shut, like my lawyer said. But I was sweating.

"The autopsy report saved me. It said the body had been dead since Friday night, not Saturday. That's twenty-four hours longer than anyone guessed. There were fly eggs, but the flies didn't develop very far. They were killed by the Vikane.

"But the autopsy said Page Turner did not die of Vikane poisoning." He was checking gauges on the Vikane cylinder.

"Well, no. He had a knife in his back," Margery said.

"But that knife didn't kill him, either. The coroner said he was smothered with a pillow. While drunk."

"That's why we didn't see any blood," Helen said.

"The stab wound in the back was inflicted after death," Trevor said. He sounded like he'd memorized the autopsy report. "A butcher knife had been found in the body, and there were prints on the knife, but the police didn't tell me who they belonged to. I was just happy they weren't mine.

"Page Turner had died Friday night, before the Vikane was ever pumped into the building. I can't tell you how relieved I felt. I had nothing to do with that man's death.

"Also, he'd been moved. The blood had pooled in the lower body. The police found evidence the body was kept in the closet and dragged out later. They believe that we passed right by the closet where the body was stashed. It was covered by some long bridesmaids' dresses."

"Glad somebody found a use for those things," Margery said.

Helen and Trevor ignored her.

"The man was probably murdered between eight and midnight on Friday, and that's what saved me. I was coaching my church's softball team. We won the division finals and had a victory party afterward. I was not only in the photos, I was in the video, with a time-and-date stamp. It was two a.m. when I finally went home. Page Turner was long dead by then. Besides, the police could find no connection between me and Turner."

"So you were off the hook," Helen said.

"Mostly. But the police knew I knew something. I made a deal with them. My lawyer and I explained why I'd delayed informing the police about the dead body for twenty-four hours. I got a lecture and was released."

He checked the gauges again and the clear plastic hoses. Helen heard the hissing of the Vikane gas, releasing more death. She wanted out of there. She and Margery congratulated Trevor and left.

On the ride home, Helen said, "I knew Trevor didn't do it."

"Oh, really?" Margery said. "You were ready to convict him when he called his lawyer."

Helen wasn't proud of that. "I heard the cops found the tapes with all Page's naked girlfriends," she said, hoping to change the subject. "That will keep them busy for years. We have nothing to worry about."

But Margery looked worried indeed.

Chapter 8

"You don't know anything," the woman said.

"Ma'am, I need either the title or the author," Helen said. "I can't find the book without one or the other. Please give me more information."

"I saw that book in your store last month. It had a blue cover," the woman said triumphantly, as if she'd produced a crucial fact.

"I'm sorry, but we have a hundred thousand books," Helen said. "Lots of them have blue covers."

"You're an idiot," the woman said, and turned her back on Helen.

I must be, Helen thought, to take this abuse for six seventy an hour. She used to think bookstores were genteel places to work. Now she knew how mean some customers could be. They seemed to get almost physical satisfaction from insulting clerks.

It had been a bad day at the store. She'd also had to deal with a young weasel who tried to return a stolen Bible. Helen had watched him shoplift it, sliding it into his backpack. The Bible was the store's most shoplifted book. Now he had the nerve to come up to the counter, take out the boosted Bible, and claim he lost the sales receipt. The weasel spat four-letter words at her when she confiscated the Bible and refused to give him any money.

"Thou shalt not steal," she told him. He took the Lord's name in vain. Then the Bible stealer left.

The bad customers looked like animals today, she thought, weasels and pigs with the dispositions of wolverines.

The nice customers were worse. They asked the questions Helen wished she could answer: When was Page Turner's funeral? Would the store close for the service? Would it close permanently? Who was in charge now? Albert was the day manager, but he didn't know any more than Helen did. He stood around in his starched shirt, sweating and wringing his pale hands, afraid to make the smallest decision.

A blonde came up to the counter with *Tuesdays with Morrie*. She was stick-thin with balloon breasts, sexy sandals, and a silver toe ring. "I'm devastated by Page's death," she said softly, and Helen noticed her red, swollen eyes. "He once told me this was the best book when you lost someone you cared about, but I never thought I'd need it for him." Her voice faltered for a moment, then steadied. "We used to talk about books for hours upstairs in his office."

Helen saw how the blonde filled out her white halter top. Another pigeon, she thought.

"They had such lovely literary discussions," said the little brown mother hen with her. "You don't find many men who can talk about books in South Florida. And to die in such a senseless way."

"We're all sorry, ma'am," Helen said, sliding the book into a bag.

But she wasn't, and neither was anyone else who worked

at Page Turners. Helen felt like a fraud as she made fake sounds of sympathy to the customers.

Only Matt, the bookseller who'd walked off the job when his paycheck bounced, came out and said it. He stopped at the store the morning after Page Turner's murder hit the news. Matt's dreads were as luxuriant as ever, but his usual white T-shirt was black.

"You're out of uniform," Helen said. "What's with the black? You in mourning for Page?"

"I'm not wasting any tears over that man. I heard you found the body."

"It was dreadful. He had a butcher knife in his back."

"I told you he'd pay," Matt said. "The man passed, but it wasn't easy. He's gone and I'm glad."

Helen was, too. But she couldn't bring herself to say so. This store has pigs, pigeons, hens, and weasels, she thought. You can add another animal to the menagerie. I'm a rat. I've got to get out of retail. I'm beginning to hate the human race. I need a nice desk job. Someplace without a cash register. I need to get off my feet.

Before Helen started at Page Turners, she had no idea how physically hard a bookstore job could be. Booksellers were not allowed to sit when they worked the cash register. Cheap Page did not carpet the cashiers' area. He wouldn't even spring for rubber mats. After eight hours of standing on concrete, her feet hurt so badly she could hardly walk home. Her back ached and kept her awake at night.

"The key to survival," Gayle told her, "is to get the ugliest shoes with the thickest soles you can find."

Helen spent sixty dollars she couldn't afford for cushion-soled lace-ups too styleless for her grandmother. Gayle was right. The thick soles helped. But the pain never really went away.

Now that she was cut back to thirty hours a week, Helen had time for a serious job search. She'd had an interview with a good prospect after work. An accounting firm wanted an office assistant.

The office was in a new building four blocks from the Coronado. Helen saw herself sitting at a clean, well-lighted desk with a comfortable chair and a potted philodendron. The pay was better than the bookstore: eight fifty an hour. The requirements would be laughable anywhere but South Florida. *Must have neat appearance and speak fluent English*, the ad said. Local standards could be delightfully low. Helen hoped she could persuade the owner to pay her in cash off the books. She'd settle for eight dollars an hour.

At four-thirty, Helen put on fresh lipstick, combed her hair, and checked her panty hose for runs. No doubt about it, she looked neat. She walked confidently to what she hoped would be her new job. The door to the office suite was a solid slab of mahogany with a discreet silver plaque: THE HANSELMEYER COMPANY. The old corporate part of her responded immediately and approved. The receptionist's desk was equally impressive, and the woman behind it was a dignified fifty instead of some fluffy young chick. Another good sign.

The owner, Selwyn Hanselmeyer, looked like a snake in a suit, but Helen figured she could put up with him. He had a flat face, yellow eyes that never blinked, and a large bulge in his midsection. Helen wondered if he'd swallowed a piglet for lunch.

Just beyond his door, she glimpsed the office cubicles, padded with soft gray fabric to deaden sound. Even ordinary office workers had big leather executive chairs. She longed to sit in one. On the closest desk, she saw a framed baby picture and a philodendron in a blue pot. The throne-like chair was empty. It was waiting for her.

Please let me get this job, she prayed. I'll work for a snake. It won't be so bad.

Hanselmeyer was so short, she suspected he'd jacked up

his chair to make himself look taller. He did not rise when Helen entered the room. He probably didn't want to be measured against her six feet. Instead, she looked down on his elaborate comb-over. She wondered if it hid a diamond-back pattern.

Helen recognized his first questions as part of the standard employee interview. He wanted to know her goals and past experience. Helen lied about both. She truthfully said she was skilled in all the right software.

When Hanselmeyer asked what job she wanted in ten years, Helen knew not to say, "Yours." The snake asked when she would be available.

"Tomorrow," she said.

Could she could work overtime? "I love overtime." Yes! she thought.

Then he hissed, "Do you hear that old biological clock ticking?"

"I beg your pardon?" Helen said. She wasn't sure what this had to do with typing and filing.

"I know I shouldn't ask, but are you planning to have children?"

"I'm not married," Helen said.

"Unmarried women can have children," Hanselmeyer said, pointing to the empty desk. "That girl out there had herself a turkey-baster baby because she was afraid time was running out. Now she's off half the time taking care of the kid. It's always sick. Got croup today. I can't fire her or I'll have the libbers all over me. Maybe it's a little illegal to ask, but are you going to have kids?"

Helen wasn't. But she could feel her anger burst in her brain in a red-hot shower. How dare he? He only asked because she was powerless. He knew he could get away with a question that was piercingly personal and definitely illegal.

"Oh, dear, I wouldn't want you to do anything illegal, Mr. Hanselmeyer," she said. "So I won't answer that."

Oh, damn, she thought. There goes my chance to ask the snake to pay me in cash under the table. That's illegal, too. Well, I couldn't work for the slithering SOB, anyway.

She stood up and said, "Thank you for your time."

On the way out, she gave the desk with the leather chair one last lingering look.

Helen dragged herself home to the Coronado, tired and discouraged. Margery poked her gray head out her door and yelled, "Pick your face off the sidewalk. That boyfriend of yours is on the phone."

"Rich?" she said. She'd asked Rich never to call her landlady unless there was an emergency.

"You dating someone else?" Tonight, Margery's shorts were a militant mulberry. They clashed alarmingly with her plum sandals and crimson toenail polish.

Helen picked up Margery's phone with a fluttering heart. "What's wrong?"

"I couldn't reach you all day." Rich sounded whiny, her least favorite male mood. "I called the store six times. No one answered."

"I'm sorry, Rich. We were swamped because of Page's death. When that happens, the phones go unanswered."

"How are you?" he said. "Are you avoiding strange men at the store, like I told you?"

She wanted to tell him not to be so foolish, but she wasn't going to fight on Margery's phone.

"Look, I don't want to tie up Margery's phone. She may be expecting a call."

"Then let's talk tomorrow night. We could go to my place. I'll pick you up after work and throw a couple of steaks on the grill. You can meet Beans and Sissy."

His pets—at his place. For Rich, meeting his animals was like meeting the family. Beans was a basset hound

who'd been brought to the clinic with terminal flatulence.
The exasperated owner wanted to put the gasbag to sleep,
but Rich adopted the dog instead. Helen thought that was
sweet. Sissy was a regal gray Persian. Helen had not been
to Rich's home yet, so she'd only heard about the animals.
This was a step forward in their relationship.

"Helen," he said, "why don't you let me buy you a
phone?"

Helen did not want to be in any phone company computer. She'd be too easy to trace.

"Thanks, Rich, but I'd rather not."

"Don't let your pride get in the way. I know you can't afford one, but I can. You can keep it with you and then I can
talk to you anytime I want."

Anytime he wanted. The phrase lodged uneasily in
Helen's mind. Would that also be anytime she wanted? She
could see Margery in the kitchen, pacing impatiently back
and forth, smoking a cigarette, the red tips of her fingers
and her cigarette glowing in the evening shadows.

"I can't talk now, Rich," she said. "I'm tying up
Margery's phone. I'll see you tomorrow night at six. Your
roses were still gorgeous this morning." She hung up.

"Everything OK with lover boy?" Margery said. She
blew a wreath of smoke.

"Just fine." Helen had a feeling her landlady knew she
was lying. "Gotta go." She almost fled out the door to
avoid talking about Rich. She ran straight into a wall of
heat. Even at six-thirty, it was a force. Helen liked it better
than artificially chilled rooms. She was ready for a cool
drink by the pool.

Pete and Peggy were already out there. Helen waved at
them, but Peggy didn't respond. She was staring into space.
She hadn't been herself since the murder.

Why should she? Helen thought. Peggy had found a dead
man in her bed. Once the police tape came off the door,

would Peggy ever sleep in that soft, sensual bed again? Or would she always share it with a bloating corpse?

Helen was worried about her friend. Peggy seemed drained and lifeless. Her dark red hair was flat, and her long elegant nose seemed more beaklike than ever. Maybe a glass of wine would cheer her up.

"Want a drink?" Helen called across the courtyard.

"Yes," Peggy said. She sounded like she was sleepwalking. Pete let out a raucous squawk. "Don't bring any crackers. He's getting fatter."

Helen opened her apartment door and was hit with the funeral-parlor scent of dying flowers. She'd turned off her air conditioner when she went to work that morning, to save money. The heat must have roasted her roses. The dropped petals looked like spots of blood on her coffee table. Rich's gorgeous gift was dead too soon.

Helen sighed, threw the roses in the trash, and dumped the water down the sink. Then she slipped into shorts, found two wineglasses, and pulled a new box of wine out of the refrigerator. Out by the pool, she poured them both drinks.

Peggy took a sip and made a face. "What flavor is this?"

"'Blush pink,'" Helen said, reading the name on the box.

"It should blush if it's trying to pass itself off as wine. Tastes like Kool-Aid. Who made it—Jim Jones?"

"Guess that explains why it was on sale," Helen said.

Peggy set her wineglass down by her cordless phone. "I'm expecting a call," she said. "I've got this great idea for winning the lottery, this special system. I'm waiting for some information so I can choose my lucky numbers."

"Another system?" Helen asked. "Why is this one different?"

"Because I'm going to win this time. I've figured out what it takes. I don't want to jinx it by talking about it before it comes true. But this phone call will change my life."

The more she talked about the lottery, the livelier Peggy became. When the phone rang a few minutes later, both women jumped. Peggy grabbed the phone and scrambled to hit the talk button. She listened a moment, then said, "Yes, I am." She stared at the phone for a second before she snapped it off.

"Wrong number," she said. "Some woman asked, 'Are you Margaret Freeton?' When I said yes, she hung up."

"That doesn't make any sense. If it was a wrong number, why would she know your name?" Helen said.

"You don't suppose it's a burglar or something, calling to see if I'm at home?"

"Could be. I'd tell Margery to be safe. She'll keep a watch on your place when you're not around."

They heard car doors slamming. Lots of them. Helen couldn't believe what happened next. A small army of police officers fanned across the yard, taking combat positions. Two men in plainclothes materialized. Helen and Peggy stared at them, openmouthed. Helen saw Margery's door open. Their landlady looked equally shocked.

It's a drug bust, Helen thought. The cops have finally busted Phil the invisible pothead.

The plainclothes officers were homicide detectives Clarence Jax and Tom Levinson. Helen wondered what they were doing on a drug bust.

"Margaret Freeton?" Detective Jax asked.

"Yes?" said Peggy.

"We have a warrant for your arrest."

"What?" Peggy said. She didn't understand what was happening. Neither did Helen. Margery was marching toward them, a purple-clad protector, demanding, "What is the meaning of this? What are you doing on my property?"

The detectives ignored her. "You are being charged with murder in the first degree in the death of Page Turner III,"

Jax said. He read the Miranda warning and started to cuff Peggy's hands. Pete bit him hard.

"Get that damned bird away from me or I'll wring his neck."

Peggy freed the detective's bleeding finger and gently handed Pete to Helen. The parrot struggled, but did not fight Helen. He stayed perched on her hand and she stroked his feathers with one finger to soothe him. The detective cuffed Peggy's hands behind her back.

"Is that necessary?" Helen said.

"It wasn't necessary for that bird to bite me," he said.

"I didn't kill Page Turner," Peggy said.

"We'll get you a good lawyer," Margery said. "Don't say a word until she shows up."

"Please take care of Pete," Peggy cried. "His birdseed is in your cabinet. It's the red box. Don't overfeed him. He's on a diet."

"Shut up," Margery said. "Promise me, not another word until your lawyer gets there."

As the police took Peggy away in handcuffed shame, Helen could hear her phone ringing and ringing, with the call that was supposed to change her life. Madame Muffy's prediction was complete. Death, destruction, and murder had buried Peggy in a dark landslide.

A dazed Helen said, "How could they arrest Peggy for murder?"

"Because she probably did it," Margery said.

"Peggy didn't even know Page Turner," Helen said.

"Of course she did," Margery said. "They were engaged."

Helen was too stunned to say anything. The woman at the bookstore was right, she thought. I am an idiot. And I don't know anything.

Chapter 9

"Tell me why you think Peggy did it," Helen asked Margery.

The question had been hanging over them for the last two hours. Margery had been working the phone to find a lawyer for Peggy. She called friends and called in favors. She asked everyone, If you were in trouble, who would you call?

It came down to two lawyers: Oliver Steinway and Colby Cox. "Both are good. But Steinway's defended so many killers that hiring him is practically an admission of guilt," Margery said. "Colby is a little more low-profile. We'll go with her."

Then Margery called more numbers, until she found Cox at her home. It was now nine p.m. "She doesn't live far away. She's on the Isle of Capri. Want to come with me?"

Capri was one of several small islands connected to Las Olas by causeways. The residents were connected by lots of money. On the drive over, Margery said, "That Detective Jax is damn smart. He came back again today, batting his eyes and saying he needed to confirm the times when everyone arrived and left the barbecue Friday night. He didn't seem interested in one particular person, but I should have known."

"Known what?" Helen said.

"That he was after Peggy. She was the only one who came late and left early." Margery hit the steering wheel with her hand. "I'm an old fool. I told him the times. I could have said I didn't remember, but no, I had to prove I had such a great memory. I hope I haven't talked that poor girl into the electric chair."

She thinks Peggy is guilty, Helen thought, but she was too frightened to say the words. Margery swung her big white car into the driveway of Cox's tract mansion, a pink stucco affair the size of a hotel. The small forest of royal palms sheltering it was lit like a stage set. As they drove up, the security gates swung open. Cox must be one successful lawyer.

"Wait out here," Margery said. "I'll just be a minute."

Helen suspected Margery was writing a sizable check and didn't want her to know. Waiting in the Cadillac was like sitting in a plush lounge, but Helen could not relax. It all seemed so surreal. Peggy would be on trial for murder. The police had said first-degree murder. Was that the bad one? Florida was a death-penalty state.

She heard the front door open. Margery walked out slowly, as if she didn't want to deliver her news. She pulled open the car door and sat down heavily on the seat. "Cox will see Peggy tonight at the jail, but there's no way she can get a bail hearing before morning. She said Peggy may not get bail, period, because this is first-degree murder."

"Margery, lawyers are expensive," Helen said. "Peggy's my friend, too. I've got seven thousand dollars in cash. You're welcome to that." It was all the money she had in the world.

"Don't be ridiculous," Margery said.

Helen had read somewhere that a full-blown murder trial

could cost the defendant half a million dollars or more. She wondered where Peggy would get that kind of money. She'd have to win the lottery for sure.

On the drive back, in the wan glow of the streetlights, Margery looked exhausted. Her gray hair was limp, her skin sagged along her jawline, and her purple shorts set was wrinkled. She caught herself in the mirror and said, "I look like particular hell. Why don't you come back to my place for a drink?"

When the landlady flipped on her kitchen light, Pete's squawk sliced through their ears like a chain saw. He had overturned his water dish and dumped his birdseed on the floor. Helen cleaned up the wreckage from the one-parrot riot. Margery made herself a screwdriver that was a glass of vodka with a shot of orange juice. Helen had white wine out of a bottle with a real cork. It sure beat box wine.

"Now," she said when they were settled at Margery's kitchen table, "tell me why you think she did it."

"You know Peggy dated Page Turner," Margery said.

Helen did not. That still had her reeling. "I can't believe it. The only male I've ever seen her with is Pete."

"Believe it. Her problems started before you came to town. She and Page dated for almost a year. Peggy thought they had a serious relationship. She really believed he would marry her. He gave her a ring, a fire opal, and she wore it as an engagement ring. I told her opals were bad luck.

"One morning, after Page got out of her bed and went to work, Peggy went outside for the newspaper. She opened it up and there was an announcement of Page Turner's engagement to this society babe in Palm Beach, Astrid somebody. Peggy went crazy. She screamed and shouted and threw things. Then she went storming over to the bookstore, still in her nightgown, and threw the ring in his face."

"I heard about that," Helen said. "But I didn't realize the woman was Peggy."

She thought of languid, laid-back Peggy on the chaise longue by the pool, and tried to imagine her as a screaming shrew in a nightgown. Was it possible?

Then Helen saw herself in St. Louis the afternoon she caught her husband, Rob, naked with their next-door neighbor. He always said he hated Sandy. He's a bare-assed liar, she'd thought irrelevantly as she watched Rob's hairy rump. That was just before she picked up the crowbar and started swinging. Helen had been so cool and controlled until that moment. Then something snapped inside and it started an avalanche of snapping outside.

"I could see Peggy being angry," Helen said. "But this happened two years ago. Why would she kill him now?"

"Because Peggy said, 'I'll get you. But it will be when you least expect it. Then I'll stab you in the back, just like you stabbed me.' Everyone at the bookstore heard it."

"Oh," Helen said.

"Peggy was never the same after Page Turner. She swore off men forever. That's when she got Pete and began buying lottery tickets. She hasn't had a date since."

They were both silent as they sipped their drinks. It had been more than a year since her ex-husband had betrayed her and Helen began her zigzag flight across the country. Did she still want to kill Rob? Helen didn't think so. Her fury had flared up and then burned to ashes. Now she only wanted to stay away from her ex. She'd made another life for herself. She was beginning to forget his betrayal. She thought again of her hot weekend with Rich and melted inside.

"I don't believe Peggy would kill him after all this time," Helen said. "That story is a Las Olas legend. It would be easy for anyone to find out the jilted woman was Peggy and plant Page's dead body in her home. Is that all the police have?"

"The butcher knife in Page's back had Peggy's fingerprints on it," Margery said.

"Of course it had her fingerprints. It was in her kitchen."

"That's not what the cops think."

"How do you know what the cops think?"

"I have my sources," Margery said smugly.

"You still haven't answered my question: Why would Peggy go after him now?"

"Page has a video of her." Pete squawked in protest, and Margery threw the cover over his cage.

"He has—or had—lots of videos. Peggy has plenty of company, if the stories I heard are true."

"Peggy has company in this video. She was with two men and a lot of coke." Margery knew the most surprising things and said them without the slightest disapproval.

"Peggy? In a threesome? She lives like a nun."

"Now. But she used to be a wild one, honey. You've got to promise to keep this next part quiet. I'm only telling you because you're her friend and maybe it will help you understand what she's up against."

Some friend, Helen thought. I talked with her three or four nights a week and didn't know anything about her.

"When Peggy was going out with Page, she often partied in his office. It was a pretty spectacular place."

"I saw the couch and his fabulous first-edition collection."

"You didn't see the half of it," Margery said. "Peggy told me there's a back playroom with a bed, a fireplace, a fur rug, and a closet full of toys you don't buy at FAO Schwarz."

"There is?" Helen said, feeling dumber still. "I didn't know anything about that."

"Peggy did. She said there were cameras all over. She knew he was taping some of their sessions. Page said it made sex more exciting. Young women are so trusting today. We used to ask for our love letters back when we broke up with a man. Now, they let guys videotape them."

She shook her head at modern gullibility and took a swig of her screwdriver. "One night after the store closed, Page asked her to do a threesome. She was so crazy in love, she said yes. The third party was a much younger guy named Collie. Peggy said he was cute and clean-cut."

"Wait a minute. Wouldn't she have had the threesome with another woman?" Helen's worldly knowledge came from *Cosmo*.

"Not this time. Peggy was very nervous and did a lot of coke before she got there. She did even more at Page's place. Peggy said the tape made *Basic Instinct* look like *Bambi*."

Helen and Rob had rented that movie, and Rob had raved about Sharon Stone for weeks. Helen didn't remember any cocaine. Oh, wait, the scene with the murdered guy. He had coke on his . . . Helen could feel herself blushing. Sometimes, she was so Midwestern.

Margery didn't seem to notice. "The coked-up Peggy passed out and woke up the next morning in her own bed. She didn't know how or when she got there.

"She turned on the TV and heard the news bulletin: State Senator Colgate Hoffman III's son was found dead in a Fort Lauderdale hotel room of a suspected drug overdose. He was Colgate IV, Collie for short. Peggy recognized him as the cute guy in Page's office. She realized that he must have died sometime during their party or soon after.

"Peggy was terrified. She begged me to help her. She expected to hear from the police any day, but they never showed up. She was lucky. You know anything about the senator?"

"He's one of those law-and-order, war-on-drugs types," Helen said.

"That's right. His son Collie had a long history of drug abuse. Hoffman's political opponents charged that the investigation into his son's death was covered up. The public's sympathy was with the senator. People felt he'd suffered enough and should be left alone in his grief.

"Collie was buried and so was the scandal. Peggy was relieved. I could see her starting to get over her fright. She and Page patched things up. She was still seeing him. I told her that was a bad idea, but she didn't listen to me. All she saw was that ring on her finger. Then she discovered that creep was engaged to another woman. She remembered all the things he'd talked her into, all the false promises he'd made. She ran to the bookstore in her nightgown and made a scene."

"What did she think Page would do—dump Astrid and marry her?" Helen said.

"She didn't think. Period. She just wanted Page to hurt as much as she did. She managed to embarrass him big-time. That was a mistake. He got her upstairs in his office. When there were no witnesses, he told her he'd made a tape of her and Collie and a lot of coke.

"'So what?' Peggy said. 'You're in it, too. It was a threesome.'

"'Not on my tape,' Turner said.

"Peggy was frightened. She could be charged with manslaughter at the very least, based on her coking with the soon-to-be-dead man. Page told her that she'd let Collie die. He didn't mention his own role. He didn't say how Peggy got home and Collie got to that hotel. Peggy couldn't contradict him. She had only the haziest recollection of that night. Page's threat shut her up permanently."

"Poor Peggy. She must have been shattered." Helen knew how you could go off the rails when you loved the wrong man. She and Peggy were sisters in experience.

"She never saw that bastard Page Turner again," Margery

said, "or any other man. That's a waste of a fine woman. The only good thing was, she went into rehab and got herself off the nose candy."

The long speech made Margery thirsty. She took a deep drink of her screwdriver and lit a cigarette.

Peggy had often told Helen that she was through with men for good. Now Helen knew why. No wonder Pete was the only male she trusted.

"Her life was nice and quiet. Then, all of a sudden, Page threatened to give that video to the press. Peggy was afraid she'd wind up in prison. Murder has no statute of limitations."

"But that's crazy. Why would Page do that after keeping quiet for more than two years?"

"Does he need a reason? The man was drunk, mean, and hated women. He's so rich he can do what he wants. I don't know why. But I know she was desperate."

"Did the police find the tape?"

"No. Not yet. But they found five others he made of her. And they know one video is missing. My source says Page put the women's first names on the videos and then numbered them—Peggy one, Peggy two."

"Quite the little librarian," Helen said.

"Page had six of Peggy, and the third one is missing. I hope to God the cops never find it. They've got enough on her.

"I love Peggy. I'll do my best to defend her. But I think she did it." This judgment was delivered in a hellish haze of cigarette smoke. Helen refused to accept it.

"Lots of people hated Page Turner," she said. "They had equally good reasons to kill him."

"Name two," Margery said.

"There's Albert, the day manager at Page Turners. He's worked there for thirty years. Now the store is probably going to close. Albert will be out of a job with no severance, no health insurance, and no way to support his old mother."

"And killing Page would stop the store from closing?"

"No. But it was a lousy thing to do to Albert," Helen said.

"Hell, it was a lousy thing to do to you. And you didn't kill Page Turner."

"No, but I thought about it. Gayle, the night manager, hated the way Page treated women."

"That's why she killed him? To save a bunch of women she didn't know?" Margery snorted more smoke. Even Helen thought her reason sounded stupid.

"Probably not. Gayle did warn off a woman so she wouldn't star in another one of Page's videos."

"Then she could warn the others."

"How about his wife, Astrid? She called Page a son of a bitch on the phone."

"If every wife who did that killed her husband, there wouldn't be a man left in Florida."

"Madame Muffy, the preppy psychic, could have done it. I heard her arguing with Page the day he died."

Margery snorted like a mad bull. "Muffy said on TV she was warning him about his terrible fate."

"I know. But there's something weird about her."

"Of course she's weird. How many psychics wear deck shoes?" Margery took a last swig of her screwdriver.

"It could be someone or something we don't know anything about," Helen said. "What if Page Turner was blackmailing the senator?"

"And the senator, who is surrounded by security night and day, slipped out and killed him?"

"He could have had someone do it for him."

"Right. One of the senator's preppy aides offed Page. Come on. That's a bit much even for Florida." Margery blew a fantastic plume of smoke.

"How about the other women in those sex videos? The police took away boxes of tapes."

"Some of those tapes are old. They even predate Peggy. Why would those women kill him now?"

"For the same reason the police think Peggy wanted him dead."

"Maybe, but none of them went running to the bookstore in her nightgown, threatening to kill him."

"I know she's innocent." Helen wondered if she was trying to convince herself. "She's innocent," she repeated, this time with conviction. "I'm going to prove it."

"I hope so," Margery said as she stubbed out her cigarette. "Because I'm tired of that damned bird throwing seed all over my kitchen."

Chapter 10

Page Turner was buried the next day in Palm Beach. No one bothered to tell the bookstore staff. Helen saw the story in the morning paper. We don't exist for the Turner family, she thought. We're another store fixture, like the cash registers.

"Why aren't we closing for the funeral?" Helen asked Gayle. The night manager was running the store now.

"Astrid said he would have wanted it that way." His widow was probably right. Page never missed a chance to make a buck. His whole family loved those ringing registers. They didn't even hang a mourning wreath on the bookstore door, in case it discouraged sales.

"I gather we aren't invited to the funeral," Helen said.

"It's private. Family members only," Gayle said.

"We need closure," Brad said. "We should hold our own wake for Page Turner."

"We're dressed for one," Gayle said. All three booksellers were in black, although Helen didn't think Gayle's Doc Martens were standard mourning attire.

Albert and the new guy, Denny, were working the registers up front. Gayle, Brad, and Helen were in the dingy break room. They didn't start work for another twenty minutes. Page Turner may have had a luxurious office, but he stuffed his staff into a grimy closet. The break room smelled of microwaved pizza and old Taco Bell takeout. It was furnished with broken chairs and a folding table covered with crumbs, napkins, plastic forks, and old magazines.

The rest of the space was taken up by cases of Bawls. The distinctive cobalt bottles were piled to the ceiling, shutting out the light from the single window.

Gayle broke open a case of Bawls and gave Brad and Helen each a blue bottle, and took one for herself. She found an opener in the mess on the table and popped the caps. Then she said the first words in memory of their dead boss:

"Page Turner was a cheap bastard."

"Amen," Helen and Brad said.

The three employees clinked their bottles together in a toast. Helen took a sip. Bawls was clear and slightly fizzy, with a strange, subtle flavor. At first it tasted like nothing at all. Then she detected a distinctive, almost citrusy tang that was like nothing else. She guessed that was the much-touted guarana, an exotic Brazilian berry. Delicious—and it had a caffeine zing. Too bad it was almost two bucks a bottle. She couldn't afford to drink it.

"He never gave a damn about us," Brad said. "When I broke my foot, he wouldn't let me sit down. I still had to stand at the cash register. My foot never did heal right. He was heartless."

"Hear, hear." They clinked their blue bottles and drank again.

"He said ugly things to us," Gayle said. "He degraded women. He embarrassed our customers with his crude remarks. He was vicious."

They toasted for the third time. Helen remembered Page

roaming the store, broad-shouldered and big-bellied, red-faced and richly dressed, a modern Henry VIII. She heard him yelling "Who's got Bawls?" at gentle Mr. Davies until the poor man blushed. Page never understood that Mr. Davies was blushing for him.

"He was a bully," she said. "And he made the staff clean the toilets. I hope he's cleaning toilets in hell."

"Oh, Lord, grant our prayer," Brad said reverently. He had the face of a depraved acolyte. He was so thin, Helen saw his ribs under his tight black knit shirt.

"He bounced our checks. He closed two stores and never gave anyone a dime of severance. He could have afforded it. He sure can't take it with him," Gayle said. She threw her bottle into the big metal trash can. Brad hurled his bottle after hers. It hit the first, and broke in a shower of sapphire glass. Helen tossed her nearly full bottle of Bawls on top, and a geyser of guarana flared up.

Then, in a bitter rush of malignant energy, the three staffers started ripping open the cases of Bawls and heaving the bottles into the trash, breaking each one. Blue glass and fizzing guarana water splashed and shattered and slid down the walls. The tower of Bawls toppled. Sunlight poured into the room. It seemed even shabbier.

Soon the trash can was overflowing with broken dark blue glass, a miser's horde of cobalt. They still had not broken all the Bawls. They each grabbed a case and carried it outside to the Dumpster. The summer heat hit them in the face. The sun glared down. The garbage stink was powerful. Nothing stopped their destructive frenzy.

The three booksellers slashed open the cases like hungry predators and hurled the bottles into the Dumpster. When they broke those cases, they went back inside for more, until there was nothing but dust where the Bawls used to be. They smiled as the last bottles broke on the sides of the

Dumpster, splintering in bursts of deep blue. The exotic, expensive drink perfumed the putrid air.

They watched it ooze into the soggy trash.

"Who's got Bawls now?" Gayle said.

Helen cleaned off the sticky splashes of Bawls on her clothes, put on fresh lipstick, and combed her hair. A sliver of blue glass clinked to the floor. She heard her name being paged, "Helen, line one. Helen, line one."

It was Rich. Sometimes, he called her at the bookstore four or five times a day. "I'm just checking to see how you're doing," he said.

"I'm doing the same thing I was doing an hour ago. Trying to keep my job without getting fired. Rich, I know you mean well, but I can't take personal calls at work."

"But I'm worried about you," he pouted. She hung up. When she was younger, she would have found his calls romantic. Now she felt smothered. She was used to being on her own.

I'm a fool, she told herself. He's a good man. (But maybe not a good man for you.)

While she was at the phone, she called Margery. "What's the news on Peggy?"

"It's all bad." Margery's voice was flat, drained of emotion. That scared Helen more than her landlady's words. Margery couldn't—or wouldn't—continue.

Finally Helen said, "What is it?"

"First-degree murder. She's in detention pending trial. There's no possibility of bail."

"No!" Helen said. She couldn't picture the elegant Peggy sharing a jail cell with an open toilet and a tattooed biker chick. She saw that sumptuous bed again, with the pale sheets and pillows. What was Peggy sleeping on now?

"It's worse. The prosecutor may ask for the death penalty."

Helen couldn't say anything then. Finally, she managed, "That's horrible. Peggy didn't murder Page Turner."

"She sure doesn't deserve to die for it," Margery said. That wasn't a vigorous defense of Peggy's innocence.

"Peggy is no murderer," Helen said.

(And your ex wouldn't cheat on you. And you wouldn't pick up a crowbar and wind up on the run. Not a nice little number cruncher like you.)

"Can I see her?"

"The lawyer said Peggy doesn't want to see anyone right now. This is a fairly common reaction. Don't worry. She'll want to see you in a day or two. Give her time to get used to it."

"Margery, I'm supposed to go to Rich's tonight. He's picking me up after work for a barbecue at his place. Maybe I should cancel."

"Why? You can't do anything about Peggy. Go on. Do you need someone to look in on your place?"

That was Margery's oblique way of asking about Thumbs. She would not say the C-word.

"I left him extra food and put the lid up on the emergency water supply. He'll be fine."

Margery was a woman of contradictions. The Coronado had a no-pets policy. Margery would not rent to anyone with an animal. But she turned a blind eye to Pete and Thumbs, maybe because she liked Peggy and Helen. Her landlady also hated drugs. Margery had refused to transport Phil's pot to the beach motel. But she ignored the perpetual cloud of marijuana smoke around Phil's door. Typical Florida. If we don't have to confront a problem, it doesn't exist.

"Is there anything I can do for Peggy? Does she need food, clothes, a toothbrush? I don't feel right leaving her alone there."

"Helen, she'll have these problems a long time. You

didn't make them. Go out with your boyfriend—unless there's some other reason you don't want to be with Rich."

"No, no," Helen said.

"Then go. There's nothing you can do for Peggy."

Margery hung up the phone, but her words lingered, There's nothing you can do . . . But there was. Helen could find out who murdered Page Turner.

Yeah, right. A clerk who stumbled over the cash register keys knew more than the police. But she did. She saw and heard things at the bookstore the police didn't know. And she knew Peggy. Well, she didn't know her. But she knew she didn't kill Page Turner.

"Uh, Helen, can you help me?" She recognized that frantic tone. Denny, her new coworker, had a problem with his tricky register. His line was backing up. "How do you ring up a special coupon?"

Finally, someone knew less than she did. Helen felt good showing him the intricate combination of keys. The line of customers snaked around the store. Once again, everyone in the store had decided to buy a book at the same time.

Denny was so young he didn't shave. He had a slim body and a face like a Renaissance cherub, complete with silky auburn hair that curled fetchingly on his forehead. He looked like a rock star, before the sex and drugs. He seemed to have no idea he was beautiful. The women customers didn't seem to mind waiting in his line.

When the crowds finally abated, Helen asked, "Is this your first job at a bookstore?"

"First job ever," Denny said. "I got hired in a special deal by the guy who got killed, what's his name?"

"Page Turner."

"Yeah, Turner was friends with the judge."

"What judge?"

"My juvie judge. I beat up a teacher at school." Denny looked about as vicious as a new puppy.

"Anyway, my old man paid the teacher's medical bills and bought him off with a settlement for pain and suffering, and the judge sentenced me to get a job."

Only in Florida, Helen thought. She was surprised work wasn't considered cruel and unusual punishment.

"How long do you have to work here?"

"Six months." Denny made it sound like a life sentence.

So much for meeting a better class of people in a bookstore. The late and unlamented Page had found a way to stop staff turnover—convict labor. He wouldn't have to worry about Denny complaining if his check bounced. The kid would clean toilets under court order. At least he wasn't handcuffed to the cash register.

She wondered how much damage Denny had done to the teacher, and what those medical bills were for. Was Denny dangerous? She hoped not. He was so beautiful, she tried not to stare. And he worked hard. He even volunteered to go on a slush run. Maybe he just wanted to get away from starchy old Albert, who came back from lunch in a snit.

"Who threw away those cases of Bawls?" Albert said. "Do you have any idea what they cost? I would have taken them."

There was no way to explain their Bawls-busting frenzy. "The family wanted it that way," Helen lied. That shut Albert up. He still worshiped the Turner family.

A businessman in a dark gray suit and rep tie reverently placed *Jesus CEO* on the counter. Helen wondered if the guy realized this CEO had been crucified by the competition.

Denny came back with a stack of slush books and said, "Red alert. Wild children are tearing up the kids' department."

Helen paged Gayle, who said, "I'm tied up in receiving. Will you check it out?"

The Children's section looked like a small tornado had

sucked all the books off the shelves. The little tornado was industriously tearing the pages out of a Harry Potter pop-up book. *Rip.* A Hogwart's tower vanished. *Tear.* A witch disappeared. *Tug.* A cat came loose. The little girl gave Helen an angelic smile and mashed the book into the rug.

A slightly older boy let out an earsplitting shriek, then leaped over a kiddie chair. His chubby foot caught in the chair back and he fell into a Dr. Seuss display. He burst into startled sobs. Helen helped the boy up and checked him out. Angry tears ran down his cheeks, but he appeared unhurt.

The children's mother was sitting in the midst of the chaos, reading an Oprah book and ignoring both children. She was heavily pregnant.

"Ma'am," Helen said, "I'm afraid your little boy might have hurt himself. And your little girl is tearing up a very nice book."

The mother finally looked up. She said indignantly, "Come along, Gabrielle and Justin. It's obvious they don't like children here."

Not when they destroy the store, Helen thought. She was still picking up the pieces when Gayle appeared, a dark angel in Doc Martens. "Can you believe that?" Helen said. "The mother sat there and let the little bastards rip up the books."

A mother in flowery Laura Ashley heard Helen and pulled her child closer.

Gayle smothered a smile. "Maybe I'd better have you collect slush in Fiction. I'll finish here. The murder mysteries need work, too."

"Speaking of murder, do you remember the night Page Turner died?" Helen asked.

"Do I ever," Gayle said. "It was a full moon and the customers were nuts."

"I remember that. I saw him leave, too, although I didn't

know it was for the last time. He was drunk," Helen said. "Did he have anything with him? Did he drive away in his car or did someone pick him up?"

Was she asking Gayle too many questions? Apparently not. "Let me think." Gayle closed her eyes, as if she was seeing Page's final exit in her mind. "He walked out carrying his briefcase, which the cops never found. He left his car here. The police impounded it. They think someone picked him up."

"Did you see who?"

"No. It was too crazy."

Great interrogation technique, Helen thought. That got a lot of useful information. At this rate, Peggy will be in jail until she's ninety. (If she's lucky, a mean little voice whispered.) Helen tried to hush it by working harder.

Fiction was chaos. Since the staff hours were cut back, no one had time to check the shelves. Jane Austen had been shoved next to James Patterson. Skin magazines were piled on top of Mark Twain. Danielle Steel rubbed shoulders with William Faulkner. Helen straightened the long rows of shelves. She saw Mr. Davies sitting in the book nook by the back window, the favorite reading spot for the store's oldest inhabitant. He had a pleasant view of a palm garden—and Page's private parking spot. He might know who picked up Page Turner.

"Mr. Davies, do you remember Page Turner's last day?"

"Oh, my, yes," the small, squirrellike man said. His bright eyes gleamed. He was enjoying the attention.

"Very sad when a young man dies. Very sad. I knew his grandfather since the 1960s. He was nothing like his grandson, nothing. A great lover of books, was old Mr. Turner. His grandson saw himself as a great lover."

The old man chuckled at his joke. Helen tried to steer the conversation back to the topic. "Did you see who Page drove off with?"

"Yes, indeed. I don't miss much, especially not a pretty girl. Woman, I mean. I'm trying to raise my consciousness and say the right thing. But I'm not so old I don't notice a pretty female individual. And this one was hard to miss. As I told the police, she had unusual dark red hair and a most imposing nose. It gave her character, you know. She was very attractive."

Helen's heart sank as Mr. Davies talked. "Did you see what she was driving?"

"Oh, yes. A little green car with a funny name. Always makes me think of Vietnam. I remember, it was a Kia. KIA meant killed in action in the war."

Peggy, Helen thought. Peggy drove a green Kia. She picked up Turner the night he died.

"I also told them—" Mr. Davies said, but Helen could not listen to any more of the old man's chatter. She was heartsick.

"I'm sorry, Mr. Davies," she interrupted. "I have to go back to work."

Chapter 11

Did Peggy drive Page Turner to his death?

Where did she take him, just before he was murdered? And why?

Helen had to know. She needed answers now. She was not going to wait until Peggy felt like seeing her. Women prisoners were at the North Broward facility, way out west near the turnpike. Helen did not want to beg a ride from Margery or Sarah. This was between her and Peggy. She would take the bus. It was an hour-and-a-half trip one way.

Helen called the jail's information number on her break. Visitors may not bring in "drugs or weapons of any type," the recording said. No problem there.

"Visitors are subject to search." She expected that, too.

"Inmates are permitted one two-hour visit per week." That surprised her. She'd thought jail would be like a hospital, with daily visiting hours.

She could not take Peggy anything—no food, books, flowers, or candy. "Visitors may not give anything to or take anything from an inmate." That was sad. She wanted to bring her friend some comfort.

Then she heard, "Photo identification, such as a driver's

license, military identification, passport, or state-issued ID card must be presented by each visitor."

ID? Helen didn't have any identification. She had to stay out of the government computers.

"Visitors who do not have proper identification will not be permitted to visit," the recording continued relentlessly. Helen panicked and hung up.

How was she going to get ID? Would Sarah lend Helen her license? No, Helen wouldn't ask. She couldn't involve her friend in a fraud. Besides, she couldn't tell Sarah why she had no driver's license. She could buy a fake ID on the Internet, but that would take weeks.

Then she remembered the bookstore's lost-and-found. She rooted around in the unclaimed sweaters, flowered umbrellas, scratched sunglasses, wrinkled scarves, and . . . what was a purple suede glove doing in there?

Ah, there it was. The driver's license. A woman had left it on the counter about two months ago. Gayle had mailed it to the address on the license, but it came back "addressee unknown." It was probably a fake, but Gayle had tossed it into the lost-and-found limbo.

Helen looked at the battered license. It was for Kay Gordy, a cute blonde, age thirty-eight, height five-eight, weight one-forty-five. Helen was four inches taller, four years older, and fifteen pounds heavier. She was also a brunette. Well, no woman looked like her driver's-license photo. It would have to do.

Helen felt calm enough to call the jail recording again for Peggy's visiting day. She nearly dropped the phone when she heard it was today. Today? If she missed it, she'd have to wait another week. Visiting hours seemed designed for working people—that was one blessing. They were three-thirty to ten p.m. She got off work at three. She could catch the bus and make it back before her date with Rich at eight o'clock.

It seemed like a good plan as the bus crawled through the late-afternoon traffic, but her courage began to fail as she got closer. The landscape around the North Broward jail was flat, barren, and hot, more like a desert than lush South Florida. The jail looked like a warehouse surrounded by razor wire.

As Helen approached, she saw cops of all sorts: locals from Fort Lauderdale, Hollywood, Pembroke Pines, and Dania Beach. Police from Miami to the south and Delray Beach to the north, state cops, and gray-suited FBI agents, all watching her with hawklike eyes. Even in her worst nightmare, she'd never imagined this. When she ran from St. Louis, Helen changed her name, but not her face. Did the court send her description to Florida?

White female, age forty-two, weight approximately 150 pounds, height six feet, brown hair, brown eyes, no distinguishing marks . . . ? Had these cops seen her photo? They had phenomenal memories. Would someone remember her and send her back to St. Louis?

She put her head down, hunched her shoulders, and tried to make herself invisible. But there was no way she could erase herself. Any odd behavior would make her more noticeable.

I'm being ridiculous, she told herself. I'm twelve hundred miles from St. Louis. I'm here to help my friend Peggy. Who's going to recognize me?

She felt trapped in the security line. There was a police officer behind her, so she couldn't even bolt. She put her purse on the conveyor to be X-rayed and walked through the scanner. Something on her set it off. The guard waved the wand around her. She held her breath until she passed.

Helen presented her driver's license and signed her fake name, Kay Gordy, then sat and waited. An elderly woman sat down next to Helen, then moved away. I must stink of fright sweat, she thought. Or maybe the woman just wanted to be alone.

Finally, she was shown to a narrow cinder-block booth with a Plexiglas window set in the wall. Peggy sat down. Redheads were supposed to look good in green, but Peggy's green jailhouse scrubs seemed to drain all the color from her face. Her dark red hair was too vivid, as if it belonged to a more flamboyant woman. It did—the old Peggy who sat out by the pool with Pete. She looked forlorn without her parrot.

Helen wanted to reach out and touch her friend. Instead, she picked up the phone receiver on the wall. Peggy's first words were, "How's Pete? Is he eating OK?"

Peggy had not been eating at all. She was thin and tired. Helen did not know how she would survive in here until her trial. And after the trial, if she lost . . . She wouldn't go there.

"Pete's fine," Helen said quickly. "He misses you."

She did not mention that Pete was driving Margery nuts. He squawked constantly and demanded to be let out of his cage. When Margery had let him out, he'd chewed up her living room curtains. Now Pete was in jail, too, life without possibility of parole. He threw his seed on the floor and spilled his water in fury.

"How is everybody at the Coronado?" Peggy said, as if she were asking about her family.

"The same. Margery is still into purple. Phil is still into pot. Cal is still cooking up smelly suppers of boiled broccoli and Brussels sprouts."

"And you're still seeing Dr. Rich?"

"Tonight's my first visit to his home. I'm going to meet the animals, Sissy and Beans."

"I never liked a man enough to take him home to Pete," Peggy said.

Helen found this attempt at ordinary conversation unbearably sad. It felt strange talking on the phone to someone you were looking at, someone separated only by a sheet of Plexiglas. She sneaked a peek at her watch. She'd have to start back soon. They had not discussed anything important yet.

"Peggy . . ." Helen began, and then stopped. She did not know how to go on.

But Peggy knew what she wanted to ask. "I didn't do it. I hated Page Turner. But I never killed him."

"A witness says you picked Page up at the bookstore the night he died."

"I did," Peggy said. "Did Margery tell you why? I thought I could get that video back."

"The one with the senator's son?" That was tactful, Helen thought.

"The senator's dead son. If that video got out, I'd be the Monica Lewinsky of Florida. Only it would be a hundred times worse. I not only had coke-snorting sex with an antidrug senator's son, I killed him, or let him die. At least that's what Page said."

"Did you?"

"I don't think so. But I was so fucked-up back then, I don't know." This didn't sound like the Peggy Helen knew. I talked to her almost every day, Helen thought, and she told me nothing about herself. But then what did I tell her about me? People in Florida did not discuss the past. They moved here to get away from it.

"I didn't know you were engaged to Page Turner," Helen said.

"It wasn't anything I was proud of," she said. "I hoped when we broke off" (Helen noticed that *we* instead of *he*) "I could start with a clean slate. I hoped my new friends wouldn't know about my old life. I should have known better."

"What did you see in him?" Helen asked. It was a rude

question, but this didn't seem the place for ordinary politeness.

Peggy shrugged. "Page was different from the other men I'd dated. He was funny. He was rich. We did things and went places. We'd sail to Miami for dinner or fly to New York for a play. On Monday morning, I'd go back to my dull little job and my dull little life. Being with Page was like having a secret life. It was exciting. I knew if he ever left me, I'd have nothing. Then he started with the cocaine. That was another exciting secret. I felt so good, so mellow, so alive that first time. I never felt that way again, but I kept trying. First drugs are a lot like first love.

"Coke changes people," she said. "It made Page meaner. It made me do crazy things I'd never even thought about before."

Like a threesome with a senator's son.

"I loved him," she said. "I thought we were getting married. Page gave me a ring for my birthday. We were going to fly off one weekend and go to the Elvis chapel in Las Vegas. But somehow, we never got around to it. Then one morning, after he got out of my bed, I opened up the paper and there was the announcement for his society wedding in Palm Beach. You know what happened next."

Helen did, but she couldn't picture this pathetic woman summoning up enough rage to run barefoot in her nightgown to Page Turner's bookstore. Maybe she and Peggy had both used up their lifetime quotas of anger.

"The police haven't found that video yet, have they?" Peggy said.

Helen was glad Peggy asked that question. It seemed to confirm her innocence.

"No," she said. "They're still looking. When did Page first start blackmailing you with that tape?"

"About a month ago. He'd dried out when he married Astrid and he behaved himself for a while. But then he started drinking. All he did was trade coke for booze. Soon he was back to his old ways with women, too. Last month, he got drunk, called me up, and started tormenting me about the video. I begged him to burn it. I'd get him calmed down and then he'd call again. After the last call, I didn't hear from him for several days.

"I thought I could reason with Page. I thought I could talk him into giving me the video, fool that I was. When I called him about noon that day, he seemed reasonable. He said he'd bring it in his briefcase. By the time I picked him up at the bookstore, Page was mean drunk. He was drinking something in a blue bottle."

"Absolut Bawls," Helen said. "A caffeine energy drink he dosed with vodka."

"Made him almost as crazy as coke," Peggy said. "I should have left him at the store. I knew it was useless the moment he got in my car. When he was like that he'd say no just to be contrary."

"Where did you go when you picked him up?"

"I started driving down Las Olas, toward the beach. We used to walk along the ocean when we first met. I hoped it would help him remember our old romance and he'd give me the video. We never got to the beach. We'd driven a few blocks when he asked what I wanted. He didn't even remember our conversation of a few hours ago. I told him that he'd promised me the video and he laughed at me. He said the video was his insurance."

"What could you do to him if he used it?"

"Nothing," Peggy said.

"So what happened? Why did you take him back to the store?"

"He got a call on his cell phone. He listened and then said, 'Give me ten minutes.' He demanded that I take him back to the store. By then, I knew my idea was hopeless. I was afraid to be in the car with him anymore. I was so mad,

I thought I might kill him. I dropped him off at his car. That's the last I saw of him. I swear it is. He was alive when I left him in that parking lot.

"No one believes me. The police think I did it. Margery got me a good lawyer, but she thinks I'm guilty, too."

"I believe you," Helen said. "I want to help."

"What can you do?" Peggy said, and the question laid bare their hopeless situation. Peggy, the receptionist. Helen, the bookstore clerk. Two women with no money and no power, sitting in a jail.

"I think whoever killed Page had some connection with the bookstore, either a customer or an employee," Helen said. "I work there. I see things the police don't. There's one question I think needs to be answered: Why did Page suddenly start tormenting you with that video now? He'd had it a couple of years."

"I don't know," Peggy said. But her eyes shifted and she licked her dry lips. She was lying.

"You're on trial for your life. The prosecuting attorney is asking for a lethal injection, and Florida doesn't mind killing women. Why now, Peggy? This question could save your life."

"I don't know." But Peggy's eyes would not meet Helen's.

She did know. And she'd rather die than tell me, Helen thought. Why? Was she afraid of someone? Or still hoping for help from someone?

"Please tell me," Helen pleaded. She was clutching the phone like a lifeline.

Peggy hung up.

Chapter 12

Helen awoke in Rich's arms, naked and gasping. Unfortunately, she was not breathless from passion.

"What is that disgusting odor?" she said.

"Beans has a medical condition," Rich said with as much dignity as a naked man could muster.

"Does he have to sleep on your bed? Couldn't you put him in another room?"

"Beans is part of the family," Rich said, sounding hurt. "And he loves you."

It was true. The foul-smelling basset followed her everywhere. Sissy, the Persian princess, wanted nothing to do with Helen. She glared at her now from a drink-ringed dresser. The long-haired gray cat had ignored her all night, except when she'd stolen Helen's steak off her plate and dragged it across the carpet. Rich thought that was funny. Helen ate hamburger while Sissy had steak.

The animals were here before I was, Helen thought. (And they'll be here when I'm gone.)

Her first visit to Rich's was not a success. Last night, in the moon glow, she could see things were a little dusty. When she'd asked Rich why his black socks were hanging on the bedroom lamp shade, he'd said, "My dryer is broken." It seemed funny then.

Today, in the harsh morning light, the bachelor squalor was depressing. Well, she wouldn't be moving in with him anytime soon. Helen yawned and stretched. The gray sheets felt oddly soft. Why did Rich have flannel sheets in Florida? Helen saw her hands were covered with long gray hair. The sheets, under the layers of cat hair, were actually white.

Rich saw her hairy hands. "Oops," he said. "That's where Sissy likes to sleep."

"When was the last time you changed these sheets?" Helen said.

Rich thought for a moment. "Let's see. I broke up with Sheila in March."

"It's June," Helen said, sitting up and throwing off the suspect sheets. "You didn't change your sheets for more than three months?"

"I don't think of that stuff."

"But your clinic is so clean."

"Gloria handles that. She's a terrific office manager. Sheila did the house stuff." He smiled winsomely. "I was sort of hoping, now that we're getting serious, you could take over."

"Do I look like a housekeeper?"

Helen looked like an angry naked woman. Time to fix that. She started hunting for her clothes. She wasn't about to shower at Rich's. She'd seen cleaner bus station bathrooms. She found her bra under the bed in at least three months of dust. She shook it out and snapped it on.

"Please don't be mad at me," Rich said. "I thought when a woman cared about a man, she naturally wanted to care for his house. It's like an instinct."

"Wrong," Helen said. "There's no connection between hormones and housekeeping."

She couldn't believe any man still thought that way. Then again, nobody ever called South Florida a center of advanced thinking. She put on her panties inside out, then picked up her blouse from a chair upholstered with more cat hair. She pulled on her pants and slipped on her Ferragamo loafers. They were damp.

Did she spill her drink on them? She hoped not. They were some of her last good shoes, even if they had been resoled twice. She picked up one loafer for a closer look. That's when she caught the unmistakeable odor of cat urine.

Sissy had delivered her final opinion of Helen.

Helen got home at nine-thirty that morning. Thumbs greeted her at the door. Her big-footed cat looked cuddlier than ever. He was so gentle and well mannered, compared to Rich's rude animals. She scratched his ears in appreciation and poured him an extra helping of breakfast.

As she pulled off her black Ralph Lauren pants, she saw tiny pinpricks of daylight in the seat and along the inseam. Her good pants were wearing out. She'd bought them back when she made a hundred thousand dollars a year. Now that she was working dead-end jobs, she could not afford pants that expensive. They'd cost a week's pay. She wondered if she could get by with wearing her holey pants over black panty hose.

She had to salvage her smelly shoes. Helen did not have any leather cleaner, so she sprayed her loafers with lemon Pledge. They smelled a little better, but she still caught a faint, pungent whiff. Oh, well. She had to wear her thick-soled clunkers to the bookstore anyway.

Helen kept herself busy so she would not have to think about her disastrous night with Rich—or worse, their lovely weekend together on the beach. Suddenly, she couldn't hold back the memories any longer. She saw the moonlight leaving a silver path on the endless ocean, and the two of them walking along the shining sand.

The tears came and she could not stop them. She cried for all that she had lost long before she knew Rich. She could not change the past, but she would not repeat it. She'd let her ex take her for granted. That would never happen again. Could Rich believe that a woman naturally wanted to clean house for a man? She would not be any man's unpaid housekeeper, no matter how good the sex.

She thought of her grandmother, a short tanklike woman who'd supported herself with dead-end jobs, watching other people's children and cleaning other people's houses. Grandma never got a weekend on the beach with a man who looked like a shaggy Mel Gibson, but she kept going.

She was tougher than I am, Helen thought. She seemed to hear her grandmother's voice now: Pull your socks up and quit whining. She dried her tears and checked the clock. It was time to go to work.

When Helen walked into Page Turners shortly before eleven, the phone was ringing. "It's for you," Albert said, and frowned. "It's a personal call. Again." He pursed his mouth in irritation. Helen hoped his starched collar would strangle him.

The caller was Rich. "I can't talk now," Helen said.

"Don't hang up," he said desperately. "I'm sorry."

"You certainly are," she said, slamming down the receiver.

He called every half hour after that. Helen didn't know if she or Albert was more annoyed. She begged Rich to stop, afraid she might be fired. Finally he quit calling. At one o'clock, a florist arrived with an enormous bouquet. Rich had sent two dozen red roses.

Forgive me, the card said. *P.S.: I've hired a cleaning service.*

"You've got yourself one romantic dude," Denny said.

The newest bookseller smiled cherubically. He didn't look like a nose breaker. But then, she didn't look like someone on the run.

"I guess," Helen said.

She wished Rich had not spent so much money on something that would be dead in three days. The roses cost almost as much as a new pair of pants. I've got to stop thinking like this, she decided. Being chronically broke was ruining her sense of romance.

She wanted to take the roses to the break room, but Denny set them on the counter, "So we all can enjoy them."

"Those roses are beautiful," gushed a gray-haired woman.

"Her boyfriend sent them," Denny said.

"You are a lucky young woman. Not many men send roses anymore."

He doesn't care about me, she thought. He had them delivered here to make a big public splash. But Helen was glad to have the Rich problem. If she was mad at Rich, she wouldn't have to think about Peggy, in jail and on trial for her life, hiding the one fact that could save her.

Helen was convinced that Peggy did not kill Page. Then who did? That was the problem. The list was endless. She would have to write down all the suspects. But the day was taking its own slow pace. At the store, the lines of book buyers went on endlessly.

A tall woman with long blond hair and a soft blue blouse said, "May I write a check?"

"Sure," Helen said. "If I can see a picture ID."

The check said Willamena Delgarno. Her driver's license said William Delgarno. The address was the same. The photo was the same, too, except William was not wearing makeup and had a military buzz cut.

Helen looked at Willamena again. Under the makeup she

had a five-o'clock shadow. Helen hoped the surprise did not show on her face.

The next person in line was undoubtedly a man. In fact, he looked like a Viking recruiting poster. He was tall, with narrow hips, a tight T-shirt, and long strong legs in form-fitting jeans. He was wearing work boots and a tool belt, but he had a natural air of command, as if he carried five stars on his shoulders.

Helen felt a definite *ka-zoing!* somewhere south of her belt. She also heard warning bells go off. She'd had a disastrous date with a perfect man not too long ago. She looked at the Viking again. She was relieved when she saw his blond hair was receding. His front teeth were yellow from cigarettes and a little crooked. His stomach was not quite as flat as it first appeared. Perfect—he wasn't perfect after all.

The Viking handed her two books, *Building Your Dream Home* and *The Red Tent*.

"Guess you must wonder what I'm doing with a woman's novel," he said, and blushed. Helen thought it was charming in a man so big. "My sister talked about it so much, I thought I'd better read it. Do you think that's stupid? I mean, a guy reading a woman's novel?"

"I think more guys should read woman's novels. And vice versa."

Helen's hand accidentally brushed his as she picked up the books, and it was her turn to blush. His arms had little golden hairs and big muscles. He was not wearing a wedding ring.

"Uh, are you single?" he asked her.

"Divorced," she said.

"My name is Gabriel," he said.

Gabriel, she thought. And he looks like an angel. A balding, slightly paunchy angel.

"But you can call me Gabe."

"Any children?" she said.

"Never wanted any."

"Me, either," Helen said. This man was a soul mate. At least on that subject.

"Listen, am I rushing things? Would you like to go out? Maybe for coffee or a drink or something?" Gabe said.

Or something, Helen thought. "Coffee," she said. She really wanted a drink, but coffee was a safer choice. "How about the café here?"

"Sounds good," he said. "Six-thirty tonight?"

"Tomorrow night," she said, not wanting to be too available.

The woman behind Gabriel politely cleared her throat.

"I better go, I'm holding up the line," he said.

Helen apologized to the woman, who winked and said, "No problem, but I've got to get back to work."

The customer line was gone suddenly as a summer shower. But there was one thundercloud. Dr. Rich Petton, her erstwhile boyfriend, came up to the counter.

"Why were you flirting with that guy?" he said. "You don't know him. It's dangerous. You could get yourself killed. What if he's a serial killer? This is Florida, home of Ted Bundy. At least find someone who knows him before you start flirting with that man."

"What business is it of yours?" Helen said in a hissing whisper, so her colleagues wouldn't hear.

"I care about you."

"I'm a grown woman, Richard. I don't need a chaperon."

"You were making a date with him. You were picking up men in bookstores."

"I can take care of myself," she said.

"You don't need another man," he said. "You have me. Didn't last night mean anything?"

She looked down. His strong callused hand was clamped on her wrist like a handcuff. She felt the pain shoot up her arm. He was hurting her.

"Let me go, Richard," she said coldly, trying to keep control. "I'm not a dog on a leash. I won't follow your commands."

"Helen, please, I didn't mean it." He let her go. There were red marks on her wrist where he'd grabbed her. They would turn into bruises. "I'll do anything. I got a cleaning service for you. I'll see a counselor. I'll—"

"Good-bye," she said. Her wrist throbbed. She'd been manhandled. That scared her.

Helen felt only relief when Dr. Richard Petton walked out of her life. Relief and regret that she did not feel more.

Chapter 13

Helen picked up the knife carefully. Her wrist hurt from where Dr. Rich had grabbed her. She wore a bracelet of bruises and a long-sleeved blouse to cover them. No man had ever treated her like that, not even her ex, Rob. She seethed with anger.

Crack! A peanut-butter cracker crumbled into pieces. She imagined it was Rich's bones. She should have hit him. She should have killed him. She picked up the plastic knife and plunged it into the heart of the peanut-butter jar. It snapped off. So far she'd broken two knives and six crackers. She had a pile of peanut-butter-smeared pieces, but nothing she could eat.

Helen was alone in the Bawls-less break room with her anger and her lunch, a jar of crunchy peanut butter and a box of crackers. She was still furious after that humiliating scene with Rich yesterday. He hadn't called her since. She almost wished he would, so she could tell him what she'd thought of him. She'd carried his roses home and thrown them in the Dumpster. Her only revenge was her date with Gabriel. Well, she couldn't call it a date exactly. It was coffee at the Page Turners café, under the watchful eye of Gayle.

"That's your lunch?" Gayle said, opening the break room door. She'd brought back a lovely little salad Nicoise from a nearby French restaurant. She brushed cracker crumbs off the table and sat down in the second least wobbly chair. Gayle was wearing black, as usual. Her metal belt buckle looked like it belonged on a blast furnace.

"It's one of the few things I can cook," Helen said.

"You call that cooking?"

"I opened the jar myself."

"Look out, Emeril. Doesn't the break room look better since we got rid of all those cases of Bawls?"

"It's bigger, anyway," Helen said, looking around the dingy room. It still smelled like Taco Bell takeout. "Did Astrid tell you anything about Page's funeral?"

"It was short and sweet," Gayle said. "They had him underground in record time."

"Any of his old girlfriends show up?"

"Not a one. That's why Astrid kept the funeral service private. She didn't want his weeping bimbos there."

Helen wondered if the other women in Page's videos would weep for him. Peggy was just one of many in that locked cabinet. Maybe one wanted him dead. Maybe they all did. She imagined a scene like something from *Murder on the Orient Express:* A dozen flossy-haired beauties held a pillow over Page's face while he struggled helplessly.

"Did you know any of the women who starred in his videos?" she asked Gayle.

"You mean besides the one who was arrested? Because I have to tell you, Peggy was here more than the rest combined."

Helen winced. Gayle didn't notice. She was picking the tuna off her salad.

"I knew most of them. They usually came into the store when I was on nights. Let's see . . . there were Cheree and

Maree, two skinny blondes with long straight hair. Very striking, those two. They looked like twins, although I don't think they were. They always showed up together. They wore identical black dresses and black studded dog collars. I expected Page to walk them on a leash. I think they were pros.

"Then there was Liza. She was a sweet little thing, curly brown hair, big brown eyes. She moved back home to Pittsburgh and married a dentist. You see any pepper over there?"

Helen dug in the pile of leftover ketchup, mustard, and sugar until she found a pepper packet. Gayle ate her peppered salad methodically. First all the tuna. Then the tomatoes. She was working on the string beans when she said, "Jamie was a sad case. She OD'd on heroin last year.

"Shelly was the smart one. She left Page for another man. Her new boyfriend got them a great gig on a yacht. She cooks, he crews. Last I heard they were headed for Brazil.

"I'm sure there were more, one-night stands or women who showed up after hours, but those are the ones I knew about."

Five women, a typical South Florida sampling: Two thrived on the corruption here, one ran back home, one ran away to sea, and one died. Cheree and Maree wouldn't care about sex videos. They'd consider them good advertising. Jamie was dead, and couldn't be hurt any more. Shelly had left the country. That left one candidate for blackmail. How would the Pittsburgh dentist feel about a wife who starred in Page's private porn library?

"Liza, the one who went back home, are you in contact with her?"

"I get a card from her at Christmas," Gayle said, intent on spearing an escaped string bean.

"Could you find out if she heard from Page recently?"

"Why?" Gayle stabbed and subdued the slippery green bean and began working on the potatoes.

"Because I think Page may have been blackmailing those women."

Gayle waved a forkful of potato as if it were a pointer. "Page Turner was a lot of things, most of them bad. But he wasn't a blackmailer. Why bother? He didn't need the money."

"Rich people never have enough money," Helen said.

"He certainly wouldn't get it from the women in those videos. None of them had two nickels to rub together. Astrid was the only woman he dated with money. I think that's why he married her."

"Then he did it because he could," Helen said. "He liked the power."

"I never thought I'd hear myself defending Page Turner," Gayle said, "but I'll say it again: He's not a blackmailer. I'll call Liza for you, but I'm not sure she'll tell me anything. We weren't close. I knew Peggy better."

Gayle put her fork down and looked at Helen. "She's your friend, isn't she? That's why you're asking these questions."

"Yes," Helen said. There was no point in hiding it. "Page was blackmailing her. I think he may have been blackmailing the others, too, if not for money, then for pure meanness."

"Page was always motivated by money. Always. How would he get money from Peggy? I don't think Page's sex videos are any big deal. The cops will watch them and snicker, but that's all. Peggy is lucky there's no video of the day she stormed into the bookstore in her nightgown. That was your blackmail material. I never saw anyone, man or woman, so angry. If she'd had a knife instead of a newspaper, she'd have stabbed him on the spot." Gayle ran her fork savagely through the last potato.

"But that was two years ago," Helen said.

"You don't get over a hurt like that right away. Maybe not ever. He made a fool of a smart woman."

Gayle threw away her salad things and wiped the crumby tabletop with her napkin. "I'll call Liza in Pittsburgh. But don't expect anything."

That should have been the motto for the whole afternoon. A badly used blonde with a big chest wobbled up to Helen's cash register with a stack of coin-collector folders. Either the blonde was wearing bourbon cologne, or she was trashed. She tried to pay with two rolls of quarters. Helen groaned. She'd have to count all the coins.

"Hey!" the woman said, and slapped Helen with a wave of bourbon. "Why yuh taking 'em out of the wrappers? I already counted 'em for you."

"Because half these quarters are Canadian," Helen said, and slid them back across the counter. The bourbonized blonde was hanging on to the counter and swaying. Helen felt seasick.

"Oh, yeah." She looked sheepish and shrugged her shoulders, a bad move. Her right breast nearly slid out of her halter top. She stuffed it back in, and the other breast almost escaped.

"Shit," said the drunken numismatist.

"Can I help?" said the man in line behind her. Helen eyed his wedding ring and glared at him. "Er, maybe not." He took a step back.

The blonde was trying to subdue her slippery breasts. Helen spotted a star-and-dagger tattoo during the struggle, which threw off her quarter count. The line kept getting longer. She paged Brad for backup. The little bookseller eyed the pile of coins and whispered, "How exactly do you think she earned all those quarters?"

"Who cares?" Helen snapped, her patience strained. "Now start ringing."

She finally determined that the woman had $17.25 in U.S. quarters. "You're a dollar twenty-three short."

The tipsy numismatist produced a roll of dimes from a large, limp leather purse. The count started again, but this time it went quicker. Helen found twelve U.S. dimes in the welter of Canadian coins. To heck with the three cents. The woman belched delicately, let go of the counter, and lurched out the door.

The next customer was a round-faced, smiling teacher who looked like a Chaucer goodwife. She had a two-foot stack of bargain books. Even with her teacher's discount card, her purchases came to $99.81. She handed Helen a hundred-dollar bill. Helen gave her back a pathetic nineteen cents.

The teacher threw up her hands and said, "Thank God! Now I can have the operation."

Helen was still laughing when the woman bustled out.

"Glad something's made you happy," Gayle said. The line had vanished, and they could talk again. "I found Liza. It wasn't too difficult. She's pregnant and the doctor's ordered bed rest until the baby comes. There's no way she was being blackmailed. She didn't even know Page was dead. She sounded completely surprised."

"Maybe Liza's a good actor," Helen said.

"Liza was always a bad liar. She's telling the truth. Look, I did what you asked. Now maybe you need to ask yourself: If Page really was a blackmailer, why only Peggy? And why now?"

Good questions. Helen tried to come up with answers all afternoon. She also asked herself why Peggy was holding back information. None of it made sense. Her brain raced like a gerbil on a treadmill, going round and round, getting nowhere, while she rang up books and watched the clock.

At six-thirty she clocked out. It was time to meet Gabriel in the store's café. She would even buy her own coffee, thank you. She wasn't starting this relationship off on the wrong foot.

Denny was working the café tonight, baking chocolate-chip cookies between latte orders. The heat from the oven made his auburn hair curlier and flushed his skin. There was something about a man working in a kitchen that was irresistible. Helen stood in line behind a painfully thin woman with red hair and tight Moschino jeans.

"Black coffee and a bagel. Can you scoop out the bagel?" Ms. Moschino asked.

"No," Denny said, "but you can." He handed her the bagel and a spoon, and she gutted the center, leaving behind a thick rope of bread.

"Why did she do that?" Helen asked when Ms. Moschino left.

"She's on a diet."

"Why not just eat half a bagel and take the other half home?"

"Beats me," Denny said. "We got people in here who get mad because they don't want cheese on their sandwiches. I tell them I can't take off the cheese, they have to do it. It's health-department regulations. They yell at me, saying, 'I'm paying all this money for a sandwich and I have to take off my own cheese?' Yes, sir. I can't move the cheese, I can't scoop the bagel, and I can't figure any of them out."

"Ah, Denny, you sound as unhappy as the rest of us. Welcome to the wonderful world of retail."

"Thanks. What do you want?"

"A double latte and a chocolate biscotti."

"Whipped cream on that latte?"

She looked at the too-thin woman picking at her gutted bagel. "Absolutely."

Helen was sitting at a table by the window when Gabe walked in. Heads turned, male and female. The skinny red-head stopped in mid–bagel bite. Gabe, with his blond hair and massive muscles, drew all eyes. But Helen looked first for his imperfections, her guarantee of a good relationship. When he smiled at her, she saw his teeth were still crooked. He ordered a cappuccino and a slab of double chocolate cake. Good. That would maintain the slight paunch. Nothing would stop the natural hair erosion. She smiled when he sauntered over with his coffee and cake. He seemed so easygoing compared to Dr. Rich.

They talked books, then South Florida theater. "Most people don't realize it, but South Florida is overrun with Shakespearean actors," he said. "Want to see *A Midsummer Night's Dream* at the Shakespeare in the Park Festival in Hollywood?"

It was a real date. Helen wasn't sure she wanted to say yes. She warily studied Gabe's strong hands for signs of a wedding ring, but saw no tan line. "Are you in a relationship right now?"

"Not really," Gabe said.

Helen had made three major mistakes with men since she'd moved down here. Before that, there was her ex-husband Rob, one giant step backward for mankind. If she had to interview Gabe like a prospective employer, she would.

"What happened, if you don't mind me asking?"

"Nothing, really," he said with a charming shrug that sent muscles rippling across his shoulders. "We just drifted apart."

Drifted apart. That sounded nice and neutral. Not, "I followed her to work and called her fifty times a day." They drifted apart, two ships in the night. A gentle ending.

Gabe's cell phone rang. He checked the number and turned it off, scoring more points.

"Sorry," he said. "I hate these things, but I need it for business."

Helen continued to probe. She'd been burned by Rich. No, bruised. She flexed her battered wrist. "I guess you make lots of phone calls when you're going out with some-one."

"I'm not sure what you mean." Gabe looked endearingly puzzled, like a golden retriever who'd lost his toy under the couch.

"A cell phone is a good way to keep track of someone you're dating."

"You mean like constant phone calls? I've got better things to do and so does she. At least I hope she does. I don't believe in hog-tying a woman with a phone cord. You either have her or you don't."

He's got me, Helen thought.

"I'd love to see the play," she said, as her last fears were put to bed.

Chapter 14

The store's doors were locked. Clusters of customers stood outside, noses pressed against the windows like abandoned puppies.

The group inside looked even more forlorn. Gayle the manager was dressed in her usual black, but today it was not a fashion statement. It was an undertaker's outfit. Gayle didn't actually say the store was closing. But even the youngest bookseller, Denny, figured it out.

"We're fucked," he whispered to Helen. "We're going to wind up shoveling fries at Mickey D's."

"If we're lucky," Helen said.

Albert glared at them, and they lapsed into guilty silence.

"So, to recap before we open this morning." Gayle began counting on her fingers. "One, no new stock will be delivered. We will not be getting any new books until further notice.

"Two, we will not be receiving any more new magazines." Brad's sharp face went red with anger. The magazines were his domain. He managed the section, fussed over the stock, worried about the snowfall of subscription cards. Now he was demoted to an ordinary bookseller.

"Three, staff hours will remain reduced.

"Four, there will be no new hires, even if someone quits.

"And five, if customers ask if the store is closing, the answer is no."

Helen didn't believe that. In her experience, business declines were rarely reversed. Page Turners was on a downward slide. They were enforcing Page's destructive last decisions and had made more bad ones. She had to find another job.

Albert stood there, shell-shocked. He did not ask if the store was closing. Even his optimism was dead. The starch had gone out of his white shirt, and his tie was spotted. Helen heard him muttering, "At my age, what am I going to do?"

When she went to the break room to get her name tag, Denny was putting on his café apron. His normally curly auburn hair stuck out in porcupine spikes. His innocent face was troubled.

"Here's what I don't get," he said. "We have people lining up to buy books. Look at the crowd waiting for us to open. It will be like that all day. In the café, I'll be cranking out five-dollar coffee drinks and selling four-buck slices of cake nonstop. But they're acting like the store is a loser. Where's the money going—up someone's nose?"

Maybe once upon a time, when Page and Peggy romped in the upper room. But Page had stopped using coke when he'd married Astrid. Gayle said the late owner was all about money. Where did the store's money flow? Was it an underground river, diverted to some unknown source? And what—if anything—did it have to do with the penniless Peggy?

Gayle opened Helen's cash register, unlocked the doors, and greeted the customers with her usual smile. But they were not fooled. They knew Page Turners was in trouble.

A skinny elderly man who smelled of cigar smoke and

solitary soup lunches waved a newspaper clipping in Helen's face. "Why don't you have that book? It's on the *New York Times* best-seller list." He pointed out its place on the list, as if that could make her produce it.

"Our shipment was delayed," Helen lied.

"You're supposed to be a bookstore," he said. "Where are your books?" He threw the clipping on the counter and stormed out.

Behind him was an unhappy old hippie. His bald dome tapered off into a pony tail. His red eyes were dilated from weed. "Don't you have more of these music books? That's a pathetic selection, man." The Grateful Dead biography he handed Helen was well thumbed and sticky with spilled whipped-cream coffee.

"That's our only copy, sir. But I can check with the manager. We could sell it to you for ten percent off."

"I can't give this as a gift," he said, leaving the stained book on the counter next to the newspaper clipping. "Hey, no prob. I'll go to one of the chains. I just wanted to support your store."

Brad mourned the fact that the floors were no longer strewn with subscription cards. "The new magazines come out this week," he said. "These magazines are so old all the cards have fallen out. That *People* magazine story on J.Lo is four weeks old. I have to get my news about her on the Internet."

"What's wrong with that?"

"You can't take a computer into the bathroom," Denny said as he passed by with a tray of abandoned café plates and cups.

Brad glared at him. "It's not like that," he said. "J.Lo is a lovely person. The Internet runs the same four photos of her."

The only bright spot in Helen's depressing day was when Sarah walked in the door. Her friend wore a long cool dress the color of lemon sherbet. A shell cameo bracelet showed off her plump, pretty arm.

"When do you get off work?" she said.

"Half an hour. I'm on a shortened schedule. Everyone's hours were cut back."

"Then you need some serious cheering up. I'll be waiting in the café."

It was two o'clock when Helen finally balanced her cash drawer. Sarah was drinking something frothy with whipped cream. "Come on," she said. "There's still time to make it."

"Make what?" Helen said.

"Butterfly World. It's better than Valium."

"Is that the butterfly preserve in Coconut Creek? How much is admission?"

"About fifteen dollars," Sarah said.

Fifteen dollars was pocket change in Helen's old life. Now she didn't have the money, unless she wanted to skip meals. She'd learned to judge costs by how long she had to stand behind a counter. A Butterfly World ticket was two and a half hours on her feet.

"I can't go," Helen said. "I can't afford it."

"I'll pay for your ticket."

"I'm not a charity case," Helen said huffily.

"So pay me off at a buck a week. Consider it an investment in your mental health."

The world looked different riding high in Sarah's luxurious Range Rover. She'd bought it with the proceeds of some shrewd investments. Sarah was smart, no doubt about it. Which was why Helen downplayed the possibility of the bookstore's closing. Sarah wanted Helen to quit her dead-end job and get something that used her number-crunching talents. Helen couldn't tell her friend why she needed to steer clear of corporate and government computers. So Sarah delicately probed and Helen dodged her questions on the interminable trip.

The long drive to Butterfly World was made longer when they got stuck behind a car with a Quebec license plate, going twenty miles under the speed limit. "Can he go any slower? Why do Canadians drive like they're on ice?" Sarah grumbled.

"Why are South Floridians so prejudiced against Canadians?" Helen said.

"Because they're slow on the road and slower to pull out their wallets. You should see the anti-Canadian graffiti on my supermarket walls: 'Canadians, give us your money or go home.'"

"Every country has cheapskates," Helen said.

"You ever met a Canadian big spender?"

Fortunately, Helen didn't have to answer. They'd arrived at Butterfly World.

Helen looked at the names of the buildings on the tour map. "Isn't this a little overdone? The Paradise Adventure Aviary. What kind of adventures can you have in an enclosed building?"

"You'll see," Sarah said. "Go inside."

Helen stood in the entrance, dazzled. She'd never seen so many butterflies. There were hundreds. No, thousands. A big white butterfly looked like a piece of flying lace. A huge electric-blue one fluttered past, glowing in the sunlight. A flock of butterflies with camouflage owl eyes on their giant brown wings feasted on bananas.

Everywhere she turned was another strange and beautiful sight. An orange-and-brown moth the size of a dinner plate clung to a green branch.

"You have a butterfly on your back," Sarah said. "One of those electric-blue ones."

"He's wearing track shoes," Helen said, as the butterfly walked up her back. "For something that looks so light, he sure stomps around."

"You do attract the good-looking ones," Sarah said.

"Yeah," she said. "But they take off in a hurry." The blue butterfly was suddenly gone.

Mozart played softly in the background. A waterfall tumbled into a koi pond.

"This is so romantic," Helen said. "Maybe I could take Gabe here."

"Gabe?" Sarah said. "What happened to Rich?"

Helen pulled back her sleeve and showed her wrist. The bruises were now an ugly yellow-green.

Sarah looked shocked. "Good Lord. That's assault. Did you report it to the police? No? Well, I hope you at least took pictures of those bruises. Are you getting a restraining order on that man?"

Helen didn't want Rich around, but she wanted the police even less. Sarah was overreacting. "It was an accident. I don't think he realized his own strength. I'm not worried about Rich. He won't bother me. He hasn't had the nerve to come near me since. If he does, I'll sic Gabe on him."

"You aren't woman enough to do your own dirty work?" Sarah said disapprovingly. "Who is this Gabe and where did you meet him?"

Helen told the story of how they met, as a pair of sunshine-yellow butterflies fluttered nearby. Helen saw the pretty pair as an omen.

Sarah listened, a frown creasing her smooth skin, her brown eyes serious.

"Look, Helen, I'm glad you quit seeing Rich. I don't think those bruises were an accident. You don't want to date any man who would do that. But I wish you weren't getting serious about this Gabe so soon."

"I'm not serious. And Gabe is the exact opposite of Rich."

"An even better reason to avoid him," Sarah said. "Do you know anything about this man except he likes books?"

"That's a good start," Helen said.

"Who are his friends? Where's his family? Where does he work?"

"He has his own contracting business," Helen said, avoiding the other questions because she couldn't answer them.

"Contractors can be one step above drug dealers in South Florida. Shouldn't you at least check with the Better Business Bureau?"

"Why? He's not remodeling my kitchen."

"No? I bet he's got some plans for your bedroom. Be careful, Helen. Rich did more than bruise your wrist. He hurt your pride. And you aren't letting yourself heal. Instead, you've run straight to another man. You've spun some fantasies around this Gabe. You need time to find out if he's the real thing before you jump into another relationship."

Helen said nothing. Sarah had never met Gabe. Once she saw his handsome, open face and easy manner, she'd change her mind. Right now, Helen would change the subject.

"Look at that," she said. "A butterfly lounge."

A dozen red-and-black butterflies rested on a leaf the size of a hubcap. Butterflies with stained-glass wings sailed through dappled sunlight, sipped nectar, or sat on frilly purple orchids.

It was the last place to talk about murder. It was also the best place. Page Turner's ugly life and death seemed far away. So did Peggy's wretched jail cell. Helen recounted her sad visit to the county jail.

"Peggy is not telling me something," Helen said.

"Maybe she did it," Sarah said.

"No, Peggy said she didn't kill him. I believe her."

Helen was grateful that Sarah did not question her judgment, at least on this subject. If Helen thought her friend was innocent, that was good enough for Sarah.

"Then who did?"

"Just about everyone wanted Page dead. Look how many people hated him at the store. Even his own wife couldn't stand the man. Astrid must have known about all his girlfriends and that locked video cabinet in his office."

"Maybe they had some sort of arrangement, and he got sex elsewhere," Sarah said. "Some rich people have marriages of convenience."

"Astrid called him a son of a bitch the day he died. That's an angry woman, not an indifferent one," Helen said.

She looked up, startled, as a bright green leaf flew away. It was an emerald swallowtail. She was sprayed with mist.

"I think we're in the rain forest," Sarah said.

But nothing stopped Helen's speculations, not even indoor rain. "There's also Madame Muffy, the preppy psychic. There's something off about her, but I can't figure out what it is."

"She was at the barbecue, right?" Sarah said. "She was weird. You offered her a soda and she made a big deal about not drinking caffeine and chemicals."

"That's it!" Helen said. Suddenly she knew what was wrong. "The day Page died, Astrid called the store and wanted to talk with him. He wasn't answering his page. Rather than keep the owner's wife on hold, I went to his office. I heard people arguing inside. I knocked on the door and guess who came out? Madame Muffy, carrying an open bottle of Bawls with a straw. Bawls is laced with caffeine. So what was Miss I Don't Touch Chemicals doing with that bottle?"

"Sneaking a drink?" Sarah said. "I stayed at a hotel that had a fundamentalists' convention. All day long, they condemned dancing, fornication, and alcohol. All night long, the bar was empty, but room service went crazy delivering booze to the rooms."

Sarah was being unusually dense. Helen tried again. "I

think Muffy spiked his drink with sleeping pills or poison. She couldn't leave that bottle behind. The police would find it. So she took it with her. When Page left that last afternoon, he practically staggered out the door. I thought he was drunk. What if he was drugged?"

"OK, you saw Madame Muffy remove the evidence. Then what?"

"She's the mysterious person who picked him up after Peggy brought him back to the store. Muffy called him on his cell phone and sweet-talked him. Or offered him something he wanted."

"You're not suggesting . . ."

"Madame Muffy wouldn't be bad-looking if she took off those boring clothes."

"Thanks for that mental picture," Sarah said.

They sat on a wooden bench surrounded by palm fronds and flowers. Butterflies fluttered and darted in every direction. So did Helen's thoughts.

"It would be easy for Muffy to lead a drugged Page Turner into Peggy's apartment. The Coronado was closed for the tenting then, as Muffy well knew."

"And how would Madame Muffy get into Peggy's apartment without a key?"

"She could have crawled through an open window."

"Could she fit through those little windows?"

"I don't know. How about this? Madame Muffy lived at the Coronado. Peggy sat out by the pool most nights and left her house keys on the picnic table. Muffy could have made a wax impression of Peggy's house key. Then she could have her own key made."

"But why would Madame Muffy take Page to Peggy's apartment?"

"To frame her. Everyone had heard the story about her threatening Page."

"It's plausible. Except the Coronado was pumped full of

poison gas. How did Madame Muffy survive that? How did she open the locked door shield? And why did she want Page dead?"

"I don't know. But I'm going to find out," Helen said.

It was time to leave the butterfly paradise. Outside, they walked around a lake and a fragrant rose garden. There was a tiered fountain by the closed snack bar. Helen tossed in some coins.

"Throwing your money away?" Sarah teased.

"Wishing that Peggy would go free," Helen said.

"You don't get that by wishing," Sarah said. "You get that by working. Madame Muffy is your first target."

Chapter 15

Purple sunset clouds had drifted across the sky when Sarah dropped Helen off at the Coronado. She breathed in the warm evening air, an exotic mix of sweet night-blooming flowers, Cal's boiled broccoli, and Phil's burning pot.

The afternoon's pretty butterflies were gone. Now leathery-winged creatures were flapping in her stomach, stirring up her anxieties. Helen had work to do if she was going to save her friend. She needed to get into Madame Muffy's apartment, and Margery was the key. She had to persuade her landlady to do something illegal.

Margery was slouched in the same chaise longue where Peggy used to sit, smoking and staring into space. Her shorts set was dappled with purple butterflies. Helen took that as a good omen.

"You look thoughtful," Helen said.

"I've been thinking of wringing that blasted parrot's neck," Margery said. A rude squawk came from Margery's home.

"He misses Peggy," Helen said.

"We all do," Margery said, and blew out a dragon tail of smoke. "I've tried to think how I could have headed off this disaster, but I didn't see it coming. Now I can't see how to fix it."

"I do. I'm going to find Page Turner's killer. I think Madame Muffy had something to do with his murder."

"That's the best news I've heard all week," Margery said. She sat up straight, suddenly bright-eyed and alert. "You really think we can pin it on that obnoxious preppy?"

Helen told her about Madame Muffy and the bottle of Bawls. Margery smoked and listened. Finally, she said what Helen hoped: "Muffy's definitely mixed up in something. We need to take a look inside her apartment. I have a passkey. I can use it in case of emergency."

"Is this an emergency?" Helen said.

"It's a matter of life and death. I'm going to kill that parrot if he doesn't shut up. I want Peggy cleared so she can take Pete home."

Margery pointed to the lights in Madame Muffy's apartment. "She's home," she said. "It's only seven. We'll wait and see if she goes out tonight."

Margery smoked her way through half a pack by ten o'clock. Helen paced nervously by the pool until Margery said, "Sit down, will you? You're wearing out the grass."

Madame Muffy didn't budge.

"What's wrong with that young woman? She should be out enjoying herself," Margery said. "I don't think she's going anywhere tonight. What time do you go into work tomorrow?"

"Eleven a.m."

"That will work. Muffy usually leaves about eight-thirty and doesn't come back until late afternoon, unless she has a palm-reading client. We'll search her place at nine o'clock."

The next morning was dark and humid. Thunder echoed across the sky. Lightning flashed in strobelike flares. The palm trees shook and shivered, and fat raindrops plopped on the concrete. Helen was soaked by the time she ran over to Margery's place. She saw Pete's cage still had the cover on. He was asleep and silent.

"Good," Margery said, surveying the wretched weather from her kitchen window. "The rain will keep nosy Cal inside. Phil's no problem. He minds his own business."

She put her coffee cup in the sink and stubbed out her cigarette. "Let's go."

The fat drops had turned into a downpour. They splashed across the courtyard and up the steps to 2C.

"Take off your shoes," Margery said as she unlocked the door. "You don't want to track in anything that will make her suspicious." She produced a towel from under her top. "Dry yourself off with this. You don't want to drip, either."

Helen felt a guilty thrill as she stepped inside Madame Muffy's apartment.

"Breaking and entering is better than sex," Margery said.

"When's the last time you had sex?"

Margery shrugged. "It's been awhile. Maybe I've forgotten."

The bleak morning made Madame Muffy's apartment shadowy and mysterious. A crystal ball glowed in the dim light like a pearl. Helen looked into it.

"What do you see?" asked Margery.

"My nose. It's really big and shiny."

"We'd better get to work, in case she comes back early."

Muffy's apartment was still the same depressing combination of cheap furniture with cardboard-box accents. Muffy used two boxes as end tables next to the lumpy couch. Three boxes served as a coffee table. Three more were stacked into a bedside nightstand. They opened them all and found beige and brown sweaters, old boots, and astrology books. They found star charts, tarot cards, lists of clients, and lucky lottery numbers.

"Maybe I should keep these numbers for Peggy," Helen said.

"Maybe you should look for something to spring Peggy. Then she'd really be lucky."

They checked under the bed, under the mattress, and in the toilet tank. They read the opened piles of mail. Nothing.

"Where would you hide something in here?" Margery asked.

Helen thought about where she kept her cash stash. "Have you tried the utility closet?"

Inside were empty suitcases and extra blankets. But Helen was sure something was hidden in that closet. The water heater sat there, fat and dumb. Helen threw her arms around it.

"Ha. Even I'm not that desperate for something big and warm," Margery said.

Helen felt nothing. Then she realized she was about six inches taller than Madame Muffy. She moved her arms down and found what felt like a fat envelope taped to the back of the water heater. She ripped it off and pulled it out.

"It's stuffed with letters from a lawyer in Connecticut," she said.

Helen read them slowly. She couldn't believe what she was reading. Flamboyant Page Turner and mousy Madame Muffy? Helen was holding a fat motive for murder.

"Well, well. Madame Muffy sees money in her future."

"Who's she suing?" Margery asked, reaching eagerly for the letters.

"Nobody. Yet. Madame Muffy is trying to prove that she is the natural daughter of Page Turner. She wants his DNA for a test."

Margery whistled. "He died without any children. I can practically see the lines of salivating lawyers. They'd try to overturn the will. Muffy would be worth a fortune, even if the Turner family bought her off out of court."

"That argument I overheard in Page's office the day he died makes sense now," Helen said. "Muffy was yelling, 'You are. I know you are. My mother said so.' She was talking about Page being her father. Page told her, 'Your mother's crazy. And so are you. Get out.' Page Turner refused to acknowledge her as his daughter. He had the money for a real legal battle."

"It will be easier now with him dead. Think her lawyer will get Page's body exhumed for the DNA test?"

"Nice," Helen said. "First she gets him planted, then she has him dug up."

"I think we can have an interesting conversation with Madame Muffy this evening," Margery said, solemnly handing her the papers. They were a death warrant.

"I get off work at seven," Helen said. She retaped the envelope on the back of the water heater. They tiptoed out and Margery locked the door.

"Meet me at my place when you get home," was the last thing Margery said as she headed for her place. Suddenly, she looked ten years younger.

The day was longer than a public-radio fund drive, but finally Helen was at Margery's home. At seven-thirty that night, the two women knocked on the little psychic's door. Madame Muffy was at the wobbly patio table in the palm-reading parlor, finishing a rare steak. Helen thought she should be eating tofu and sprouts.

"Can I help you?" she said. "Would you like your palm read?"

"We're more interested in the past than the future," Helen said. "What were you doing in Page Turner's office the day he died?"

"Warning him about his terrible fate."

"Bullfeathers," said Margery. That bird must be driving her crazy if she was cussing with feathers, Helen thought.

"You told him you were his long-lost daughter," Helen said.

Madame Muffy turned pale. "You were listening at the door."

"What was in that Bawls bottle you took out of his office?"

Muffy looked puzzled. "In it? Nothing."

"Why did you take it?" Margery said.

Madame Muffy gave a little yip.

"I'll tell you why," Helen said, double-teaming her. "You drugged him so you could kill him."

Muffy turned whiter still. Now she was the color of dingy teeth. "What? I didn't want him dead. He's my father."

"Not according to him. He said you were nuts."

"That hurt," Muffy said. "But I knew my father would change his mind once he was presented with the proof. That's why I took his bottle of Bawls. I wanted his DNA off the straw."

The straw. Of course. She'd shipped it off to the lawyer. Now she was waiting on the lab report. She didn't care what was in the bottle.

"Why do you think Page Turner is your father?" Helen said. Actually, it wasn't an unreasonable assumption. Muffy was young enough to be Page Turner's daughter, and he could have fathered half of Fort Lauderdale.

"My mother said that she had an affair with him. Page wouldn't marry her when he found out she was pregnant. My mother married another man, who raised me as his child. After Daddy died, she told me who my real father was. The spirit voices told me I would come into a lot of money."

"You actually hear voices?" Helen said.

"Not all the time. But I heard them about Peggy, and look what happened to her. And I heard them this time. I heard the number nine hundred and the word 'book.' When I saw an article in *Forbes* magazine that Page Turner was worth nine hundred million dollars, I knew it was a sign my mother was telling the truth. I was Page Turner's daughter. I was entitled to my share of the Turner family fortune."

"I saw that article," Margery said. "That's the family's combined business fortune, if you count all their holdings. Page's share is only worth about ten million."

"It's still a lot of money," Muffy said. "It would have been easier for me to get it when he was alive. Then he could have acknowledged me. Now I'll have to contest the will."

"How'd you get in to see him at the bookstore?"

"I have a sexy voice on the phone. I said I'd always admired him and wanted to meet him. Of course, he was disappointed when he met me, but he's not supposed to be attracted to me. He's my father."

"Where's your mother fit into this? Won't she testify on your behalf?"

"My mother has Alzheimer's, so her word would not be good. But DNA would tell the truth. I got a lawyer who said I needed a DNA test to prove my case. So I stole the bottle of Bawls from my father's office.

"But I couldn't have killed him. I was reading palms at the Sunnysea Condo get-acquainted party. They expected me to dress up in scarves and beads like some carnival act. It was demeaning, but at least they paid me."

Muffy's eyes grew narrow. "And in case you're trying to accuse me, I was there until midnight the night my father died. I had about a hundred witnesses."

She handed Helen a pink flyer announcing *A Palm-reading Gala by Madame Muffy, Psychic Extraordinaire, From Eight p.m. Until the Midnight Hour.*

"You really have to lose that name," Margery said as Helen pulled her out the door.

Helen would check, but she knew the psychic's story was true. Their best chance was dead. Helen did not have to be psychic to see Peggy's hopeless future.

"You still believe she's innocent, don't you?"

Sarah called Helen at work the next day to find out how the Madame Muffy search went. She did not seem as discouraged by the results as Helen.

"Yes, I do. But Muffy was our best candidate," Helen said.

"But not your only one. You have to check out all the people who hated Page Turner."

"There's too many," Helen said. "And I didn't travel in his social circles. I couldn't get in any doors in Palm Beach."

"The last door he walked out alive wasn't in Palm Beach," Sarah said. "It was at that bookstore on Las Olas. Something happened there that led to his death. You have to find out what it was. Check out everyone at the store who had a good reason to kill Page Turner."

"But that could take years," Helen said.

"Peggy will be on death row a long time," she said.

Chapter 16

"There are two people in the large stall in the women's rest room," the woman said. She was forty-something, with the look of a no-nonsense mom. "One is a teenage boy about fourteen. The girl is about the same age. You can't miss them. The boy has blue hair."

"I'm sorry, ma'am," Helen said. "You shouldn't have to put up with that."

The mom shrugged. She seemed immune to teenage folly.

Anyone who believed bookstores celebrated the life of the mind didn't know about the bathrooms. Weird things happened there. People got naked. People got crazy. People had sex and drugs in the stalls. They pried open shoplifted CDs and buried the packaging in the rest-room trash. Public bathrooms were the bane of a bookseller's existence.

Helen spotted the kid when he came out into the store a few minutes later. He was all nose and bones, with hair the color of blueberry Jell-O. His plump girlfriend was dressed in black with dead-white skin and bug-blood nails. The pair left. That problem took care of itself, Helen thought.

But it didn't. Half an hour later, Blue Hair and the girl in black were back, heading for the bathroom.

"Oh, sir," Helen said loudly. The boy stopped.

"This time you might want to use the men's room," she said.

Blue Hair's face turned bright red. His girlfriend giggled. He made a U-turn and walked out the front door, the snickering girl following. Helen didn't think he'd be back soon.

Twenty minutes later, another woman was up at the cashier's desk. She had gray hair in a short sensible cut and wore a comfortable blue cotton dress. She looked smart, practical, and in charge. A nurse possibly, or a teacher. She said, "There's a man in the women's rest room. He's in the handicapped stall."

"Skinny kid with blue hair?" Helen said.

"Preppy in a pink shirt. I got a good look at him through the space in the door. He's about twenty-five, sandy hair, wearing khakis, boat shoes, and no socks. I didn't see a knife, gun, or other weapon, and he wasn't talking to himself."

The woman knew her Florida crazies. "Thank you for handling this so well," Helen said. The woman gave a short nod, like a superior officer acknowledging a sergeant, and marched out.

Helen paged Brad, and it was several minutes before the little bookseller came up front, loaded with books. He steadied the towering stack of slush with his chin.

"Brad, watch the register, please," Helen said. "There's a problem in the women's bathroom. Some preppy in a pink shirt is hiding in a stall."

"At least he's dressed," Brad said. "Last week, I got the naked guy drying himself in front of the men's-room hand dryer, holding his own wienie roast."

The bookstore bathrooms were at the top of a long corridor. At the other end were the steps up to Page's office. That section was roped off and had a PRIVATE—NO ADMITTANCE sign, but it was easy to step over the flimsy barricade. Helen saw the pink-shirted preppy in the hall, on the wrong side of the green velvet rope. He was coming from the direction of Page Turner's office.

"Excuse me, sir," Helen said.

"Do you want something?" he said, as if Helen were the one trespassing. He had blond hair and a built-in sneer.

"A woman reported that a man answering your description was lurking in a stall in the rest room," Helen said.

"The old biddy needed glasses," he said. "I'm here in the hall. And I'm not lurking. I'm lost."

"You're in a restricted area."

"I made a wrong turn," the preppy sneered.

"Maybe you'd better show me some identification."

"I don't have to do anything of the kind."

"No, you don't. You have another choice. I can call two strong booksellers and they can hold you here until the police arrive. Then we'll charge you with trespassing."

The preppy reluctantly pulled out his wallet. Instead of a driver's license, he produced a picture ID that said he was Harper Grisham IV, legislative assistant to State Senator Colgate Hoffman III. Were all those Roman numerals supposed to intimidate her? And why was that name familiar?

"You're a little far from Tallahassee," Helen said. "So why don't you go back where you belong?"

"Gladly," he said. Helen wanted to wipe that sneer off his face. Instead, she stood in the doorway and watched Harper the preppy stroll through the store. He walked at a stately pace, as befitted a future political mover and shaker. Finally, the preppy prowler was gone.

An hour later, Gayle was at Helen's register. She was not her usual cool self. Her blond hair stuck out at weird angles. Her black turtleneck was dotted with packing lint. She was definitely upset.

"Page's office has been broken into," she said. "I've called the police."

"Did they get anything?"

"I can't tell. I noticed the break-in when I took the last cash pickup to the safe. The office lock was jimmied. I've never seen such a mess. The place is ransacked. Astrid has been through so much, and now she'll have to deal with this."

"Why? I know she's the owner, but you know what's there better than she does."

Gayle ran her fingers through her hair, and sent her bangs up in more spikes. "I thought the police made a mess, but that was nothing. Papers are tossed all over the floor. The file drawers are open. The couch is slashed. Things are broken and overturned. The locked video cabinet door was bashed in, too. I guess someone didn't know the police took all the videos. Either that, or the thief wanted it to look that way. There's a lot of damage."

"I caught a guy in the back hall about an hour ago," Helen said. "I have his name. He's a legislative assistant to State Senator Colgate Hoffman III." As soon as she said the name out loud, she knew why it was familiar. The thought rocked her.

"Why would a senator's assistant break into Page's office?"

Helen knew, but she couldn't say why. Peggy had starred in the missing video with the senator's late son.

The women's rest room was right next to the rope barricade. Someone must have come along when the preppy prowler was trying to break into the office and he ducked in there. It was the closest hiding place.

The store was soon overrun with police. Helen expected the evidence technician and burglary detectives. But she didn't expect to see Homicide Detective Clarence Jax. He spent most of the afternoon with Gayle, while she tried to figure out what was missing. Helen rang up the customers and gave vague answers to their curious questions about the police.

Gayle was her capable self the next time Helen saw her. The punk-stress spikes were gone. Her black clothes were lint-free. She was a gunslinger in Doc Martens.

"Nothing's missing," the manager concluded. "Whoever did it trashed the place. I think it was a pissed-off staffer. But Detective Jax wants to hear about your preppy prowler."

Jax peppered her with questions that made Helen feel like she was lying, even when she wasn't. "And you actually saw the senator's aide in the women's bathroom?" he said. Did he think she was making that up?

"No, I didn't. A woman customer reported him there."

"Do you have her name and number? Do you have a description of her?"

"I didn't take her phone number. She was about fifty, on the chunky side, short gray hair. A sensible-looking woman." Helen hoped that would make Jax believe her.

"Did she pay for a purchase by check or credit card? We could find her that way."

"She didn't buy anything," Helen said. "She reported a strange man in the women's bathroom and I went back to investigate."

"And then she left? Without buying anything?" Helen thought she heard more skepticism in his voice. "Did you see this man in the rest room?"

"No, he was in the hall, in the restricted area."

"Did he say why he was there?"

"He claimed he was lost, even though he'd have to step over a velvet rope with a PRIVATE sign on it."

"Did you see him near the office door? Did he have anything in his hand?"

"No. He was coming from the direction of Mr. Turner's

office, but I didn't actually see him touch the door. He didn't seem to have anything with him."

Because he didn't find anything, Helen thought.

"What was his demeanor?"

"Arrogant," Helen said.

"But he didn't seem furtive or guilty?" Jax said. "He didn't appear to be hiding anything?"

"No, I asked for identification. He showed me his legislative assistant's ID, as if that was supposed to impress me. He left when I asked him."

"So at the time, you didn't think his actions were suspicious enough to report him to the police?"

"No," Helen said. "That was before I knew about the break-in."

"Well, we'll talk to him," he said.

He doesn't believe me, Helen thought. She wanted to scream in frustration. She knew why the preppy prowler was in Page's office, and why he could brazen it out. He didn't find the video with Peggy and the senator's dead son. He came away with nothing. Helen wondered if the ambitious little twit was acting on the senator's orders, or if he thought he could advance his career with a timely burglary.

But Helen couldn't mention the video to Detective Jax. Yes, it would explain why the pink-shirted prowler was in Page's office. But it would also give the police an even stronger motive for Peggy to commit murder.

There was only one good thing about the break-in: It proved Peggy was innocent. She was in jail when it happened. For the first time, Helen felt hope.

Detective Jax stopped by the bookstore the next day. He flashed his badge and his smile at a woman waiting in line, and stepped up to Helen's cash register. Once again, he had those aggressive movements, that fiery red hair and air of righteousness. Jax had arrested her friend for murder, but

Helen recognized a man who believed he had done the right thing.

"Mr. Harper Grisham IV says he was never in your bookstore. He produced two witnesses who say he was on the beach with them in Fort Lauderdale all day."

"And you believe that?" That preppy scum had lied.

"They all have sunburns," Jax said.

"This time of year, you can burn in ten minutes. He was here. Why would I make up that story?" Helen could feel her rage building. The angry heat rose out of her core and seemed to travel up her spinal column.

"He says you're politically motived. You're a liberal trying to hurt Senator Hoffman's chances of reelection."

Another lie, even more outrageous. Her anger level was rising. "I never laid eyes on him before I found him wandering the bookstore hall."

"Maybe he is lying," Jax said. "But you're not telling me the whole truth, either. You're holding back something about this prowler. I know it. I want to know what it is."

Helen pretended to be interested in her cash register keys. Mentioning that video would sign Peggy's death warrant.

When she thought she could talk without her voice shaking, she said, "You've got to reopen Page Turner's murder investigation. This break-in proves Peggy was innocent. She was in jail when it happened. She couldn't have done it."

"The break-in has nothing to do with Page Turner's murder," Jax said. "The investigation is closed. Ms. Freeton killed him. I can't investigate a case that's going to trial. It's over."

Red rage surged up and boiled over in her brain. It was the same rash anger that destroyed her St. Louis life. "Your mind is made up," she said. "Don't confuse you with the facts. You'd rather send an innocent woman to her death.

Tell me this, Detective Jax. Why would Peggy kill that man and leave his body in her bed?"

"Because her brains were fried on coke. People who use drugs don't make sensible decisions. And she does use drugs. We have her on tape."

"Not anymore. She's clean. She was framed. But you'd rather railroad an innocent woman, because you need that case cleared. Page Turner was an important man. Peggy's not important. But she is my friend, and she didn't kill him."

She regretted her outburst instantly. She waited for Jax to lash back. Instead, he picked up a delicate gift book from a counter display, *What Is a Friend?* Its cover was garlanded with pink ribbons and roses. He coolly paged through its flowery sentiments.

"Loyalty to a friend is a beautiful thing," he said, holding up the book. "But some loyalty is misplaced. I can't see a nice woman like you being friends with a coke dealer."

"No," Helen protested, but that small word didn't seem strong enough to ward off the ugly accusation. The thought made her sick. "Peggy may have used it years ago, but she never sold cocaine."

"That's not what I heard," he said. He tossed the open book on the counter and walked out.

Helen picked it up and read the page: *A friend is someone who can tell you anything—and everything.*

Chapter 17

"He's a damn liar," Margery said. Her face was purple with rage. It set off her violently violet shorts and purple tennis shoes. She'd been skimming dead leaves out of the Coronado pool when Helen came home from work that afternoon.

Now Helen's landlady held the long-handled net like a warrior's spear and declared, "Peggy's no coke dealer. Do you think for one minute I'd tolerate drugs at the Coronado?"

The scent of Phil's pot smoke wafted on the warm air. Helen's nostrils quivered. "Phil's different," Margery said. "Anyway, he's not a dealer."

"Then why would Detective Jax say that?"

"Cops lie," Margery said. "They aren't sworn to tell the whole truth and nothing but the truth during an investigation. They'll lead you on with a little falsehood and feel it's in a good cause. If Jax can turn you against Peggy, you may give him more information to nail her. At the very least, you won't be a character witness for her in court."

Some character, Helen thought. I couldn't testify on her behalf if I wanted.

"I thought I could get him to start asking himself questions, so he'd reopen the investigation."

"He can't reopen the investigation," Margery said. "Don't you understand? Once Peggy was arrested, he couldn't investigate anyone else for that murder. Do you know what a good defense attorney would do with that? 'Tell me, Detective, is it not true that you continued to look for another suspect even after my client was arrested and in jail pending trial?' "

"How do you know so much about how the police operate?" Helen said.

"You live as long as I do, you learn things. The hard way," Margery said, and the door slammed shut on her past again, locking Helen out. She put the leaf net away, then uncoiled a green garden hose and began cleaning off the pool deck. Helen slipped off her shoes, rolled up her pants cuffs, and got her toes wet in a poolside puddle. She smelled the ozone rising off the warm wet concrete and felt the sun on her back. They soothed her.

"I never understood why the police arrested Peggy," she said. "It's obvious someone put Page's body in her place to set her up. How could Peggy go into a tented building filled with tear gas and poison gas? She isn't Superwoman."

Margery adjusted the nozzle. A stream of water drove the pool deck's dirt and debris into the grass. "Did you know what your wine-drinking buddy did for a living?" Did. Margery used the past tense, as if Peggy was never going back—or she was dead.

"She's a receptionist for some company off Cypress Creek Road," Helen said.

"Do you know the company's name?" Mist rose from the hot concrete as the hose squirted it.

"NECC. ENCC. Something anonymous. Peggy said her job was as dull as the name."

"The company is National Environmental Cleanup Corp. They get called in when there's asbestos in a building, or there's a toxic spill or some other environmental cleanup problem."

Helen felt sick. She knew where this was heading.

"They have SCBA breathing equipment. Keep it in a locked room. Peggy had the keypad combination taped inside her desk," Margery said.

"Of course she did. She worked there."

"Yeah, well, the police think she took her work home with her."

Margery turned off the water and coiled up the hose. Helen could feel her own fear coiling inside. I'm not wrong. Peggy didn't kill him, she told herself. I knew her. At least, I thought I knew her. "How do you know this stuff about the investigation?" she said.

"Never mind how I know. I've lived here a long time. I have friends."

"I thought Peggy was my friend. Why didn't she tell me where she worked?"

"She learned not to talk about it," Margery said. "Florida's not exactly famous for protecting the environment. When people found out she worked for a bunch of tree huggers, she'd get some crazy reactions. She had to listen to a lot of lectures."

"Taking out asbestos is a tree-hugging activity?"

"Around here it is," Margery said.

"But she didn't actually use the equipment at work. She wasn't cleaning contaminated sites. She answered the phone and typed letters."

"Peggy's not stupid. If she was around the equipment on a daily basis, she'd know how to use it," Margery said.

"Okay, even if she had access to SCBA equipment, how did she get into her apartment when the building was tented?" Helen said. "She's bigger than Muffy. I don't think she could fit through those little windows."

"She had a key, what do you think?"

"But she didn't have a key to that big metal shield they put on the doorknob," Helen said. "Only Trevor the fumigator had those. Peggy couldn't get into her own apartment even if she wanted." Helen felt better just saying it. It was more proof Peggy was innocent.

"Maybe we should ask Trevor," Margery said. "I'll take him some of my brownies. Come in and cool off while I change my shoes."

Margery opened her kitchen door to a blast of chilled air. She slipped off her tennis shoes and started walking across the floor. Her feet made an odd crunching sound, as if she was walking on eggshells. She pointed to Pete's cage. "I've got to get that seed-slinging monster out of my kitchen. I'm sick of my floor crunching with birdseed. And feathers are everywhere."

Pete screeched. The sound was an icepick in Helen's ear.

"Oh, yeah," Margery said. "The noise. How could I forget? He never shuts up."

"He's lonesome," Helen said.

"I'd like to give him your cat for company."

Helen tried to soothe Pete by petting him, but he snapped at her finger. Instead, she swept up the spilled birdseed. Green fluff and feathers floated on the air. The little Quaker parrot was pining for his Peggy. Helen sighed. She put away the broom when Margery clattered out in purple ankle-strap slides. "It's all set. I called the office and got the address where Trevor is tenting. He'll be there until six."

Margery took a dozen brownies out of the freezer and microwaved them. "They'll smell like fresh-baked," she said, wrapping them in foil. Helen followed Margery out to her big white Cadillac. Helen was sure that once you collected Social Security, the state of Florida automatically issued you a big white car.

"We're in luck. He's at a hardware store in Pembroke Pines." Margery drove at a stately pace. They didn't need to check the address. They could see the building, covered in flapping canvas, a block away.

"Do you think he'll talk to us?" Helen said.

"No man can resist my brownies," Margery said.

Certainly not Trevor. "Fresh-baked," he said when Margery handed him the warm package. Helen felt rather baked herself, standing in the hardware store's parking lot in the four-o'clock heat. Trevor looked cool in his pressed uniform. The man didn't sweat.

"I wish I could help you," he said after he stashed the brownies in his truck. "I'd like to set an innocent free, like I was set free. But those door-shield locks are mostly for show. You could pop them with a screwdriver."

Helen said nothing on the drive back. There was nothing to say.

It all went back to Peggy. She had the answers. Helen had to ask the questions. She caught the bus after work.

This time Helen had no fear of the police when she visited the North Broward jail. She had put on her cloak of invisibility. The ugly thick-soled bookstore shoes and sensible clothes turned her into a faceless clerk. She presented her fake ID without fear. You can get used to anything, she thought. Even talking to your friend through Plexiglas. But nothing could protect her from the sight of Peggy.

Peggy wasn't just losing weight. She was shrinking. She seemed to be collapsing inside her baggy jailhouse suit. Her pale skin was an unhealthy yellow. Her large elegant nose had become a bony beak. For the first time, Helen saw gray in Peggy's dark red hair.

Now Helen was going to add to her misery. She took another look at this new, frail Peggy and almost stopped. But it had to be done or she'd never get Peggy out of here.

She picked up her phone and said, "A legislative assistant to Senator Hoffman was at the bookstore. I found him wandering in the restricted area. I can't prove it, but I know he's the one who broke into Page Turner's office. The place was trashed. Whoever did it was obviously looking for something. They even broke open the locked video cabinet—although why anyone would bother to lock an empty cabinet, I'll never know."

A single tear rolled down Peggy's cheek.

"What is it, Peggy? What's going on? You've got to tell me. How can I help you if I don't know?"

"They don't have it," Peggy said. "I thought they did. That's why I kept quiet. But they don't have it."

"Don't have what?" A deputy walked by. Helen realized she was almost shouting into the phone.

"The video. That horrible sex video." Peggy was crying harder now. Helen had trouble understanding her. "It would have destroyed me, but the fight wasn't about me. It was about two powerful men. I was caught in their cross fire. Page Turner never blackmailed me. I wasn't important enough."

Peggy stopped and began plucking at a loose string on her top until Helen thought she would scream. "Tell me, Peggy. Please."

Peggy wiped her eyes and took a deep gulping breath. "You know about the video with the cocaine and Senator Hoffman's son."

Helen nodded.

"There was some ugly stuff on that video. Not just the sex. Collie hated his father. He said things like, 'My father's big on law and order—for other people. When I get caught, he calls in his fixers. If I did crack in Homestead instead of coke in Lauderdale, they'd lock up my ass and throw away the key.' "

"And he said this while snorting the white stuff?" Helen said.

Peggy nodded. "There was a lot more. It's like he made this tape to get even with his father. And then . . . there was the sex. You must think I'm a real slut." She was picking at the loose thread again.

"I think you're my friend, and I'm sorry you're in this mess."

Peggy quit torturing the thread. "Collie's death was my wake-up call. I went into rehab and got Pete and played the lottery."

She laughed bitterly. "Doesn't sound like much of a life, does it? But I was happy. Or at least I didn't hurt anymore. Then Gayle found out that Page was planning to use the tape to ruin Senator Hoffman. She warned me."

"Gayle? How did she know?"

Peggy shrugged. "She must have overheard something at the bookstore."

"Why would Page do that? Was he drunk or crazy?"

"Neither," Peggy said. "Senator Hoffman cost Page Turner several million dollars. He talked him into investing in some energy stock."

"Enron?"

"No, that's not the name. But it tanked like Enron. Unfortunately, the senator neglected to tell Page to sell the stock when it started diving. Page lost about three million. He was going to have to close the bookstores because of the losses. He'd used their working capital."

Finally, the store closings made sense. The stores weren't losing money. Page had taken their cash and blown it on bad investments.

"He'd embezzled from the stores."

"Well, he owned the stores, so I don't know if you'd call it embezzling. But the family wasn't going to bail him out. Gayle said they hushed it up, but he was stuck with the losses.

"Page tried to get the senator to cover his losses, but

Hoffman said he couldn't do anything about it. That's when Page vowed to ruin him by turning that tape over to the press. It would make the senator a laughingstock."

"Right," Helen said. "Hoffman's running on a family-values, antidrug platform. If the voters saw his coke-snorting son saying what a hypocrite he was, the senator couldn't run for a bus."

"Page hoped to get his money back by threatening Hoffman with the tape. But it would also ruin my life. I'd be a national joke, worse than Monica Lewinsky. At least she didn't have sex with a man who turned up dead the next day. I'd kill myself before I went through a scandal like that. I called Page and tried to appeal to his better instincts."

"So you picked him up at the bookstore," Helen said.

"I told him it wasn't fair. I would be destroyed because he was angry at the senator. Page laughed at me. He said this was payback for when I ran into the store in my nightgown."

"And then what?"

"I knew it was hopeless," Peggy said. "He got that cell phone call. I drove him back to the bookstore. I hated him. I wanted him dead.

"Then someone who hated Page even more killed him and left him to rot in my bed."

Chapter 18

"Wanna dance on the table with gorgeous men?" Sarah said when Helen answered the bookstore phone.

"Best invitation I've had all day," Helen said. "Where are these dancing men?"

"They're the waiters at Taverna Opa, a Greek restaurant in Hollywood. The female servers are good-looking too, but they're not my type. Anyway, the staff dances with the diners on the tabletops. The music is loud, the food is good, and the male waiters look hot in tight white T-shirts. It's tough getting a table on the weekends, but tonight we should have no problem."

"I have a problem," Helen said. "I don't have any money."

"Oh, come on. You can afford an appetizer and a drink. You're turning into a mope."

"Sarah, I'd love to go, but when my hours were cut, so was my pay."

"So let me buy."

"No," Helen said. "I'll pay my own way, or not go at all."

"This isn't charity. It's friendship."

"Friends should be equals," Helen said.

"It's just money," Sarah said, irritated. "Look, it's ten a.m. Call me if you change your mind."

Did she slam down the phone, or did Sarah? Helen used to think it was just money, back when she made six figures. Now that she had to struggle, she knew money gave you peace of mind and independence. (But not happiness, a voice whispered. It gave you a lying, cheating husband.)

Helen sighed and looked around at the nearly empty bookshelves. With no new books coming in, the shelves were growing bare. The booksellers had covered the empty spaces by turning the books face-out, like the letter tiles in a Scrabble game. It worked for now. But as those books sold, Helen wondered what they would do. Maybe the store would be closed by then. She had to keep looking for a job.

At lunch, Helen ate a Luna bar, bought a cup of coffee, and went out for a free paper. She found a bench under a palm tree and read the want ads. The only jobs that paid anything were for telemarketers, and Helen hadn't stooped that low. Yet.

Then she saw something promising: *Watch this spot for the job jamboree at Down & Dirty Discounts. The new Triple D on Federal Highway near Broward opens soon. Jobs galore for eight dollars an hour and more.*

Good money within walking distance. The upstart Down & Dirty was giving Wal-Mart a run for its money. Helen would apply for a job as soon as the stores started accepting applications. She walked back to work with a spring in her step, admiring the warm blue sky, the pink and red impatiens blooming around the tree trunks. She saw something greenish gray on the sidewalk. Wait! Was that what she thought it was? Did someone drop a dollar? She bent down and picked up—

A hundred-dollar bill! Half a week's pay was at her feet.

Helen couldn't believe her luck. The most she'd ever found had been a Georgia quarter. Now Ben Franklin was smiling coyly at her. The redesigned currency made the founding father look like a Grateful Deadhead. She wanted to kiss him.

She saw two young men elbowing each other and thought, They want my hundred. They're going to say they dropped it. Helen wasn't going to let anything happen to her windfall. She shoved the bill into the inside zip pocket of her purse, then hurried into Page Turners to call Sarah.

"God wants me to go to Taverna Opa," she told her friend.

"The devil is more like it," Sarah said.

"Nope. God must be a woman. She put a hundred-dollar bill right in my path, so I can see the natural beauties of Florida. Take me to Taverna Opa."

"I'll pick you up at seven," Sarah said.

Just the thought of that much free money was liberating. Helen felt inspired. She would save Peggy. She would find out who killed Page Turner. She'd love to pin Page's murder on the preppy prowler, Harper Grisham IV. But he wouldn't give her the time of day, much less tell her where he was the night Page died. There had to be a way to make him tell her.

"Son of a bitch," said Brad the bookseller, as he came back from lunch. "I got a twenty-dollar ticket. All because this place is too cheap to give us free parking."

Parking was scarce on Las Olas. The lot behind the bookstore cost four dollars an hour. Most booksellers were not about to spend half their pay on parking. Instead, they found free parking five or six blocks away.

"What happened?" Helen said.

"The ticket says I was in a no-parking zone," he said. "I

didn't see the yellow paint on the curb. First my hours were cut, now this. I don't know how I'll make the rent."

The little bookseller's shoulders were hunched, and his head hung down in defeat.

"I'm sorry, Brad," she said. But Brad's misfortune was her gain. She knew now how to question the preppy prowler. It was risky. If he had caller ID, she would be fired, but this job wouldn't last much longer anyway.

When there was a lull in the customers, she asked Brad to cover for her and headed for the break room. She dialed Senator Hoffman's Tallahassee office and said, "Hello, may I please speak to Mr. Harper Grisham?"

After a brief wait, his arrogant voice was on the phone. "This is Harper Grisham."

Helen held her nose to make her voice nasal. "This is the city of Fort Lauderdale," she said. "You have an unpaid parking ticket for two hundred dollars, plus fifty dollars in court costs and overdue fines. We are issuing a bench warrant for your arrest."

"You're joking," Grisham said. His voice was relaxed, affable, as befit a future ruler of the free world.

"I am completely serious, sir," Helen said, still pinching her nose. "The ticket was issued June second at eight p.m. You were ticketed a second time at eleven-thirty p.m. for nonremoval of your vehicle." She was making up the charges as she went along.

"I was in Tallahassee that night at a rally for Senator Colgate Hoffman," Grisham drawled. "I can have my office send you a news clip that shows me on the platform."

Suddenly the affability was gone, and there was a lash in his voice. "But if I have to do that, I'll have your job, you incompetent moron. What is your name?"

Helen hung up and let go of her nose.

The preppy prowler wasn't guilty of murder. Too bad. Helen would have loved to administer that lethal injection herself. She wondered how she was going to help Peggy now.

Sarah pulled up in her green Range Rover at seven on the dot, wearing a green linen Ralph Lauren pantsuit that set off her curly brown hair, and square-cut emeralds at her ears and throat.

Helen whistled. "Wow, you look good. Mind being seen with me?" She was suddenly ashamed of her clunky bookstore shoes.

"You look fine," Sarah said. "But if you want to change your clothes, I can take you home first."

"Naw, I'll just slip off my shoes if I dance on the table-top. Ben Franklin is burning a hole in my pocket. Let's eat, my treat."

The line for Opa was out the door at seven-thirty. "Not bad," said Sarah. "On the weekends, the crowd is lined up across the parking lot."

In fifteen minutes, they were inside, where they were hit with a blast of Greek music. It seemed to vibrate off the floor and slam into the ceiling. A twenty-something waiter who looked like a Greek James Dean was dancing on the table with a woman of forty. She was shaking her hips like an exotic dancer, and he was matching her move for move.

Everyone at the table was cheering—except for one surly-looking man. Her husband? Helen wondered.

Across the room, a woman server of about twenty was dancing on a long table with a white-haired man of seventy, while his family yelled "Opa!" and applauded. His moves were stiff and too slow for the music, but he looked so happy Helen laughed out loud.

The host showed Helen and Sarah to a table on an open gallery running along the main room. It had a view of the water on one side and the table dancing on the other. Suddenly, the dance was over, and the waiters went back to running drinks and hauling huge trays of food.

The dark-haired James Dean brought a wooden bowl of chickpeas to their table and, using a pestle, mashed them into hummus. Helen and Sarah spread it on crusty bread. It was strong with garlic.

"This is good," Helen said.

With the hundred burning a hole in her pocket, she ordered lavishly: caviar spread, roast lamb, grilled sea bass, Greek salad with snowdrifts of feta cheese, lots of wine to cut the olive oil.

Periodically, the waiters would jump on the wooden tables on the main floor and start dancing. One or two brave diners would join them, while their friends clapped and hooted.

"Are you going to dance?" Helen asked Sarah.

She looked at their wobbly plastic table and said, "Do you really think this will support me?"

"How about the wooden tables in the main area?" Even now, a sizable woman was shaking her hips over plates of moussaka.

"Right," Sarah said. "I can see me now. 'Excuse me, sir. Could you move your sea bass? I'd like to climb on your table and dance with your hunky waiter.'"

Helen laughed. "It's a spectator sport for me, too."

They talked and laughed and ate until Helen felt better than she had in months. It was fun to have money again, even for one night. Over strong black coffee and sweet flaky baklava, Sarah asked, "How are your efforts to save Peggy going?"

"Not so good. Everything I find out just makes it worse." She told Sarah about Peggy's job and the videotape. "I'm a little hurt, too. Why didn't Peggy tell me anything about herself?"

"She probably didn't want to look bad. You're a good

person, Helen. One look at you, and you can tell you don't do drugs or know anything about the police. Peggy was probably ashamed of her old life and thought you wouldn't understand."

She doesn't suspect, Helen thought. None of them do. If I told Sarah I was on the run, hiding from my ex and the courts, she wouldn't believe me. What right do I have to be hurt by Peggy hiding her past? What have I told her or Sarah about me?

"I want to help her," Helen said. "But I'm spinning my wheels. Today, I found out the preppy prowler had a decent alibi. I would have loved to pin it on him."

"Don't give up," Sarah said. "You have a lot of work to do. You have to check the alibis of anyone in the bookstore who wanted to kill him."

"That's a lot of people, Sarah. I can't just ask them, 'Where were you the night Page Turner died?'"

"You won't have to. It's like love. Just let it happen naturally."

"I've not had much luck in love, either," Helen said.

"How are things going with your contractor?"

Helen was irritated that Sarah wouldn't say Gabriel's name. "Just fine. I'm taking it slowly. We had coffee at the café. He's taking me to the Shakespeare festival on Sunday to see *A Midsummer Night's Dream*."

"You know any more about him?"

"I know a man who likes Shakespeare is a rare find in Florida."

"Just because a man likes culture doesn't make him a good person. Hitler loved art and opera."

"Sarah! Are you comparing Gabriel to Hitler?"

"No, I'm just telling you to be careful. This is South Florida."

"Anything else, ladies?" said their James Dean waiter. His white T-shirt was sweaty from his last dance. It clung to his muscular torso, revealing well-developed pecs. Helen thought of a few answers to his question, but said, "It's time for the check."

The bill for their meal was $79.82. That was the end of her hundred-dollar bill, she thought. But it was a glorious meal and an entertaining evening, except for Sarah's last lecture. And her friend did care about her. She was just overly concerned. Maybe Sarah needed a date, Helen thought.

She pulled out the hundred-dollar bill from the zippered compartment where she'd stashed it. It felt odd. Lighter or thinner or something. Helen looked at it in the waning evening light. No, that was definitely Ben Franklin. The man may have said a penny saved is a penny earned, but he looked happy on a hundred.

But the bill felt wrong. Helen turned it over. The back side was blank white paper. Printed in heavy black ink was *Sucker!*

Helen felt the blood drain from her face. She thought she was going to lose her hundred-dollar dinner. Suddenly, the scene with the two young men nudging each other took on another meaning. They didn't want her bill. They were laughing at her. She was a stupid greedhead.

Sucker! indeed.

"Helen, are you OK? What's wrong?"

Helen showed her the fake hundred-dollar bill. Sarah burst out laughing. "It's a color Xerox copy. I've heard of these. They're the latest scam. Crooks have been putting them on high-grade paper and passing them off as real bills to busy cashiers. Some copies are good enough, if they aren't inspected too closely. This one is not bad. Leaving the fake bill on the sidewalk is a new twist. Trust Florida to invent it." Like many residents, Sarah seemed proud of the endless creativity of the local scam artists.

"I feel like such a fool," Helen said. "I only have two dollars." She apologized until Sarah begged her to stop.

"Forget it," she said. "It was worth the entertainment value." She whipped out her credit card and cheerfully paid the bill, leaving a generous tip. "Ready to go?"

Helen nodded. *Sucker!* the fake bill screamed at her. Helen tore it up.

But she felt like the word was branded on her forehead.

Chapter 19

"Excuse me, I need some help here."

A lean woman with bad skin and dead-black hair plunked four paperbacks down on the counter at Helen's register. They weren't the usual women's reading: *Letters to Penthouse XIV, XV, XVI, XVII.*

"I'm not sure this is what I want," she said. "I need a book on talking dirty. Can you see if you have any books like that?"

Helen typed *talking dirty* into the bookstore computer and got several hits. She read the titles out loud.

"No, that's not quite it." The hard-faced woman had a surprisingly soft voice. "How about 'talking sexy'?"

Helen typed in those key words. "I get a lot of books, but they're about relationships."

"I don't want a relationship."

"Can I ask what you do want?" Helen said.

"I'm going back to work doing phone sex. It's been a couple of years and I'm out of practice. The new place does not allow scripts. I need some backup in case I go dry."

Helen typed in *phone sex.* Bingo. "Here's *Confessions of*

a Phone-sex Queen. We don't have the book in stock, but I can order it."

"I'll take it," the woman said.

Another satisfied customer, Helen thought. "What's your last name?"

"Retner," the woman said. That name was familiar.

Helen typed it in and saw three other Retners had ordered books in the last thirty days. One was Albert. Helen wondered what kind of book the prissy, bad-tempered manager would order.

Curiosity overcame her. After the phone-sex worker left, Helen looked in the computer. Albert had ordered *Smother Love: The True Story of a Serial Killer Who Smothered His Victims to Death.*

Interesting.

Helen checked the publisher's information on *Smother Love.* She read: *Darryl Eugene Crow was shy and quiet, but he had no problem finding women. The relationships never lasted. When love died, Darryl Eugene's lovers died, too. He would ply his soon-to-be lost loves with alcohol, then end their lives with a pillow. This compelling study of . . .*

End their lives with a pillow? That was how Page Turner died. He was drunk, too.

When did Albert get this book?

Helen looked at the computer record. The book arrived three weeks before Page Turner died.

Helen couldn't see Albert killing someone with a knife or a gun. That would be messy. He might get blood on his hands. But something sneaky, like smothering a defenseless drunk, that was his style. She could imagine him pressing down that pillow. It would be neat and quick. Albert wouldn't even get his starched shirt wrinkled.

"Did Albert work the night Page Turner died?" Helen asked Brad.

The little bookseller looked skittish. "No, he got off work at six with me."

"Where did Albert go after work?"

"Why don't you ask him?" Brad said. "Excuse me, I have to go." He seemed anxious to get away. Had she offended him? And how could she ask Albert such a personal question? The thought made her head throb, and that gave her an idea. Helen waited till he returned from lunch, then clutched her forehead dramatically. She knew she couldn't count on Albert to ask what was wrong. If she fell over on the floor, he'd reprimand her for lying down on the job.

She said, "Do you have any aspirin, Albert? Ever since Page Turner died, I've had the worst headaches."

"I don't dispense medication," Albert said. "I read where a woman at a store was sued because she gave an aspirin to a customer."

"For heaven's sake, Albert, I'm not going to sue you. I have a headache. Didn't Page Turner's murder bother you?"

"Well, it has affected my colitis," he said. "Just this morning . . ."

You asked for it, Helen thought, as Albert gave her the intimate details of his ailment. At least they were bonding. "I've never had an attack so explosive," he finished. "It's gotten much worse since Mr. Turner passed on. Stress, you know."

"That's terrible," she cut in quickly. "His death seems to have caused so many problems. When Page left the store that Friday, I had no idea it would be the last time I'd see him alive. I went to a party, like it was any other day. Where did you go?"

"What I do on my own time is my business," Albert said, and his lips zipped. So much for bonding.

He's hiding something, Helen thought. And I'm going to find out what it is.

But not tonight. Tonight she had another task. It was even worse than listening to Albert. She had to call her mother in St. Louis. Once a month, at seven in the evening, she made the call. And dreaded it the rest of the time.

At home, Helen prepared herself. She shut the miniblinds and locked the door, then opened her utility closet and got out the battered Samsonite suitcase that held her seven-thousand-dollar stash. She rooted around in the old-lady underwear until she found the cell phone and a piece of pink cellophane from a gift basket.

She'd bought the cell phone in Kansas when she was on the run. She'd sent her sister Kathy a thousand dollars and hoped that would cover the bills for a long time. Her air conditioner was rattling so loud, it sounded like it was about to take off and join the mother ship. She had to turn it off so she could hear on the phone.

"Hi, Mom. How's everything?" she said.

"Just fine," said her mother in a high, clipped voice that signaled disaster. "Absolutely peachy. Kathy—you remember your sister?—was in the hospital with emergency surgery. I'm taking care of the kids. Of course, I couldn't call you, because I don't know where you are, and you won't tell me."

"Surgery? Oh, my God. What's wrong?" Not Kathy, the only person she trusted.

"She had her gall bladder removed," her mother said. She was dragging it out, reveling in Helen's remorse and guilt.

"The doctor was able to do the so-called easy surgery, but her recovery has been slow. It didn't help that you weren't at your sister's side when she needed you, because you're busy ruining your life for a stupid, stubborn reason."

"It's not stupid," burst out Helen. "Rob betrayed me—with Sandy, a woman he said he couldn't stand."

"He made a mistake. Men do that."

"A mistake! Mother, that man didn't have a job for *five years*. He lived off me during that time. He was supposed to be oiling the patio furniture. I came home from work early and caught him with our next-door neighbor."

"And instead of handling the situation with dignity, the way a daughter of mine should, you went crazy with a crowbar."

Helen was not getting into this argument again. "Is Kathy home? I'd better call her before it's too late."

"You can't hang up," her mother said. "I want to talk to you. Helen, what if Kathy had died? What if something had happened to one of her children? Or me? You need to—"

Helen crinkled the pink cellophane. "Sorry, Mom, you're breaking up. Bad connection. Good-bye, Mom, I love you."

Now she really did have a headache. She was sweating heavily, and not just because the air conditioner was off. Helen dialed her sister's number with shaky fingers.

"I'm fine, Helen," Kathy insisted.

"You don't sound fine. You sound weak."

"I was asleep. Really, I'm OK. Tom has been making me dinner. Mom has the kids. I'm enjoying the rest. I may malinger a little longer."

Helen wished she could see her sister so she'd know for sure. Instead, she resorted to their old childhood code. "Cross your heart and hope to die?"

"Cross my heart, Helen. You know Mom. She makes every scratch into a fatal illness."

"I don't think gall-bladder surgery is a scratch."

"It's not that big a deal. I had the keyhole surgery. You should see my scars. I've had bigger mosquito bites. I'm more worried about you, Helen. Are you OK? There are a lot of murders down there in Florida."

"There are a lot of murders up there in St. Louis."

"Yes, but mostly in the black part of town."

Helen sighed. Kathy was good at closing her eyes to reality.

"Helen, are you happy?" Kathy said. "I can't see you living in two rooms with some old 1950s furniture, when you used to have a twelve-room mansion in St. Louis. You had Ralph Lauren fabrics and—"

"Yes, Kathy, I had all that. But you know what? It wasn't me. I worked until eight or nine every night so I could buy things I didn't want. For recreation, I went shopping, which got me in more debt.

"When I was divorcing Rob, I used to walk around the house at night and say, 'I could live without this. I could live without that.' I'd go through the house room by room. I could live without the dining room that seated twelve. Twelve people from the office I didn't really like but wanted to impress. I could live without the formal living room, where I rarely relaxed. It was a showcase for parties to advance my career.

"Or the guest room, which never had any guests because I was too busy to stay in touch with my out-of-town friends. One day, I realized I could live without it all.

"Now I sit out by the pool here in Florida and drink wine and watch the sunset. It's a better life for me. I'm much happier."

"You're sure?" Kathy said. "Cross your heart?"

"Cross my heart. Stay well, Kathy. I love you."

She hung up. Helen missed her sister with an almost physical pain. Kathy understood her. She had stood by Helen during the divorce. Her ultra-Catholic mother wanted her to get back with Rob. Not Kathy. She'd told Helen, "I'm surprised you only took the crowbar to his car. I'd have broken every bone in his body."

The memory of a naked Rob, running for his Land

Cruiser, could still make Helen smile. He had abandoned Sandy and locked himself inside the SUV. Helen picked up a crowbar and smashed the windshield. By the time a terrified Sandy had called 911, Helen had trashed every inch of the vehicle.

There was no law against that. The car was registered in her name. She'd paid for it.

The police had laughed themselves silly at her bare-assed husband, cowering in the broken glass. He and Sandy did not press assault charges. They didn't want Sandy's husband to find out. He did anyway.

Helen filed for divorce. That's when things went really bad.

Rob claimed that she earned her six-figure salary because he was a loyal house husband, subject to her wild mood swings. As proof, his lawyer showed photos of the beaten SUV and the police report. Rob's many girlfriends testified that he'd done a lot around the house. A lot of screwing, maybe, but no hammering and sawing. He never finished any of his home-handyman projects. Helen had to pay contractors to undo his lousy work.

Throughout this fiasco, Helen's high-priced lawyer sat there like a department-store dummy. He wouldn't let her say a word. He didn't want to upset the judge.

In the end, the judge gave Rob half their house, even though she'd made all the payments. She'd expected that. What she didn't expect was when the judge gave Rob half her future earnings, because her successful career was based on his "love and support."

That was when a red rage flamed up in Helen. She stood up in court, picked up the familiar black book with the gold lettering, and said, "I swear on this Bible that my husband Rob will not get another nickel of my salary."

Later, the Bible turned out to be the *Revised Missouri Statutes.* But Helen considered the oath binding. She packed a suitcase and ran from St. Louis, driving a zigzag course across the country to throw the law and her ex off her trail. She wasn't sure how far the courts would go to track down a deadbeat wife, but Rob would work hard to avoid work.

On the road, she sold her silver Lexus to a crooked used-car dealer. He gave her a clunker that died in Fort Lauderdale. That's how she wound up in South Florida, working dead-end jobs to avoid the corporate and government computers. Even if Rob found her, he'd get only half of her miserable paycheck. That wouldn't keep him in imported beer.

Only her sister Kathy knew where she was. Helen couldn't trust her mother. Rob would sweet-talk her address out of her mother.

It wasn't a bad call, Helen lied to herself. She'd had worse. She packed away the phone and stretched out on the bed for just a minute. When she woke up the next morning, she was still in her work clothes, clutching her cat, Thumbs, like a teddy bear.

Helen went warily to her date with Gabriel. She had the warnings from Sarah and the knowledge of her own failures with men. The production of *A Midsummer Night's Dream* was spellbinding. Even in an outdoor amphitheater, the ancient words overpowered the modern distractions of thumping car radios and traffic noise. She applauded vigorously when the actors took their bows. Then she and Gabe walked around downtown Hollywood. Helen liked the way his eyes crinkled. She was a sucker for eye crinkles.

"Can I show you something?" Gabriel asked. "It's only a few blocks away."

They walked to a pretty residential neighborhood with older homes. He stopped at an empty lot landscaped with

fan-shaped palms and a fish pond. In the center was a concrete foundation.

"This will be my dream house," he said. "I'm finishing it
a little at a time. What do you think the perfect house
needs?"

Two people who love each other, Helen wanted to say.
Instead she discussed fireplaces, hardwood floors, and
granite countertops. They walked and talked, then drank
cold beer and ate spicy peanut noodles at a Thai restaurant.

At last, he took her home to the Coronado. The night was
thick with her neighbor's cannabis fog. Helen knew Phil's
dreams were smoke. Gabriel's dream was solid concrete.
Maybe they could build on it together.

"Let me in," Gabe said quietly. "I've shown you my
dream. Let me be part of yours." He kissed her, and his lips
were soft and warm and his body was hard and insistent.

Helen unlocked the door.

Chapter 20

Helen woke up alone.

She was sure last night was a dream, a wonderful dream, until she saw the blond hair on her pillow. Gabriel had definitely been in her bed, and this morning he was a hair balder. She smiled and stretched. She did not want a perfect man, but she'd had a perfect night.

She padded out to the kitchen. On the sink was a chocolate croissant, fresh-squeezed orange juice, and a single red rose. Gabriel definitely understood a woman's needs.

There was also a note:

> *Dear Helen,*
> *I hated to leave you, but I had to be on the job at six this morning. I'll be working late into the night, but I'll think of you all day. Thanks for letting me share my dream house with you. I'll stop by the store tomorrow, but if you're too busy to talk, I'll understand. See you soon, dream lover.*
> *Gabriel*
> *P.S.: Your air conditioner was rattling, so I fixed it.*

Helen sighed. This man was too good to be true. So sensitive. So understanding. It wasn't until her cat nearly tripped her that she realized Thumbs had been weaving through her legs, demanding breakfast.

"Sorry, boy," she said, giving him a pat. "I'm in a daze here."

She fed Thumbs, made coffee, then took her breakfast outside to the table by the pool.

"Well, well, somebody had a good night," Margery said. She looked like a grape Popsicle in a purple shorts outfit that showed off her tanned legs. At seventy-six, Margery had legs most women would envy.

Helen took a big bite of croissant so she wouldn't have to answer.

Margery sipped her coffee, lit a cigarette, and said, "How's the investigation going, Sherlock?"

"I think I have a lead." Helen didn't mention that everything she found out so far made Peggy guiltier. "It's Albert. When I asked him where he was the night Page died, he got angry and refused to tell me."

"He sounds guilty, all right. Albert the one with the stick up his ass?"

Helen nodded.

"Those are the worst kind." Margery blew a massive cloud of smoke. "What's his motive?"

"He's fifty-six, has an old mother to support, no health insurance if he loses this job, and no prospects for more work."

"Turner took everything from him. A stupid thing to do. How will you find out what this Albert was doing?"

"I'll think of something," Helen said, licking the last of the chocolate croissant off her fingers. "I'd better get to work. I'm due in at nine."

It's like love, Sarah had told her. Just let it happen naturally. Well, love had happened last night. Maybe Albert's alibi would happen, too.

"He's so vicious," Brad said. "Do you know what Albert did?" The little bookseller was in the break room, trembling with anger. His color was a dangerous red.

"He showed me this." He had a magazine, rolled up as if he was going to swat a puppy.

"I didn't even know it existed." Brad looked ready to shred the magazine with his bare hands. "This piece of trash makes fun of J.Lo's . . . demeans her . . ."

"Her what?" Helen said.

"Her derriere! How can they do this to a sweet, sensitive woman?"

He unrolled a *MAD* magazine. Helen hadn't read one since she was a kid, but it didn't look much different. Brad found the offending page with shaking fingers, a satire called "People Who Should Have Won This Year's Nobel Prizes."

MAD gave an honorable mention for the Nobel prize for chemistry to "Jennifer Lopez . . . who in conjunction with Du Pont, developed a synthetic fabric capable of containing her ass." The cartoon showed Lopez with PASS and DON'T PASS signs on her bulging bottom.

For Brad's sake, Helen suppressed a smile.

"It's so sexist," said the skinny bookseller, whose own rear was flat as Nebraska. "J.Lo is not fat. She's not like these half-starved actresses. She's a grown woman with curves."

"That she is," Helen said. "If more entertainers were built like her, life would be easier for the average woman. Brad, this won't hurt J.Lo. Her fans know better."

"It's mean," Brad said. "I don't read *MAD*. I wouldn't have seen it and it wouldn't have upset me. But Albert couldn't wait to show it to me."

"Albert's gotten meaner since the store-closing rumors started," Helen said.

"Those aren't rumors, sweetie. This place will be history soon."

It was natural to go to the next topic, Helen thought. As natural as falling in love. "I know Albert hated what Page was doing. No one seems to know where he went that Friday evening. Do you think he killed Page Turner?"

Brad started, then his face lit with a malicious smile. "I know what he was doing that night. I saw him, quite by accident. He swore me to secrecy. He had to. It was awful."

"Tell me," Helen whispered.

"That would break my vow. But I can show you. Then I won't be telling you, will I? Albert doesn't deserve my secrecy. Not after what he did."

"When can I see?" said Helen.

"Tonight. He can't stop himself. He does it three or four times a week. Meet me in front of the store at nine p.m. And wear black."

Wear black? What was Albert doing at night? Was he a burglar? A grave robber?

The hands crawled around the clock. Finally, it was nine and she was in black, waiting in front of the bookstore. Brad picked her up in a rusty little blue car that looked like a running shoe. They chugged into the lot of a chain bookstore. A sign at the door announced, OPEN-MIKE POETRY NIGHT—9:00 P.M. TONIGHT.

"What are we doing here?" Helen said.

"Shhh. Don't talk," Brad said. "Sit in the back row on the floor and keep your head down. If he spots you, he'll bolt."

About forty black-clad poetry lovers were perched on folding chairs or sprawled on the floor. A young woman with luminous white skin was standing in front of the microphone, reciting her poem in a flat, uninflected voice.

"My milk is the feast of goddesses. My right breast is Juno. My left is Hera," she droned.

"Aren't they the same person?" Helen whispered.

"It's about feelings, not facts," Brad said. People gave them dirty looks. Brad shut up.

"And from my womb flows Venus and rebellion," the poet said in a monotone, then stopped. The audience applauded loudly. The poem was over.

A thin man who looked like Ichabod Crane in a beret stepped up to the microphone. He was dressed entirely in black, like a Beat poet of fifty years ago. It was Albert. Helen hardly recognized him without his stiff white shirt. He adjusted the microphone and began reading in a high, thin voice:

"Pain.

"Pain.

"Pain is a red scream in my head.

"Pain is a cry in my heart . . ."

"Pain is listening to this," Helen whispered.

"I told you it was awful. Page Turner deserved to die. The English language does not deserve this torture."

"Shhh!" someone hissed.

Helen had seen enough. She and Brad scooted to the end of the row and ducked out the back.

"Lord, that was awful," Helen said. "No wonder Albert didn't want me to know what he was doing."

"At a competing bookstore, too," Brad said. "He's addicted to open-mike poetry nights. Hits all the bookstores and coffeehouses. Saturdays, he does two. "

"Why didn't anyone laugh at his bad poetry?"

"Because they'll be getting up and reading their own bad poetry."

"But I don't understand why a sensitive poet like Albert would read a true crime book called *Smother Love.*"

"Isn't that the one about Darryl Eugene Crow? He's known as the prison poet. His poetry sounds a lot like Albert's."

"Thank you for showing me, Brad. That was painful, but instructive."

"I want this book, but it's too expensive." Muffy the preppy psychic was holding a fat volume called *Cooking with the Stars: A Guide to Astrology and Food.* She was dressed almost like the preppy prowler in a pink shirt and khakis. The pink made her hair look blond. She was almost pretty.

"Can you buy this for me with your employee discount?"

"No," Helen said. "I could get fired."

"But I can't afford it without your discount," Muffy said. "It's not money out of your pocket."

"I'm sorry," Helen said. "You'll have to get something else."

Muffy raised her voice so heads turned. "I can't buy the book I want. It's all your fault." Then she stomped off to the Cooking section.

When Helen saw her next customer, she didn't have to be psychic to predict more trouble. It was Melanie Devereaux DuShayne, the POD author. Helen wondered how she had the nerve to walk into the store after the Page Turner debacle. Her blond hair trailed down her back. She wore a tight, short sea foam–green sundress with a froth of polyester lace down the plunging neckline, and those clear plastic shoes.

"I got a call that my book has come in," Melanie said. Her voice trembled and her face went pink.

Now Helen knew what she was doing there. An author would endure any humiliation for her book. She checked the hold shelf. "You have two copies, actually. That will be twenty-nine ninety-five each, for a total of—"

Melanie's face crumpled. Her voice was teary. "That

much? I get a discount if I buy from the publisher, but it looks better if I order them at a real bookstore."

"I'm sorry," Helen said. "We don't give author discounts. I wish we did. We do take credit cards."

"I'm maxed out," Melanie said. "I bought the editing package."

Helen looked at her. "Editing package?"

"I wanted the best for my book, so I paid nine hundred ninety nine dollars for the deluxe package. It includes copy-editing, five free books, plus two favorable reviews."

"Where do the reviews run?" Helen said.

"On the UBookIt Web site," she said. "They're really supposed to help sales and I wanted to give my book every chance."

Poor Melanie. No one would read those reviews but other POD authors. Her book was the bastard child of the book industry. She'd been seduced by a greedy publisher who only wanted her for her money. Helen felt sorry for her.

"POD books are not returnable. You have to take both copies."

"I'll have more money next month. Can't you keep one until next payday?"

It was against the rules. But Helen figured Page Turners owed Melanie that much. She rang up one book and buried the other on the hold shelf.

"Thanks," Melanie said. "Where are your romances?"

Helen directed her to that section, and hoped Melanie could find something. The romances had been around. Helen was embarrassed to sell them.

"Helen," said Gayle, her blond hair shining like a halo in the bright sun. "My reading glasses came apart. I have to finish the weekly financial report. I'm going to run to the optometrist down the street and see if he'll fix them. Will you watch the shop for a few minutes? Albert is due in any moment. Until then, you're in charge. You and Denny can do a slush run. Brad can run the register."

Helen felt like she was on an Easter-egg hunt. She found stray books under tables and chairs, shoved under shelves, and hidden in displays. She wished it was as easy to look for Page's killer. She was running out of suspects. She was missing something, too. It nagged at her. When she turned the corner and saw Mr. Davies, the store's oldest inhabitant, in his usual chair, she knew what it was.

He'd tried to tell her something last time she'd talked with her. Except Helen had been too impatient to listen.

Now she sat humbly on the footstool at Mr. Davies' chair and said, "I cut you off last time. I'm very sorry. That was rude. On the night of the murder, the pretty redhead in the green Kia brought Page Turner back to the store, didn't she?"

Mr. Davies sat up eagerly, his bright squirrel eyes gleaming. "Oh, my, yes. I know I talk too much. It makes the young impatient. That young Detective Jax was the same way. Don't you think the police are looking younger these days? I really wonder how anyone that young can be trusted with a gun, but they say fourteen-year-olds take guns to school now. It was so different when I was young. He didn't bother listening to me."

Who? Helen wondered, then realized Mr. Davies was talking about Detective Jax.

"And he did not apologize like you did, my dear."

Helen dug her nails into her palms for patience while she waited for Mr. Davies to get to the point.

"The redheaded girl—excuse me, woman, I do try to say the right thing—the redhead was back after ten minutes. I thought Mr. Page Turner was very foolish to spend so little time with such an attractive young person. She left him at his private parking spot behind the store.

"But then I dozed off, and at first I thought it was a

dream, she was so beautiful, and I told that detective that, and he said he didn't care about my dreams, he just wanted the facts. But I wasn't dreaming. I'd been reading *The Adventures of Tom Sawyer.* I'm rereading the old classics. They are so much richer at my age. I read a biography of Mark Twain, but you can learn more about an author by reading his work—or her work, excuse me. Authors always write about themselves. The good ones are better at disguising it."

Helen suppressed a sigh and felt some sympathy for Jax. Would Mr. Davies never get on with it?.

"I'd just finished the page when this lovely blonde showed up in a silver car. A silver coach for a golden princess."

This wasn't much help. "Lots of blondes are in the store," she said.

"Not like this one. She had yellow hair and looked like Cinderella."

"Helen to the front, please, Helen to the front." She was being paged. It sounded like Denny.

"Cinderella? What do you mean?" Helen was desperate for more information.

"Helen to the front. Please come to the front!" It was definitely Denny. He sounded desperate.

"Gotta run. I'm being paged. I'll talk to you later, Mr. Davies."

"Don't worry, dear, I'll be here," he said. "I always am."

Sadly, that turned out not to be true.

Chapter 21

"What is it?" Helen said. She was out of breath, running for the cashier's desk.

"It's Mr. Goggles," Brad said. "Denny spotted him."

"Oh, Lord. Not that pervert. This store is crawling with kids."

Summer was the season of the feral children. Bands of wild teenagers roamed the bookstore until it closed at midnight, swiping CDs, shoplifting computer books, and paying for their double lattes with hundred-dollar bills.

Where did teens get that kind of money? Helen wondered. From parents who gave them everything but love? Or were they selling drugs?

Their little brothers and sisters were set free in the bookstore while Mom and Dad shopped, drank, dined on Las Olas—or sat in another section of Page Turners and read books.

The abandoned children ran through the store, tearing up books and shrieking, sitting on the floor and sobbing, sometimes even reading. Their complacent parents thought their children were safe. They never guessed a creature like Mr. Goggles was lurking nearby.

Mr. Goggles haunted local libraries and bookstores. Librarians and store managers called the cops or threw him out when they saw him, but Mr. Goggles slipped in like mist on the ocean and drifted back to the Children's section. No one knew how he was able to move about stores without being noticed.

Mr. Goggles was an evil creature. If you opened up the dictionary and looked under "pervert," you would see him. Mr. Goggles wore swim goggles. If that wasn't strange enough, he was a small, misshapen man with mismatched clothes that looked like they'd been stolen from the Goodwill bin: an orange dress shirt and plaid walking shorts.

In some countries, the people would stone Mr. Goggles. In South Florida, he'd been in and out of jail and various institutions. But he always returned to haunting bookstores and libraries.

Even the most inexperienced bookseller knew there was something wrong with Mr. Goggles. Young Denny recognized the goblin man as a destroyer of innocence. He came running up to Helen and said, "There's this weird guy playing with himself in the Spider-man section. He's one row from the kids' books."

"Call nine-one-one," Helen told Brad. "I'll grab Mr. Goggles. Denny, guard the Children's section and make sure he doesn't run back there."

Helen quickly collared Mr. Goggles. The little man struggled, but he was easy to subdue. Helen was six inches taller and forty pounds heavier. She bent his arm behind his back, and shuddered when his hand touched hers. She knew where it had been.

Mr. Goggles smelled like fried eggs and unwashed hair. Helen wanted to let go of him and take a shower. In Lysol. "You should be ashamed of yourself," she said.

"I'm sorry. I didn't mean it," he whined. "Don't be mad at me."

"Shut up or I'll break your neck and do the world a favor."

Helen was grateful that the Spider-man section was in a secluded book nook. Mr. Goggles was too scared of Helen to make any noise, and he'd stopped struggling. The police were on the way. She heard the sirens and started to relax. They would haul him away soon.

That's when a little boy said loudly, "Mommy, that man's wee-wee is showing."

It was the child who'd torn up the Children's section, along with his book-ripping sister. Helen would never forget those little monsters, or their heavily pregnant mother. She'd sat there and read Oprah best-sellers while her offspring destroyed the place.

Mom had her nose buried in another Oprah pick. But her son's words must have set off some special mommy alert. She put her trade paperback facedown on the table, cracking its spine.

"Justin," his mother commanded, "go read about Clifford, the big red dog, with your sister."

She stood up. My Lord, that woman is pregnant, Helen thought. She must be due any day. She looked like a fertility goddess in a white, high-waisted dress, her long brown hair trailing down her back.

Mr. Goggles saw the woman rise to her full height and girth and backed into Helen for protection. Helen nearly threw up as she got a wave of fried egg and oily hair. The pregnant woman lumbered over to the law books and picked up a *Black's Law Dictionary*. It was the deluxe leather-bound edition, more than seventeen hundred pages. The thing was the size of a lawyer's briefcase and a lot heavier.

"Stand back," she ordered Helen.

"No!" Helen said. But she saw the fire in the outraged mother's eyes. She was not going to get squashed saving

Mr. Goggles. She moved aside, and the woman walloped him on the head.

"Ma'am, it's OK, the police are on their way," Helen said. But Justin's mom pounded Mr. Goggles like a pile driver. Helen hoped the police took their time. The pervert deserved it.

Another mother in a denim jumper grabbed *Jane's Fighting Ships of World War II* and slammed it into Mr. Goggles' private parts. He shrieked in agony.

"Shut up, you nasty man. You'll scare my child," the woman said, and got him in the groin again. This time, he moaned softly and fell to the floor.

All around Helen, mothers were arming themselves with monster tomes. Helen abandoned Mr. Goggles to his fate. By the time the cops arrived, there was a full-scale parental riot. Mothers were beating Mr. Goggles with bigger and bigger books. He was clutching his groin. It would be a long time before he used that area for recreation.

As the cops dragged Mr. Goggles away, a woman screamed, "I hope you throw the book at him."

That's when Gayle returned from the optometrist. "I'm gone fifteen minutes and there's a riot. What the hell happened?"

"Mr. Goggles," Helen said. "He got what he deserved."

Gayle picked up the battered *Black's Law*. The title page was ripped and smeared with blood. Other pages were torn. "Justice has a high price," she said. "This book goes for ninety-six bucks. I can't sell it or return it in this condition."

Gayle and Helen squatted on the floor, gathering up far-flung books and assessing the damage. *Black's Law* was beyond repair. *Jane's Fighting Ships* might sell if they slipped off the torn dustcover. Helen spotted a *Webster's Third New International Dictionary, Unabridged* under a display table. It weighed twelve and a half pounds, but it had been tossed aside like a paperback. If Mr. Goggles got hit with that baby, he would hurt for a while.

She crawled under the table to the abandoned dictionary and saw that it was resting near two paint-spattered work boots. She followed them up to a pair of superbly tanned legs, blond hairs glistening in the afternoon sun. She knew those legs and the rest of that muscular body. It was her all-around handyman, Gabe, looking cool, calm, and oh-so-handsome in this chaos. He helped her out from under the table and embraced her.

"Gabe!" Helen said.

"Daddy," said little Justin, grabbing Gabriel's leg. "Daddy, when are you coming home?"

Isn't that cute, Helen thought. He thinks Gabriel is his father.

"Daddy!" shrieked Justin's sister. Wasn't her name Gabrielle? Helen was getting a bad feeling.

The pregnant woman, now armed with a sturdy *Roget's Thesaurus*, returned to the section, fertile and ferocious, "Yes, Daddy, when are you coming home? You haven't given me a dime of child support in six months. In case you didn't notice, your third child is on the way."

"You're married?" blurted Helen.

"It's just a technicality," Gabe said.

"Technicality, my ass," said the pregnant woman, and whacked him with the *Roget's*. "You walked out, but we're still married. And your technicality is due in two weeks."

"You told me you didn't want children," Helen said.

"I didn't," Gabe said. "They just happened."

"You rat," Helen said, but two words were not adequate. She picked up the Webster's unabridged dictionary. Four hundred fifty thousand words should do it, she thought, and took aim at his—

"*Helen!*" Gayle said. Helen stopped in midswing. "Put that book down. I'll not have you ruining good books on a worthless man. You, too, ma'am. Drop that *Roget's*. Violence is bad for your unborn child."

The pregnant woman looked down at her bulging belly and slowly put the book down.

Helen had never seen Gayle look so fierce. With her golden hair and black clothes, she looked like a commando in a James Bond movie.

"Do you want me to detain this deadbeat?" she said to the pregnant woman.

"No. I don't need his money. Besides, he won't go far. He's got his little seduction routine. Takes his gullible fools to a free Shakespeare play, a cheap meal at the Thai restaurant, and a visit to his dream house."

Helen winced. He'd used all three on her.

The earth mother turned to Helen. "Bet he told you he owned some lot and was building his dream house." Helen managed a nod. "Go look again. It's not his lot. You'll see a 'For Sale' sign out front. He takes it down before he has a date."

Sucker! Helen thought.

"Don't feel too bad," the pregnant woman said, giving her absolution. "He pulled the same tricks on me. That's how I know. At least you're not pregnant. Come, Gabrielle and Justin. Let go of Daddy." Justin began whimpering, and Helen felt sorry for the little boy. He deserved a real father, not a deadbeat dad.

Gabe kept looking at his paint-spattered boots. He seemed frozen to the floor. When the children had left with their mother, Gayle turned to him. "And you, scum. Get out and don't come back. If I catch you in this store again, I'll personally throw you out."

Gabriel slouched out the door. Helen was suddenly aware that he had a full-blown pot and a silver-dollar-sized bald spot on his crown.

She also noticed that she didn't feel anything. She was

completely numb. Gayle took her upstairs to the office of
the dead adulterer, Page Turner, and tried to make her sit
down on the slashed couch. "You'll feel better if you cry,"
she said.

Helen paced like a caged leopard and stayed dry-eyed.
"I'm not wasting any tears on him." Then she burst out,
"Aren't there any good men in South Florida?"

"How would I know?" Gayle said.

"Well, at least he fixed my air conditioner," Helen said.

"Hell, I'd almost sleep with a guy for that," Gayle said.
"If you think a good man is impossible to find in South
Florida, try looking for reliable repair people."

Did Gayle really say that? Helen giggled. Then she
started laughing and couldn't stop until Gayle pounded her
on the back.

"If you're not going to cry, you might as well work,"
Gayle said. "I know you hate nights, but I need you to stay
and put the store back together after the riot. Albert had a
case of the vapors and went home. Brad can't work past
six."

"Might as well," Helen said. She didn't want to go home
to the bed she'd shared with Gabriel. She wouldn't sleep in
it again until she changed the sheets. No, she wouldn't
change those sheets. She'd burn them.

Sucker! She couldn't spot false money or a false man.
Sarah had warned her about Gabriel, but Helen didn't listen.

Sucker! She hauled heavy books back to their shelves,
hoping hard work would shut up the voice inside her.

Sucker! It screamed. Nothing drowned it out.

At eleven-thirty Denny was mopping the café floor.
There wasn't a customer in sight. Denny flipped over his
mop so the head was a microphone and sang oldies from
the 1980s. His imitation of Sting crooning "Every Breath
You Take" was hilarious. The kid danced over the tabletops

and ended his act with a soft-shoe on the café counter. All he needed was some dry-ice fog, and he could be on MTV. God, he was gorgeous, with his auburn hair flying. He was born to be a star. Helen applauded wildly.

Gayle did not. "Denny, get your feet off the counter," she said. "Now you'll have to clean it again. Helen, I found this stack of romances in the bathroom. Put them away."

As Helen headed toward the rear of the store, she remembered Mr. Davies. He was going to tell her more about the golden blonde in the silver car. She hadn't gotten back to him, and he hadn't come up front to see what caused the commotion. How could he sleep through that riot?

Well, she knew where to find him. He never left until the store closed at midnight. She put away the books, then found Mr. Davies in his secluded book nook. He was dead to the world.

Poor old fellow is really tired, she thought. His water glass had fallen over. The spilled water was dangerously close to his latest book, *The Adventures of Huckleberry Finn*. She smiled. He was still reading Mark Twain.

A ruined book would upset the old bibliophile. She bent down to pick it up and brushed his hand. It was ice-cold.

"Mr. Davies?" she said. "Are you all right?" She started to gently shake him, when he fell stiffly forward. His eyes were open.

"Please, Mr. Davies, wake up," she pleaded.

But even as she said it, Helen knew that would never happen.

Chapter 22

Helen did not shed a tear for Gabriel, but she couldn't quit crying for dear, gentle Mr. Davies. "He'll never know how *Huckleberry Finn* ended," she sobbed. Her Kleenex looked like soggy lace.

Gayle handed her a fresh tissue and said, "Helen, the man was eighty-something. It's not a tragedy when an old man dies."

Helen thought that was harsh. She sniffed and blew her nose. Young Denny patted her on the back.

"I'm just glad there weren't any customers in the store," Gayle said. "We've already had the police here once today."

Gayle had called 911 for the second time that day. Once again, they heard the sirens. "That's an ambulance pulling up," Denny said.

"I told them the man was dead," Gayle said. "What's this, the Lazarus brigade?"

The fire department paramedics came running in as if they really could save Mr. Davies. For one moment, Helen felt hope. Maybe Mr. Davies could be revived. But she remembered his skin, so cold and oddly blue, and his stiff body.

"I'll go back with the paramedics," Gayle said. "You two stay up here and lock the doors. We're closed. All we're going to get now are freaks."

The crowd gathering outside the store had hot, hungry eyes eager for a look at the body. One held up a child to see inside. The ghouls knocked on the glass, and Denny and Helen pointed to the CLOSED sign.

Helen wasn't sure how long it was before the paramedics gave up and called the police, but eventually uniformed officers pushed through the crowd. Helen and Denny let them in, then locked the door again.

The blood freaks had grown restless. Helen was glad the police were there. She and Denny stayed at their post. Sound traveled in the empty bookstore. The two booksellers could hear people talking, but they couldn't tell whether it was the police or paramedics. A woman was asking Gayle if she knew Mr. Davies' next of kin or the name of his medical doctor. A man kept saying, "I can't find any prescription bottles or Medic Alert bracelet on him. There's no doctor's appointment card in his wallet."

"I said, there's something wrong with this guy," said one man.

"Of course there is. He's dead," said a second man.

"No, look at his eyes."

"I'll be damned. Are those petechiae? Any pillows around here?"

"Over there on that couch." That was Gayle.

"I wouldn't touch those pillows with tongs," Denny whispered. "You won't believe how often I find them next to a pile of skin magazines. Have you seen the stains on those things?"

"Quiet," Helen said.

"What are petechiae?" Denny said in a small voice.

"Broken blood vessels in the eyes. You get them if you've been strangled or smothered," Helen said.

"How do you know that?"

"I watch *CSI*," Helen said. "Please shut up, or we'll never learn anything."

They heard the first man's voice again ". . . get all the pillows bagged. Have to bag his hands, too, in case he fought his attacker. We'd better get the evidence techs in here, although the paramedics have already done a great job of ruining the crime scene."

"Hey, we were trying to save his life," said an indignant male voice.

"Call homicide, too. Shit. Nothing's ever simple."

"Is something wrong, Officer?" That was Gayle, sounding worried.

"We're just being careful, ma'am."

"They're calling homicide," Denny said, sounding impressed. "They think somebody killed Mr. Davies. Who would murder an old dude like that?"

"It's all my fault," Helen said, and began to cry again. "I killed him."

"You were apparently the last person to talk with the victim," homicide detective Harold "Gil" Gilbert said. Helen liked him. A lot better than Detective Jax. Gilbert had nice hazel eyes and luxuriant light brown hair. The kind you could run your fingers through, except she was keeping her hands to herself these days.

"Now tell me about your conversation with Mr. Zebediah Davies."

Helen quit crying and looked up, startled. "His name was Zebediah?"

"What did you think it was?"

"I never called him anything but Mr. Davies," Helen said.

"'Mister' isn't much of a first name," he said. He also had a sense of humor. She could go for Detective Gilbert. If he wasn't a cop. If she wasn't on the run from the law. If she wasn't a *sucker!*

"I asked him about the night that Page Turner died," she said, wiping her eyes. Her hand was streaked with black. Terrific. Her eyeliner was running. She probably looked like a panda.

"Mr. Davies always sat in the same chair, by that window overlooking the parking lot. He was there from nine in the morning until we closed at midnight. He saw who picked up Page Turner. Detective Jax arrested my friend Peggy for Page's murder. He's wrong. I know he's wrong. I was doing my own investigation."

"That's a dangerous game. People get killed that way."

"I know. I killed Mr. Davies with my stupid questions." Helen started sniffling again and brought out the Kleenex. It was a series of interconnected holes. Gilbert offered his pocket handkerchief. When she blew her nose, it sounded like a trumpet solo. "Sorry. I'll wash it and get it back to you."

"Forget it," he said. "And you didn't kill Mr. Davies. Don't ever think that. Don't take that guilt on yourself."

Helen didn't believe him. But it was time to turn off the waterworks. She hated weepy women.

"Detective Jax thinks Page Turner drove off with Peggy and was never seen again. But Peggy brought Page back to the store, and someone else picked him up. Mr. Davies saw that person. He tried to tell Detective Jax, but Jax got impatient and didn't let him finish. Mr. Davies talks—talked—a lot, and he kind of rambles. I mean rambled."

I'm starting to ramble like poor Mr. Davies, she thought. But she could talk to Gil Gilbert. He was leaning forward as if he wanted to catch every word.

"What did Mr. Davies tell you?"

"He said a lovely blonde showed up in a silver car. He called it 'a silver coach for a golden princess.' I said there were a lot of blondes in the store. He said, 'Not like this one. She had yellow hair and looked like Cinderella.' I wanted to ask him what he meant, but then we had this problem with a pedophile."

"I heard about the Las Olas mommy riot. Those women sent Mr. Goggles to the emergency room."

"Good," Helen said. "Things got pretty hectic after that. I didn't get a chance to talk to Mr. Davies again. Then I found that sweet old man dead in his chair." She was not going to cry. She fought back the tears.

"So all he told you was that he saw a blonde with a silver car."

"It's not much help, is it?" Helen said.

"What do you think he meant by Cinderella?" Gilbert said.

"Mr. Davies had an interesting mind. It didn't work quite the same as everyone else's. Peggy drove a Kia and he called it a Vietnam car, because to him KIA meant 'killed in action,' and they used that term in the Vietnam War. Who knows what Cinderella meant?"

Gilbert had more questions, lots more. It was nearly three a.m. when the police released the booksellers. Even young Denny looked hollow-eyed and exhausted. Helen's tear-reddened eyes were twin pools of blood.

"Can I give you a ride home?" Gayle said.

"I can walk," Helen said. "I only live a few blocks away."

"You shouldn't be walking alone at this hour."

Three drunks were weaving down the sidewalk, singing "Louie, Louie." They looked harmless, playing air guitars and howling the words off-key, but suddenly Helen didn't feel so brave.

Gayle was parked in Page Turner's old spot. Astrid must have given it to her as a perk for managing the store. Page's widow rarely drove into Fort Lauderdale. Helen had seen her silver Mercedes maybe twice since she'd worked at Page Turners. Gayle moved a pile of books and papers off the passenger seat and Helen folded her legs into the little Honda. Only when she sat down did she realize how tired she was.

"You see why I hate working nights?" Helen said. Gayle managed a weak smile.

"I live at the Coronado Tropic Apartments," Helen said. "You make a left at the next street."

"I know how to get there," Gayle said. "What time do you come in tomorrow?"

"Not till eleven. And if you want me to work tomorrow night, the answer is no."

Gayle pulled into the Coronado parking lot.

"Listen, I really appreciate this," Helen said.

"No biggie. I'll see you tomorrow."

Helen waved good-bye, waiting until the silver Honda was out of sight. It was easy to get lost in these side streets. But the little car found the way back to the main highway.

The Coronado was dark and still. Even Margery's light was off. Hungry insects sang their blood songs. Predators rustled in the plants. Phil's perpetual pot smog perfumed the air. As Helen passed through, she took a deep breath and inhaled. Maybe secondhand sensimilla smoke would help her sleep.

Shoosh. Shoosh. Clunk-thud.

Helen woke up at the noise and grabbed the pistol by her bed. Too late. Her cat Thumbs sent a book sliding off her nightstand. She shot him once with the water pistol. That usually sent him scurrying for cover.

But this morning the big gray-and-white cat didn't budge. He sat defiantly on her nightstand and with his huge six-toed paw flipped the clock off the edge. Helen caught a glimpse before it went overboard. Nine forty-five.

It was hours past his feeding time. She must have slept through his breakfast cries. Now Thumbs was telling her to feed him or else. He had a system of escalation. Unbreakables like the book went first, followed by semisurvivable items like the clock. Fragile knickknacks were next. She heard the clink of china, and saw his catcher's mitt of a paw scooting the bud vase to the edge of the nightstand. She caught it and picked up the cat before he could send anything else flying off.

"All right, I'll feed you," she said, and carried Thumbs into the kitchen. He purred all the way.

"My alarm didn't go off at nine," she said as she filled his food bowl. "So I should thank you that I'm not late for work."

I'm having a conversation with a cat, she thought. But I'd rather talk to Thumbs than think about today. I dread going to the store. If I can just make it through the next eight hours, I'll have two days off.

As soon as she walked into the bookstore, she knew something was different. Mr. Davies' chair was gone, but more than that seemed missing. The store seemed barren and cold without the gentle old bookworm. He'd been so happy there, surrounded by piles of paperbacks.

She stood on the spot where his chair used to be and said, "I'll miss you, Mr. Davies."

"What were you doing back in that corner?" Albert said when she returned to the front. The prissy bookseller looked as if his starched shirt was holding him up. "I won't go near it. It's like that old man is still there."

"I wish he was," Helen said. "Mr. Davies wouldn't hurt anyone, alive or dead."

"I miss him," Brad said. "We used to talk about J.Lo. He particularly appreciated her performance in *Enough*. He said her acting was underrated, although he agreed that some of her clothes in that movie did not flatter her opulent figure."

"She's not opulent, she's obese," Albert said nastily. Brad looked stricken.

Helen intoned:

"Pain.

"Pain.

"Pain is a red scream in my head. . . ."

Albert turned dead white.

"We all have things we care about," Helen said. "We should respect them."

Albert didn't say another word about J.Lo or anyone else.

"Thanks," Brad whispered, and went back to gathering up the books scattered all over the store. He moved slower today and smiled less.

Only Gayle was her usual cheerful self, laughing and chatting with the customers. At the cashier's counter, a little boy about four proudly presented his new book to Helen. It was shaped like a fire truck.

"Here," he said. His mother put a twenty on the counter.

"Do you want to be a fireman?" Helen asked him as she rang up the book and bagged it.

"Yes," he said.

"My brother is a firefighter in Fort Lauderdale," Gayle told him. "He's very brave."

"I'm brave, too," the little boy said. "I'd like to be a fireman. Or an alligator. Then I could eat the bad people."

Helen stopped laughing abruptly. Firefighter. Firefighters have breathing gear. They could get into a tear-gas-and-Vikane building. Maybe Gayle got the SCBA equipment—or stole it—from her brother. Did she hate Page Turner enough to kill him?

She looked at Gayle with the golden hair . . . and the silver car.

What's wrong with me? she thought. How can I suspect Gayle?

How can you not? said a small voice. Gayle wasn't upset at Mr. Davies' death. That wasn't natural.

Gayle hated Page Turner. She was working at the store the night Page Turner died. She had an hour for dinner—enough time to get to the Coronado and back.

Of course, someone else could have hated Page Turner. Someone who looked even more like Cinderella.

And Astrid's silver Mercedes was a much grander coach.

Chapter 23

"I have two promising leads," Helen told Margery.

They were drinking screwdrivers in her landlady's kitchen. Margery's recipe was light on the orange juice and heavy on the vodka, with a hint of Key lime.

Helen came home from the bookstore feeling like she'd been beaten with bamboo. The booze hit her like a brick. She estimated she could down another three ounces before her lips went numb.

"Squawwwk!" said Pete. She didn't even jump when he screeched. The screwdrivers were mellowing her out.

"You really think your manager is a killer?" Margery looked frivolous in amethyst shorts and tangerine toenail polish. But her shrewd old eyes watched Helen carefully.

"I don't know," Helen said, and took another sip. Jeez, that drink was good. "I just know Gayle's very smart. Something's not right about her. She was at the store when Mr. Davies was killed, and she didn't seem very sorry that he was dead. Plus she has blond hair and a silver car."

"Ever stand on Las Olas and count blondes in silver cars? You'd run out of fingers pretty fast."

"I still want to check her out," Helen said. "But I'll have

to do my research on Gayle at the store. She's off the next two days and so am I. I thought I'd use this time to check out Astrid, the merry widow. She had her late husband underground awfully fast."

"A quick burial in a hot climate. Is that all you have on the wife?" Margery knocked back a slug that would have paralyzed Helen. The woman could pound it down.

"She had a fight with her husband the day he died. I'd like to know what that was about. And I'd really like to see if Astrid has any gentleman callers. She's a good-looking woman. My theory is she got her boyfriend to kill her husband. He'd have quite an incentive. He'd get to marry an attractive society blonde and enjoy the dead Turner's millions.

"Astrid could have been the blond bait who picked up her husband. Maybe she promised him something special when they made up after their fight. She could have delivered him to her boyfriend for the kill."

"But she didn't kill Mr. Davies."

"No, but the boyfriend could have been in the bookstore. Astrid is the type to have someone spy on the help. He could have heard me talking to Mr. Davies. During the mommy riot, he could have smothered Mr. Davies and slipped out. No one would have noticed in the confusion."

"Possible," Margery said, although she still sounded skeptical. "You planning round-the-clock surveillance of Astrid's house?"

"Not necessary," Helen said. She took a bigger sip this time. In fact, it was close to a gulp. She was feeling nicely numb, with a hint of a giggle underneath. "Astrid's no dummy. She must know the police consider her a suspect. The wife always is. She can't go to parties and dinners with her lover right now. But she must want to see him. Rich ladies aren't good at denying themselves what they want. If he's visiting her, it's going to be late at night."

"I like this," Margery said. "You're thinking. And the widow lives where, Palm Beach?"

"Right," Helen said. It came out more like "Riiiiiight." It wasn't the orange juice making her talk like that. She looked at the drink longingly, then put it back down. No more until she explained her plan to Margery. "I already have her address. From the bookstore files."

"So how are you going to get there, Samantha Spade? Hitchhike? Palm Beach is eighty miles round-trip. You don't have a car."

"Thought I'd borrow Peggy's Kia and drive up there."

"That cheap car would stick out there like a sore thumb," Margery said. "Maybe you could get by with it when the day help was around, but at night it's too noticeable. We'll take my big white boat. Half the old bags in Palm Beach drive Cadillacs like mine. No one will notice us."

"You don't mind doing surveillance?" Helen's tongue got tangled in the L's.

"Awwwwk," said Pete. Helen winced. Even the booze didn't help that time. Pete's squawk was like a stiletto in her brain. The little parrot sat on his perch, hunched and unhappy. Margery glared at him. He glared back.

"I don't mind anything that gets me away from that birdbrain," Margery said. "Parrots live even longer than Florida old farts. If you don't get Peggy out of jail, I'm facing a life sentence with Pete."

Pete screeched in protest behind his cage bars.

It rained all day, which was unusual for South Florida. Rain was usually liquid sunshine, short bursts that caught people without umbrellas. This was an old-fashioned frog strangler that flooded the flat streets.

Helen ran down to the newspaper boxes and brought back an armload. She sat at her kitchen table listening to the rain and looking at the employment ads. It was a depressing business, and the rain didn't help. Debt was a growth industry in Florida. The ads seemed to feed off the current financial crisis. Employers were looking for collection agents, credit counselors, and repo people.

If she didn't want to service the rising tide of debt and bankruptcy, there were a zillion ads for telemarketers. *Earn $700 to $1,200 weekly! . . . $12 an hour guaranteed! . . . Earn $100K,* they promised.

The more a job paid, the less useful it was, Helen decided. Selling books had redeeming social value. Calling people at dinner to peddle vacation time shares did not.

And look at this prize catch in the job pool. It paid six times what she made at the bookstore: *Spa attendants. Attractive bikini types. $1,200 a week guaranteed.*

Bet I wouldn't have to wear my ugly granny shoes, Helen thought. Or my pants with the pinpoint holes. Bet I wouldn't have to wear anything at all.

She sighed and nearly threw the paper across the floor when she saw the display ad:

> *TWO DAYS TO YOUR DREAM JOB!!*
> *Be there or be square. 10:00 a.m. till ????*
> *Interviews start for Down & Dirty Discounts.*
> *Jobs galore—$8 an hour or more at our new*
> *Federal Highway store.*

Maybe there was hope after all, she thought.

Margery's day had been equally depressing. She'd been to see Peggy.

"She looks like death on toast," Margery said. "The trial's in three weeks. Her lawyer, Colby, is supposed to be the best, but for the life of me, I don't know what she's doing. She hired a private detective to help establish an alibi for Peggy. He came up with nothing."

"What was Peggy doing after she left the barbecue?"

"She says she was driving around. But she didn't buy gas—or anything else. No one saw her."

They were in Margery's big white Cadillac. The rain had stopped, and it was nearly nine at night. I-95 was a demented dodge-'em game. Cars weaved in and out of traffic, or stomped on their brakes for no reason. Sometimes they did both at the same time.

"I remember reading an article in the 1980s that twenty percent of the people arrested for traffic violations on I-95 were on Quaaludes," Margery said.

"It explains a lot of this driving," Helen said.

"Not really," Margery said. "I think 'ludes are out. Who knows what they're on now."

The construction work started at the Palm Beach County line. The highway became a nightmare of lumpy patched asphalt and blinking barricades.

An SUV the size of an armored personnel carrier was tailgating the Cadillac. Helen could see its grille, like an evil grin, in the rearview mirror. When the SUV hit its high beams, urging Margery to get out of the way, the inside of the Caddy lit up.

"I hate when people do that," she said, and slammed on her brakes. The SUV honked loudly, then pulled in front of Margery.

"Good," she said, flipping on her high beams. "Let's give this bird a taste of his own medicine."

She tailgated and high-beamed the SUV all the way to Okeechobee Boulevard. Helen was relieved when Margery finally took that exit, even if it meant more torn-up roads in West Palm. About two blocks later, she was able to talk again.

"Can I ask a question?" she said.

"Go ahead."

"What does Phil the invisible pothead do for a living?"

"I told you, he's not invisible," Margery said, sounding irritated. "I see him at least once a month when I collect the rent."

"Well, I've never met the man and I've lived next to him almost a year. I just smell his burning weed. He's supposed to be a Clapton fan, but I never hear a note from his apartment."

"He's a considerate Clapton fan."

"Does he have a job?"

"Yes, it's something with the government. Broward County, I think. Building division, variances and permissions."

"No wonder he smokes so much dope. He must be crazy with boredom."

"He's got another five years and he can retire and do what he wants."

"What's that?" Helen said.

Margery shrugged. "He didn't tell me."

They rolled over the bridge into Palm Beach. The street looked like it had been steam-cleaned and landscaped by Disney. It was so neat, it made Helen nervous.

"We're on Royal Palm Way, which is lined with royal palms," she said.

"The rich aren't big on ambiguity," Margery said.

The late Page Turner didn't have a house on the water, but he lived only a block or so away. The sight of Turner's opulent home made Helen sick. It was a Mizner-style mansion in a shade of peach only rich people could buy. It was surrounded by a ten-foot-tall ficus hedge, but Helen could see the circular drive through the wrought-iron gates. The mansion was artistically lit, inside and out.

"Is this a hotel or what?" she said. "How many rooms does it have? Look at that. I can't believe that cheap son of a gun was whining about paying me six seventy an hour. My salary wouldn't pay for his floodlight bill."

"You wouldn't want the man walking in the dark," Margery said.

"I want him rotting in hell," Helen said.

"It's hard to sympathize with the little people when you're sitting in a Cadillac," Margery said. "Let's keep some perspective here. Now, will you put down your manifesto and help me find a place to park?"

The street signs said, PARKING BY PERMIT ONLY—9 A.M. TO 6 P.M.

"It's going on ten o'clock," Helen said. "We can park on the street. If we see any security coming around, we'll move on."

"OK, but you're going to have to do most of the watching. I can hardly see anything. My view is blocked by the hedge."

They watched for an hour with the lights off. "If we don't find a bathroom soon, I'm going to ruin the upholstery," Margery said. "I could use some coffee and a cigarette, too." Margery had made the supreme sacrifice. She didn't smoke on the stakeout.

They stopped at a convenience store on Dixie Highway. "This surveillance stuff is about as exciting as alphabetizing my spices," Margery said. "I'm beginning to miss that parrot. His squawks would keep me awake."

"It's almost eleven. You want to hang it up for tonight?" Helen said.

"No, let's go back for another hour or so."

As they sat in the dark, Helen asked, "How come the police never suspected you of Page Turner's murder? He was killed at your place."

"Why, that's so sweet," Margery said sincerely. "You don't think I'm a helpless old lady. The cops did. Also, I had an alibi. I was drinking Singapore slings with Alice, the owner of the beach motel, until two a.m. One of the guests complained about the noise."

It was eleven-twenty when a small car pulled up to the wrought-iron gates. An arm snaked out and punched in a code. The gates swung open.

"He has the combination," Helen said. "He's been here before. And look at that little car. He's no rich guy."

"This is it," Margery said. "You don't make a social call at this hour. We're about to find out the widow Turner's main squeeze."

"Main squeeze?" Helen said.

"Quiet," Margery said. "The car door is opening. Looks like a skinny guy getting out."

"That's no guy," Helen said.

"Definitely not," Margery said. "I should have put on my glasses. That's a woman."

"That's Gayle," Helen said.

Chapter 24

"More coffee, honey?"

Helen was a sucker for coffee shops where the waitresses called her "honey." This one was the real thing, a neon-and-metal diner off the highway. At midnight, the place looked like that Edward Hopper painting, *Nighthawks*. The fluorescent lights turned Margery's amethyst outfit a sickly purple and her skin an unhealthy yellow. Helen knew she looked equally exhausted. They both needed a caffeine infusion.

It was raining again and the diner's air-conditioning was on full-blast. The place was freezing. Helen spent most of the summer shivering in the refrigerated indoor Florida air. She wrapped her hands around her thick white coffee mug to keep warm.

"Maybe Astrid needed some records from the bookstore," Helen said. "Maybe that's why Gayle was there tonight."

"How does Astrid usually get the store reports?" Margery lit up a cigarette now that the surveillance was over.

"We send them by courier every Monday morning."

"Not at eleven-twenty at night," Margery said. "Not delivered by an attractive young lesbian. Who, by the way, wasn't carrying anything."

"Astrid can't be gay. She was married to Page, who was this hot stud." Helen let go of the coffee cup long enough to take a drink, hoping it would warm her insides.

"That's what *he* said," Margery said. "Ever ask any of the women if he was any good?"

"No," Helen said.

"Ha. I thought so. John Kennedy was supposed to be a stud, too, but a lot of women said he wasn't much of a lover. Don Juans rarely are. More interested in scoring than thinking about what a woman needs."

Helen took another drink while she considered this. It made sense. She wanted to ask Margery how she knew these things, but didn't dare. Her landlady probably had a fling with JFK. "I feel so Midwestern," Helen said. "Astrid was married, so I didn't expect her to have a gay lover."

"You'd be surprised by the rich women who have female lovers," Margery said. Helen really wasn't going to ask how she knew that. "In the nineteenth century, lesbianism was tolerated, even encouraged, in certain upper-class circles. Appearances were all that mattered, and it was perfectly acceptable for a woman to have a female friend."

"Even one as butch as Gayle?" Helen said. "In her Doc Martens, she could hardly mingle with Astrid's country-club friends."

"Astrid doesn't want to play tennis with her," Margery said. "I can't think of a better way to get revenge on an unfaithful husband than to cuckold him with a woman. So much for his stud rep."

"Do you think Gayle helped Astrid kill her husband?" Helen said.

"I think it's the best lead we've had so far. Let's take one more swing by the house and see if Gayle is still there. It's heading toward one a.m."

Margery drove back to Palm Beach in a pounding rain. Sometimes the road vanished completely into the wall of water. All Helen could see was the center line unwinding like a ribbon into the gray rain. She stayed silent while Margery handled the big Cadillac with considerable skill.

The rain stopped suddenly as they came over the bridge into Palm Beach. The shining moon lit the ragged clouds and turned the water into a sea of silver.

This time, the Turner mansion looked totally different. The huge house was dark and silent. Gayle's Honda was parked in the circular drive.

"Do you have to be anywhere tomorrow morning?" Margery said.

"No, I have the whole day free."

"Good. We're spending the night at a motel. I want to see something," Margery said. "Don't worry. I'll pay for it."

"You don't have to do that," Helen said. "I have money."

"I have more," Margery said. "Besides, I want that damn squawk box out of my house."

They got a no-frills motel room with two double beds in lower-rent Lake Worth. It was a smoking room and stank of stale tobacco. Helen didn't complain.

Her pillow smelled like an ashtray, but Helen was asleep as soon as her head touched it. Margery shook her awake at five-thirty a.m. and handed her a cup of coffee made in the motel room's little coffeepot. It tasted thin and bitter, but Helen was grateful for any hot caffeine.

"Throw on your clothes," Margery said. "Let's check something out."

By six a.m., they were back at the Turner mansion. Gayle's car was gone. "She's out before the day help arrives," Margery said. "They're hiding their relationship. I'd say we have a good, solid theory. Your work is cut out for you. Find out where they both were the night of the murder."

Astrid was easy. Women like her had their lives chronicled in the society columns. Helen walked over to the Broward County Library that morning, and began combing the Florida magazines and newspapers. She found what she needed two hours later in the *Florida High Life* weekly.

On the night her husband died, Astrid had hosted a benefit for the You Gotta Have Heart Association in Vero Beach, a hundred miles north of Fort Lauderdale. The newspaper photos showed Astrid at the head table, next to a well-upholstered gentleman shoving a forkful of food in his mouth. Good thing he was a major donor. The guy would need the heart association's services soon.

The photos accompanied a column called "Samantha's Society Rambles," which Helen thought was a remarkably accurate description. It was headed by a photo of Samantha, who looked like Dick Cheney in drag.

Astrid was wearing a black strapless Gucci gown, according to Samantha, who pronounced her "stunning." Helen wouldn't go that far, but Astrid was regal-looking. Her dress must have cost a fortune. More than I make at her bookstore in a year, Helen thought.

Samantha the society columnist had a positive mania for reporting the designers of all the women's dresses. Helen wondered if the charity would have made more money if the women had stayed home and donated the price of their dresses.

Samantha kept rambling, but Helen followed her to the bitter end, slogging through designer and guest names. In the last paragraph was the information she needed. Astrid had "danced till dawn to the music of Peter Duchin's Orchestra." There was a photograph to prove it. She and the well-upholstered gentleman were holding each other at arm's length, as if they were coated with anthrax.

Helen didn't know if Astrid actually stayed until the sun peeped over the horizon, but one thing was clear. She was there late. Astrid could not have slipped out for an hour to kill her husband in Fort Lauderdale. It was a two-hundred-mile round trip.

Astrid did not put the pillow over Page's face, but she wasn't off the hook. Not after what Helen saw last night. Astrid and Gayle were in it together. Astrid, as the most likely suspect, had established her alibi. Meanwhile, Gayle did the dirty work.

Suddenly, all Gayle's odd behavior made sense.

Gayle knew Peggy had threatened to kill Page. She'd been at the store when it happened.

Gayle knew where Helen lived because she'd been to the Coronado before. She took Page Turner there and dumped his body in Peggy's bed to throw suspicion on her.

Gayle was strong enough to move the body.

Gayle knew the Coronado was being tented. Helen had talked about it and asked for the weekend off.

Gayle could go into a building filled with poison gas. She had a firefighter brother with access to SCBA gear.

Gayle hated Page Turner so much, she broke his Bawls.

Gayle had golden hair and a silver car.

Gayle told everyone that Peggy was guilty. Helen was sure she steered the police her friend's way.

When Page's office was broken into, Gayle said nothing was missing. If something vital was indeed stolen, something that cleared Peggy, Gayle would never tell the police. All Gayle cared about was that the break-in would upset her precious Astrid.

And what about poor Mr. Davies, dead in his favorite chair? Gayle could have easily slipped back from her errand to hear Mr. Davies was about to spill the beans. She could have smothered him anytime during the mommy riot. She certainly didn't seem upset at his death.

Gayle stayed with the police when they were investigating Mr. Davies' death, "helping" them. She made sure Denny and Helen weren't anywhere near the scene. She could easily hide or cover up anything suspicious.

And what part did Astrid play in this? She was safely in Vero Beach, dancing till dawn in front of the photographers, while her lover made her a rich widow.

She had the money so they could live happily ever after.

Helen did not get more than four hours' sleep that night, but she didn't mind. She didn't even care that she had to go into the bookstore on her day off. Today, she would confirm Gayle's role in the murders. She would solve this case and save her friend. Peggy would be reunited with her pal Pete and live happily ever after.

Brad usually took his lunch hour at one o'clock. It was a short walk from the library to the bookstore. On the way, Helen stopped at a drugstore and picked up the latest magazine tribute to Jennifer Lopez. *J.Lo!* it said. *Twenty-four fabulous new photos! Learn her beauty secrets.*

The little bookseller was munching Miami Subs takeout when Helen walked in the break room. She had no idea how he stayed so skinny on junk food.

"I brought you a present," Helen said, and handed him the magazine.

"Is this a bribe?" he joked.

"Sort of," Helen said.

"I owe you for Albert," he said, biting into a sandwich oozing lettuce and mayonnaise sauce. "Since you recited his poem, he hasn't even mentioned J.Lo's name."

"Good," Helen said. "You remember the night Page Turner died?"

"How could I forget? He was a bastard to the end."

"Was it busy here that night?"

"Nonstop. It was a full moon, too, and every weirdo in South Florida was in the store. I was working the register. I had to call Gayle up front because some wacko wanted to order a book on devil worship, but wouldn't give us his name, phone number, or address. He was one scary dude. Dead-white skin, black clothes. Looked like he slept in a coffin. Gayle told him no phone or address, no order. I'm convinced he put a curse on us. In fact, that would explain everything that's happened to this store since." Helen thought Brad was only half kidding.

"Is that the only time Gayle came up front?"

"I think so. I handled the other crises myself. She stayed in the office the whole night, working on the accounts and the new schedule."

"Did she go out for lunch?"

"She ate an eggplant sandwich from the café at her desk," Brad said. "I saw her buy it."

"But you didn't actually see her in her office the whole night," Helen said. "You were at the front cash register. She could have easily slipped out for an hour."

"She could have, but she didn't," Brad said. He'd dripped a spot of mayo on his chin. "I hope you aren't trying to pin Page's murder on Gayle. You obviously haven't worked as many shit jobs as I have. She's a good manager. She's too decent to murder anyone. I don't really feel like reading, thank you."

He handed Helen back the J.Lo tribute. She did not think anyone could look so dignified with mayonnaise on his chin.

Helen should have felt ashamed. But she didn't. She couldn't wait to get back to the Coronado with her news.

"The wife had to have an unbreakable alibi," Helen said. "She would be the logical suspect. Gayle did the killing.

She has no alibi for that night. She was alone in the office. She could have slipped out the back door and no one would have seen her."

"Now all we have to do is prove it," Margery said. "We are going back to Palm Beach tonight, aren't we?"

"You bet," Helen said. "I've stirred things up at the store. I think we might see something interesting tonight."

This time, there was no rain on the hour-long drive. Even the traffic seemed saner. But the stakeout was just as boring. They parked in the same spot. Helen and Margery kept the same routine, watching for an hour, then driving around, then returning to their post. They encountered a security patrol, but no one questioned the formidable Margery.

After eleven p.m., they looked up hopefully every time a car came down the street. But Gayle did not arrive until twelve-thirty. The house lights went off about one a.m.

At one-ten, a hand yanked open the passenger door and pulled Helen out by the collar. She landed on her knees and found herself staring at a pair of shiny black Doc Martens. Helen could hear Margery say, in her best grande-dame voice, "Young woman, what do you think you are doing?"

"You!" Gayle said, pulling Helen up. "What are you doing here? Why is an employee spying on me?"

"I . . ."

Margery batted her eyes at Gayle and said, "We needed some privacy. Some quality time together. Surely you understand."

Helen was always astonished at how boldly and easily Margery could lie. Now she was pretending to be Helen's lover.

Gayle wasn't buying it. "Nice try. But you forgot I work with her. I got nothing on my gaydar. She's straight as an arrow. Explain yourself."

"I . . ." Helen tried again. But nothing came out. Even

Margery seemed flummoxed now. Helen knew she'd be fired.

"Let me guess. You think if you can blame Page Turner's murder on me, your friend Peggy will go free. Brad told me you asked him where I was that night. It's easy to blame the gays, isn't it? We're already doing something unnatural. Why not murder?"

"It's not like that, Gayle. I like you. I respect you."

"You like me so much you think I murdered Page. That worthless shit deserved to die, but I didn't do it."

"You have good reason to be angry, Gayle. I'm desperate, and I did something dumb. But I know Peggy is innocent. I just can't figure out who did it."

"I thought it was Peggy," Gayle said, her voice calmer. "If it's not, I haven't a clue. Don't you think I'd go to the police if knew? I want the killer in prison. Astrid and I will have to sneak around until Page's murderer is convicted."

Gayle's voice turned soft. "If Peggy is innocent, then this is a miscarriage of justice. I'm glad you're doing something about it. You're looking at the wrong person, but you're at the right place. Page Turner was his bookstore. In some way, that bookstore killed him."

Then she turned and left them, her black clothes and bright hair vanishing into the rich darkness.

Chapter 25

"Do you think she's innocent?" Margery asked.

"Either that, or she put on a good act of outraged innocence," Helen said.

They were driving back to Fort Lauderdale, both grateful for the anonymous night. Their faces were crimson with shame. Helen's still felt hot when she remembered being yanked out of the car. Both knees were bruised and she had a scrape on her hand.

"The problem is, Gayle's good at deception," she said. "No one at the store knew she was having an affair with Astrid. I wouldn't have believed it until I saw her drive up. But did she kill Page Turner? Gayle can't prove she didn't leave the store that night. I can't prove she did."

"Stalemate," Margery said. "So tomorrow—I mean today—you go back to the bookstore and start all over again?"

"Do you think she'll let me work there again, after I accused her of murder? When she tells Astrid, I'll be lucky to live in Lauderdale, much less work here. I'll call in sick this morning and look for a new job. Gayle can fire me when I show up tomorrow." Helen let out a yawn. "These hours are getting to me."

"Well, it is one a.m.," Margery said. "Got any good prospects?"

"Yeah, Down & Dirty Discounts is taking applications at ten a.m."

"Be there or be square," Margery said.

"That's what the ad said."

At nine-thirty the next morning, Helen arrived at the new discount store. Red-and-yellow flags were flying the Triple D logo. A big banner said, WELCOME TO THE FUN! Job seekers were already lined up outside the building. It was not a promising selection: skinny sunburned guys with prison tattoos, tough young women in tube tops, old men mumbling to themselves, poorly dressed people who spoke rapid Spanish and halting English. Helen, in a neat beige Ann Taylor suit and pumps, knew she was a prize.

I will get this job, she told herself. Forty hours a week at eight dollars an hour. That's another one-hundred-nineteen dollars a week, an extra four-hundred-seventy-six a month. It seemed like untold wealth after the bookstore salary; especially now that she was working thirty hours a week.

At ten-ten, the doors opened on a barnlike room furnished with long brown folding tables and chairs. Each table had a box of pencils and a stack of yellow job applications.

"Take a seat and fill out the application forms, people," said a callow young corporate type. He had no-color hair that looked like a bristle brush and a smile Helen didn't trust. "You have twenty minutes."

Helen set to work lying about her experience, her qualifications, and her background. There was no way she could list her real degrees or her former high-paying job.

A young woman in a hot-pink blouse with a plunging

neckline read her application carefully, moving her lips. Then she asked Helen, "They want to know if we have any felony convictions. Do they count if you were a juvenile?"

"Juvenile records are sealed," Helen said. She was planning to lie about her own run-in with the court.

"At the top of your application is a number," Mr. Bristle Head said. "We will call it for your interview."

Six other suits came out. Mr. Bristle Head called the first seven numbers. Nearly an hour later, Helen heard her number, sixty-three. She got Mr. B himself. "Follow me, please," he said, and walked back to a white cubicle the size of a phone booth. There was room for a chipped brown Formica table, a leather swivel chair, and an uncomfortable orange plastic chair. Bristle Head took the good chair.

"Now, Helen, your age is forty-two, right?" He talked to her as if she were a little slow. He did not bother to tell her his name.

"Yes," she said.

"And you work at Page Turners. That's very good. Can you operate a cash register?"

Helen explained her bookstore duties and skills for nearly ten minutes.

"Well, we're definitely interested," he said.

Here goes, Helen thought. This is the big test. "I'd like to work for you. But I need to make cash only."

There was only a momentary hesitation. Then Mr. Bristle Head said, "I think that can be arranged, although you might have to work for a little less. Maybe seven fifty an hour. We can arrange it through me. I'm the new store manager."

Well, well, Helen thought. This definitely was a Down & Dirty store. I'll lose about twenty dollars a week, but I can live with that.

"Fine," she said.

"We'd like you to start next Monday. The store won't be

open for another week, but we'll need help with the shelving, and, of course, we want to train you the Triple D way. Are you available to start then?"

"Yes," Helen said. Oh heck yes.

"Good. Now, there's just one more thing. We'd like you to take a little test." He handed her a piece of paper with an 800 number on it. "Just call this phone number. The prompt will ask for a special code. That's this number here."

"What's the test for?" Helen said.

"To see how good an employee you'll be," he said. "You can take it anytime, night or day. It's automated. We'll call you within twenty-four hours after you take the test. If you pass, we'll see you Monday morning."

He stood up. The interview was over.

Helen should have felt happy. She almost had the job, except for that test. But it made her uneasy. What kind of test was this? She'd ask Margery, who knew all sorts of odd things. Besides, she needed to use her landlady's phone.

Margery was sitting by the pool, painting her toenails the color of Red Hots. "Thought this color would set off my new shoes," she said. She pointed to a pair of polka-dot slides. She wore a matching polka-dot shorts set. All those white dots were making Helen dizzy.

"Very cute," she said. "I think I've got the job, but I'm supposed to take this automated phone test. Ever heard of anything like this?"

Margery studied the paper. "One of those," she said, as if Helen had handed her a palmetto bug. "It's an honesty test."

"Why are they worried about my honesty? They plan to cheat the government and pay me in cash under the counter."

"They're afraid you're going to steal them blind," she said. "The test is a piece of cake, as long as you don't follow your natural instincts. Never give a humane answer.

For instance, they'll ask something like, If you see a starving person steal a loaf of bread, you should:

"One, call the police and have them arrested.

"Two, turn a blind eye. What is bread compared to a human life?

"The correct answer is one."

"You're kidding," Helen said. "Even the nuns, who were as conservative as you could get, said it was OK to steal food if you were starving."

"We're not talking nuns," Margery said. "We're not even talking humans. Think like a robber baron. No, like an Enron executive. Never show an ounce of compassion. Screw the widows and orphans. The bottom line is what matters. If you have any doubts, ask yourself, 'What would Enron do?'"

"Right," Helen said. "Bottom line. To heck with widows and orphans. I'm ready. Can I use your phone?"

"Soon as I finish painting," Margery said. Ten minutes later, when she had foam thingies separating her red-hot toes, Margery hobbled into the house. Pete greeted them with his usual angry squawk. Margery threw the cover over the cage.

"That will shut him up. We can't have featherhead screeching during the test. You take the kitchen phone. I'll be listening on the bedroom extension if you need help."

Helen dialed the 800 number, then punched in the code. A mechanical voice asked for her Social Security number. Helen punched in her number, with two digits off, and prayed they didn't check it.

A stern female voice said, "Congratulations. You are taking the job test. Please answer honestly. Press one for yes. Press three for no." It was the voice of authority. It was the voice that said Helen did not quite measure up. She felt a sudden urge to confess she'd sneaked a cigarette in the girl's bathroom, she'd skipped school on a sunny spring day, and she'd taken two dollars off her mother's dresser. But there was no need. The voice knew every venal act.

The first couple of questions were easy.

"Are you always pleased with your job performance?" the voice asked in crisp, no-nonsense tones.

Helen pressed no. Margery kept quiet.

"If a supermarket charged you for a dozen oranges and when you got home you realized you had thirteen, would you return to the store to pay for the extra orange?"

Right. She should endure a two-dollar round-trip bus ride to return something worth ten cents—when it was the store's mistake? She could see the clerk, irritated by the extra hassle. She could see the line forming behind her, as the store tried to deal with this unprecedented situation.

Close your eyes and think of Enron, Helen told herself. They'd want every dime. She pressed yes.

"Have you ever lied about anything?"

Helen pressed yes again. It was a trick question. Everyone lies, even if it's to say, "I'm sorry, I have another engagement and can't come to your party," instead of, "I wouldn't go if you paid me."

"If a man in a bar offered to sell you a Rolex watch for twenty dollars, would you buy it?" the voice asked.

A definite no. Helen hated the guys who went around to bars late at night selling CDs and watches. Besides, it was probably a fake Rolex.

Then the voice asked, "If one of your coworkers needed money for medicine for her sick child, and you caught her taking twenty dollars from her cash register, would you:

"One, report her to your supervisor for proper disciplinary action." Ha, Helen thought, the bastards would fire her in a heartbeat.

"Two, say nothing. It's none of your business." That had possibilities.

"Three, lend her the money and remind her that pilfering is not a good idea."

Three was a little sanctimonious, but probably the best option.

Margery said, "Helen, don't you dare press three. What would Enron do?"

Damn the widows and children, full speed ahead. "Report the thieving witch," Helen said.

"Very good," Margery said.

The questions were obsessive on stealing. They asked:

"Do you think it is OK to steal from a large corporation if they won't miss it?

"Do you think it is OK to steal from a large corporation because they are stealing from you?

"Do your friends steal?

"Have you ever been tempted to steal?"

What would Enron do? What would Enron do? Helen asked herself as the voice pounded her with more questions. These people had twisted minds.

"Many companies fire someone who is caught stealing, no matter how inexpensive the item. Do you agree with this policy?"

Yes, said Helen, in full Enron mode. Unless we hang them, like they did in the good old days.

How long was this test? She glanced at Margery's kitchen clock. She'd been at it for almost an hour. Bristle Head had not told her Triple D would take an hour of her time. That was stealing, too.

"Do you ever ask yourself why you are doing something?" the voice asked, as if introspection led to nasty nighttime habits.

"Hell, yes," Helen said into the phone. "I'm asking why I want to work at your store."

"Helen," Margery said. "You've almost got this job. Don't mess it up."

The voice rolled on, relentless as a Panzer division: "Recently, bank robbers tossed thousands of dollars out of their car during a police chase. The authorities never recovered most of the stolen money. If you found a thousand dollars of the bank's money blowing down the sidewalk, would you consider keeping it?"

"Of course I would, you moron," Helen said to the phone. "I'm making two hundred and one dollars a week."

"Helen, don't do this," Margery said.

Helen ignored her and pressed yes.

The pitiless voice said, "Why do some employees steal?

"One, they're not good enough to earn a raise.

"Two, they need extra money."

"Three," Helen shouted. "You forgot number three. You drove me to it by suspecting the worst. I've never shoplifted a grape at the grocery store, but you've made me so angry I want to start slipping your CDs in my purse. I want to hand your sound systems out the side door. I want to take your cheap TVs off the loading dock. If I work for you, I'll be a thief for sure."

Helen slammed down the phone.

"Oh, well," Margery said, "the uniforms look pretty stupid."

Chapter 26

Gayle did not fire Helen.

Maybe the bookstore manager was forgiving. Maybe a reliable employee was too valuable to fire in South Florida. Or maybe Gayle and Astrid wanted to keep Helen where they could watch her.

Helen had the awful feeling door number three was the correct answer, and she didn't want to go there.

She tapped on the bookstore door at eight-fifty the morning after her Triple D encounter. Gayle unlocked it and said, "Helen, how are you feeling?"

Helen had almost forgotten she'd called in sick to go to her aborted job interview.

"Uh, fine," she managed. She stood there, waiting for Gayle to tell her to clean out her locker.

"I brought doughnuts," Gayle said. "They're in the break room. Help yourself, then I'll open your cash drawer."

Wasn't Gayle going to say anything about their Palm Beach encounter? Like, "How's your collar after I dragged you out of the car?" Or, "Do your knees hurt from when you landed on the ground?"

Gayle acted as if it had never happened. Helen found that

unnerving. But she kept her own silence. She did not tell her colleagues about Gayle's affair with Astrid. That was no one's business but theirs.

She got more silence from Brad. He didn't talk to Helen for a full day. Then the little bookseller forgave Helen those nosy questions, and told her the latest news about J.Lo.

Albert wasn't just silent—he wasn't there. He called in sick three days in a row. Helen hoped he was on job interviews.

Denny was quiet as death. He did not joke or do his Sting imitations when he cleaned the café. Mr. Davies' death weighed heavily on the young bookseller. He came to work on time. He had no choice if he didn't want to wind up in a juvenile facility. But murder was more reality than Denny wanted.

Mr. Davies' death was ruled a homicide. Detective Gil Gilbert told them the store's oldest inhabitant had been smothered. Helen thought the hazel-eyed detective looked rather like Gary Cooper in *High Noon*.

"With our couch pillows?" she said.

"Afraid so, ma'am," Gilbert said. Now he sounded like him, too. "His DNA was found on one."

"How'd it get there?" Brad asked.

"Er, fluids from his mouth and nose," Gilbert said tactfully.

"Gross, man. Snot and slobber," Denny said tactlessly.

That creeped Helen out. She could not look at the comfortable old couch without a shudder. It had held a murder weapon.

Poor Page Turners. The store had been designed as a book lover's delight, but now its cozy nooks and crannies were haunted by pedophiles and murderers, liars and rioters.

"Did he suffer?" she asked the detective.

"I don't think so," he said. "He was a frail eighty-three, and he may have been asleep at the time he was attacked."

Helen tried to take comfort in that.

Detective Gilbert questioned the bookstore staff again. By the time he finished with her, Helen did not see any further resemblance to Gary Cooper. She thought he looked like the IRS agent who'd audited her and Rob in 1988.

Helen had a question for him: "Why isn't Detective Jax here? Mr. Davies was murdered because he knew something about Page Turner's death."

"The Page Turner case is closed. The killer has been arrested."

"Do you really believe that?" Helen said.

"Can you remember any other customers who were in the store between ten a.m. and eleven-thirty p.m.?"

"You've asked me that a dozen times. I've given you every name I can think of. I want to help, but I didn't see anyone back there." And you didn't answer my question.

Helen was grateful the old book lover's murder did not make the media. The store would be swamped with curious crowds. Fortunately, in South Florida the death of an old person was not news.

She wanted to go to his funeral, but Mr. Davies' body was being shipped home to New Jersey. There was no local memorial service. His death left Helen feeling empty and restless. She'd find herself standing where his chair used to be, staring out the window overlooking the parking lot, wondering what he saw that fatal night.

Helen had to face another death. Page Turners was definitely closing. She heard it first. "I guess we need new couch pillows," Helen said, after Gilbert left. "I don't think the police will be returning ours anytime soon."

"No, we don't," Gayle said. "The store is closing. I'm making the announcement today, then putting up the 'Going

Out of Business Sale' sign. We'll stay open until the stock is sold. That should be two weeks at the most."

Helen didn't think it would take that long. The shelves at Page Turners were almost bare. Even displaying the books face-out would not cover all the holes anymore. She was ashamed to sell the survivors. They were a dog-eared lot: last year's almanacs, picture books with chocolate thumbprints, sci-fi books coated with alien slime. The cookbooks were by chefs who couldn't get cable TV shows. The children's books were gnawed. The magazines were too old for a doctor's office.

Yet people bought them. When that sale sign went up, the bargain hunters charged—and paid cash, and tried to get bigger discounts on the battered stock.

A mother came up to Helen's register with a stack of shopworn children's books. "These are half off," she said. "But this book has a bite out of it."

"That's the part that's half off," Helen said.

"We'll give you an additional ten percent," Gayle said. She muttered to Helen, "No jokes. We have to move this stock."

The mother looked pleased. "You can have two Barbie books," she said to her daughter.

"Two! Two!" The little girl did a twirling dance. "I get two. I'm double good!" She was a downy little blonde with a ruffled pink dress and a pretend princess crown.

"Don't you look pretty," Helen said.

"Yes," the little girl said. "It's my birthday. I'm five whole years old and Mom said I could have any book I wanted, and I get to wear my Cinderella shoes. See?"

She held out her small foot. She was wearing clear plastic high heels. "These are my glass slippers, except they're not, because Mom says even Cinderella didn't have real glass 'cause it's not safe. The prince wouldn't want her to get hurt."

"I see," said Helen. And she did. She saw what Mr. Davies meant. She'd seen shoes like that before, on grown-up feet.

Helen put the little girl's two books in her own special bag, which sent her into another twirling dance in her Cinderella shoes, then bagged her mother's purchase.

"You didn't have to do that. Thank you," said her mother.

"Oh, no," Helen said. "Thank you. And I do mean that."

The golden girl who looked like Cinderella.

Melanie, the print-on-demand author, wore clear plastic high heels. But she didn't get a prince. Instead she had a humiliating encounter with that toad, Page Turner.

Helen didn't know if Melanie drove a silver car. But kindly old Mr. Davies had transformed her tacky see-through plastic heels into Cinderella slippers.

Helen could see the shoes now. But she couldn't see Melanie as a murderer. Could she really kill Page Turner and Mr. Davies?

Ridiculous. Melanie wasn't a double killer. She was a double victim. She'd been screwed twice, once by her greedy publisher and again by Page Turner.

She could just see telling Detective Gilbert that fluffy little woman was a killer. OK, she wasn't that little. But with her blond hair and ruffles, she was fluffy as Flopsy, Mopsy, and Cottontail.

Mr. Davies must have meant something else. Or someone else. Maybe he saw Astrid dressed up for her society event.

She should forget all about Melanie.

Except she could not. Melanie had been badly used by Page Turner. The man had led her on, promising a signing at his prestigious store and a blurb from his best-selling writer friend, the fatheaded Burt Plank. Naive little Melanie with her Cinderella shoes and fairy-tale dreams believed those promises. Until Gayle opened her eyes.

Gayle again. The woman kept wandering through this story. Gayle told Melanie the truth about Page Turner. What was her connection? Were they in it together?

Where was Melanie the night of Page Turner's murder?

Helen knew she was in the store the day Mr. Davies was killed. She'd come in right after Madame Muffy, the preppy psychic. She'd wanted to pick up her books. Except she couldn't afford both of them. So Helen had stashed one away for her. What was Melanie's last name? Something frilly: Devereaux DuShayne. That was it.

Maybe Helen should have a friendly talk with her. Helen tried directory assistance, but there was no one listed with that name.

She checked the store's author files in the computer, but there was no mention of Melanie, more proof that Page Turner never considered giving her a signing.

The key to Page Turner was in the bookstore, Gayle had said. And the key to the author? In her book. That's one of the last things Mr. Davies told Helen. "Authors always write about themselves. The good ones are better at disguising it."

If Helen wanted to find out anything about Melanie, she would have to read her book.

Where did she hide it?

Behind the other D's on the hold shelf. Helen moved a pile of books. There it was: *Love and Murder—Forever: A Romantic Mystery or Mysterious Romance,* by Melanie Devereaux DuShayne.

The lurid cover showed a half-clad woman on a bed in the embrace of a Fabio look-alike. A bloody knife was plunged into their pillow.

Helen read the first sentence:

Jillian's gaze rested on Lance's broad chest and gentle touch.

How does your gaze rest on a gentle touch? Helen couldn't figure that out, but she kept reading.

Her heart told her this was the only man she would ever love. Jillian felt a stirring that left her moist, yielding. Lance's eyes slid down her dress.

Helen started giggling. She saw two eyes sliding down a dress, leaving a bloody trail. She closed the book. Enough.

On the back cover was a photo of Melanie holding a fat surly cat. Her biography said, *When she's not writing romantic mysteries, Melanie Devereaux DuShayne is a dental assistant at the Mr. Goodtooth Clinic in Sunnysea Beach, Florida, where she lives with her Siamese cat, Samson.*

She lives at the clinic with her cat?

No, that had to be more of Melanie's tangled syntax. But now Helen knew where Melanie worked. The Mr. Goodtooth Clinic was in the phone book. Maybe they could have that chat after all. There must be some way to casually ask Melanie where she was the night of the murder. Everything Helen thought of sounded lame. But then, Melanie didn't seem to be the brightest bulb in the chandelier.

Helen called the clinic. The receptionist said, "Melanie is with a patient. Can she call you back?"

"Uh, no," Helen said. "I can't take calls here. Could you put me on hold?"

Helen listened to a Muzak version of "Strawberry Fields" that went on forever, before Melanie answered the phone.

"Melanie, this is Helen at Page Turners bookstore," she said, and immediately wished she had been smart enough to use a different name. "We're trying to locate Mr. Turner's briefcase because it had some important business papers in it. I understand you picked him up at the store the night he . . ."

He what? Croaked? Died? Went to his reward?

Melanie's voice turned cold enough to frost the orange crop. "I was nowhere near the bookstore the night Mr. Turner died."

"Really? We have a witness who says you picked up Mr. Turner."

"Was it that old man? Because he was asleep when I . . . He always slept in that chair. You're trying to find out if I have an alibi! I can't believe this. Your store has always persecuted me, and now this!" Melanie slammed down the phone.

When she what? When she picked up Page? Put the pillow over Mr. Davies' face?

And why was Melanie talking about Mr. Davies in the past tense, as if he were dead? His death wasn't in the papers or on TV.

Helen needed to know more about Melanie. All she had was a hunch, a slip of the tongue, and a dead witness. There was only one way to learn more. It would be horrible, but she would do it for Peggy.

Helen would read Melanie's book.

Chapter 27

Helen fixed some coffee and sat in her turquoise Barcalounger, determined to read Melanie's book. Last time, she'd gotten as far as Lance's eyes sliding down Jillian's dress.

She knew Lance loved her. Lance, with his strong, sensitive hands, his sage-colored eyes, his devotion to dental science. He was her knight, the lord of her throbbing love. But Jillian was bound by law, if not by love, to the heartless Simon de Quincy, who was as rich as he was evil. Her spun-gold hair, bluebell eyes and lush, feminine body were subject to the rough, insolent caresses of another man, a man who never flossed. Jillian had toiled as a dental assistant when she first met Simon.

A dental assistant? That was Melanie's job. Mr. Davies was right. Melanie put autobiographical details in her novel. She was the heroine in this romance novel, with spun-gold hair (courtesy of Miss Clairol) and bluebell eyes (contacts). Her heaving bosom was clad in discount ruffles and laces. Her glass slippers were clear plastic.

Yet Melanie's job was ruthlessly practical. She stuck her fingers in strangers' mouths and patiently scraped the gunk off their dirty teeth. Nothing was less romantic.

Was her book a way to inject some romance into her life? Were these questions a delaying tactic on Helen's part to avoid reading this book? And what was a rich guy named Simon de Quincy doing married to a dental assistant?

> *Simon was a patient who needed his diseased gums lasered. Alas, after she married him, she realized her new husband also had a diseased soul. If Jillian ever left him, Simon would make sure she never gazed upon her darling baby Jarrod again. The corrupt de Quincys were so powerful, they could do anything, even tear a mother from her child. Night after night, Jillian endured Simon's embraces while she thought only of her true love, Lance.*

Helen read about Simon de Quincy's countless cruelties and inadequate dental hygiene until her gaze glazed and she fell asleep. She woke again at three-thirty. No woman could endure this on her own. It would take another pot of coffee. She made it extra strong. Then she resumed reading. She was 190 pages into the book. Jillian and Lance had gazed at each other sixty-seven times.

What was it about romances and gazing? Helen figured that's why it took the couple so long to get into the sack. When gazes rarely went below the neck, it took time to get down to business.

I have no romance, she thought.

Helen got up, stretched, then poured her eighth cup of the night. The caffeine buzz would keep her awake until

next week. Come on, she told herself. You have work to do.
She resumed the painful task of reading.

> *The vile Simon de Quincy was snoring on the white
> satin chaise longue, still wearing his muddy riding
> boots. The dreaded riding crop, the source of so much
> humiliation, was gripped in one hairy hand. A black
> silk tunic clutched his broad chest, just as she had
> once desired to clutch him in wifely lust, before he had
> crushed her spirit and her love. A bottle of priceless
> Napoleon brandy was beside him. It had fallen over.
> Its precious liquid spilled out on a mahogany table
> that had graced the de Quincy mansion for four gener-
> ations.*

That was another problem Helen had with romances.
Why didn't the guy wear normal clothes? You could be a
villain in jeans and deck shoes. Well, a Florida villain, anyway.

> *De Quincy's filthy snores grew louder. Jillian knew
> the utter degradation she would face when he awoke.
> Simon would beat her and force her to . . . she would
> feel his thrusting . . . he would fondle her . . . no, she
> could not endure that again. She was sickened at the
> very thought. Last night, she had forced herself to keep
> quiet as his hands slid over her tender camellia-white
> body, knowing her precious Jarrod was in the next
> room. But she swore it would not happen again. She
> felt as if an angel was leading her to their unhallowed
> marital bed, the scene of many despairing pairings.
> She picked up a lace pillow that had been embroidered
> by a de Quincy maiden two hundred years ago, and
> put it over Simon's face. He hardly struggled. When*

*the riding crop fell from his wretched hand, she knew
the man who defiled her was dead.*

*"Oh, Lance, Lance, I did it for you," Jillian cried in
an agony of triumph. And then she heard the boudoir
door creak.*

After slogging through mountains of rocky prose, Helen
had hit pay dirt. The drunken Simon had been smothered.
Just like the drunken Page Turner and poor Mr. Davies.
Maybe it wouldn't convince Detective Gilbert, but
Melanie's favorite method of murder definitely had Helen's
attention.

She set the coffee cup down and read. There was no
chance she'd fall asleep now.

Jillian got away with Simon's murder, thanks to those
bluebell eyes, which she batted shamelessly, and a devil-
may-care police investigation.

But that did not free Jillian. After Simon's death, she was
blackmailed by the de Quincy family retainer, the oppres-
sive housekeeper, Mrs. Hermione Buncaster. Mrs. B. had
photographed Jillian as she put the fatal pillow over
Simon's face. She had the photos under lock and key. It
took months of frantic searching to discover their hiding
place. Of course, the resourceful Jillian had a way to save
herself.

*Little did Mrs. Buncaster know that Jillian had be-
friended a small-time burglar named Melvin Larkey.
He, too, was a patient at the dental clinic. Jillian
taught him to floss nightly, and saved his teeth from
dreadful plaque buildup. "You showed me how to pick
me teeth proper, little missy," said Mel. "In gratitude,
I'll show you how to pick a lock."*

Jillian vowed to use her new lock-picking powers

*only for good. Thanks to Mel, she could save herself
and her innocent son.*

Jillian was a lock picker? Now that was interesting.
Helen bet this was another autobiographical detail. It took
skill and patience to wield teeth-cleaning tools. It was a
small step to picking locks. And locks didn't squirm and
yell, "Ouch."

*With nimble fingers, Jillian unlocked the door to the
housekeeper's room. Mel would have been so proud. A
Tandy DE345 lock looks difficult, but it always gives
way after a few tries. The locked drawer, which had an
old-fashioned Peerless lock, could have been opened
with a hairpin. Jillian's expert fingers knew its sordid
secret in seconds. She took one last sweeping gaze
around the room of her tormentor, then set fire to the
photos and the negatives in the metal wastebasket. She
gazed exultantly at the rising flames, and knew she was
finally free.*

Mrs. B. left town and was never heard from again. Jillian
married the honest dentist Lance at last. Helen hoped for
their future happiness that their eyes didn't go sliding anywhere.

She closed the dreadful book and thought again of dear
Mr. Davies. He may have given Helen the key to solve his
own murder. Helen was wrong about Melanie. She'd made
the same mistake as some men—if a woman was a blonde
with a big chest, she must be dumb.

The book was badly written, but Helen had learned a lot.
Melanie thought it was OK to smother dissolute drunks.
Her heroine got away with murder and lived happily ever
after.

Melanie was not disorganized. She wrote a whole

book—a bad one, maybe, but even that took effort. She knew how to construct a murder plot.

Melanie knew a thing or two about lock picking. And that meant she could have easily gotten into Peggy's tented apartment.

But even if she could get into the Coronado, where would she get the SCBA breathing gear? Helen doubted that even the most grateful patient would lend her that. Trevor said it cost two thousand dollars new. Helen didn't think Melanie had that kind of money.

Helen moved slowly around the bookstore that morning. She'd had less than three hours' sleep. But she felt she was finally getting somewhere. On her lunch hour, she bought a double espresso and walked over to the Broward County Library to check out SCBA gear on the Internet. Unfortunately, every computer was taken, and it would be twenty minutes before one was free. That might not be enough time.

Helen couldn't wait. She found a pay phone, called her friend Sarah and prayed she was home.

She answered on the fourth ring. "Hi, Helen, what are you doing?"

Helen could see curly-haired Sarah in her Hollywood beach condo, her computer set up so she could watch the ocean. "I don't have much time to talk. I have a suspect who may know how to pick locks."

"That would get him in the door."

"Her," Helen said. "But I don't know if she has access to SCBA breathing gear. Can you do an Internet search for me?"

"Sure. What do you want me to look for?"

"Can regular people buy it, or do you need a special license? Can you find it for less than two thousand dollars?"

"Want to hang on while I search?" Sarah said.

"Better not. I'll call you at two."

By the time Helen walked back to the store, her lunch hour was nearly over. At one o'clock, she opened her cash register, and watched the hands loiter on the clock face. She didn't think a court order would get them to move.

Finally, it was two. She asked Brad to cover for her for five minutes. Back in the break room, she called Sarah. "I've got good news," her friend said. "Anyone can buy SCBA equipment. In fact, after nine-eleven there's been quite a bit of interest in it. People are buying it the way our grandfathers built nuclear bomb shelters in their backyards. They're afraid of a poison-gas attack."

"If there was an attack, would you want to be one of the few survivors?"

"No, thanks," Sarah said. "I'd get stuck with the cleanup. The point is, anyone can buy this gear. It's expensive new. But you can also buy it used. You can buy used thirty-minute units for around five hundred dollars."

"You did have good news," Helen said. "I couldn't see this woman spending two thousand dollars. But she might come up with five hundred. Suddenly, Page Turner's death is positively cheap."

"OK, I did your research. Now tell me who your suspect is," Sarah said.

"Melanie, the print-on-demand author. She wears those plastic see-through heels. That's why Mr. Davies said she looked like Cinderella. She's got blond hair, too. I read her book last night. She's a terrible writer. But her character smothers the bad guy, and then picks some locks to get the incriminating photos."

"Interesting," Sarah said.

"That's because I left out the dull parts," Helen said. "Here's how I see it: Melanie, a blond, blue-eyed dental assistant, hungers for romance. She meets Page Turner and imagines this wonderful future. She'll have a mad, passionate affair with the bookstore owner. They'll have great literary discussions, and, incidentally, he'll promote her book. She falls into Page Turner's clutches."

"Did you say clutches?" Sarah said.

"It's not my fault. I've been reading Melanie's romantic mystery or mysterious romance.

"Page sees it differently. He has her for a quickie on his couch. He expected her to go quietly. But Melanie isn't like the others. She had dreams not just for herself, but her beloved book. Page Turner shattered those precious dreams. So Melanie struck back at her seducer."

"How much longer before you talk normally?" Sarah said.

"It should wear off shortly," Helen said. "What do you think?"

"It has possibilities. How are you going to get this accursed murderess arrested for her vile deeds? Please don't say you're going after her alone."

"Not me. I'm not one of those half-wit heroines who runs into the empty house looking for the killer. When I get off work, I'll go check the lock on Peggy's door. If it's a Tandy, I'll call Detective Gilbert. Even if isn't, I'll call him. But that brand will make my case stronger.

"Gilbert can get a search warrant and check Melanie's apartment for lock-picking tools and SCBA gear. He can get those Cinderella shoes and probably other evidence I can't think of. He'll have the murderer of Mr. Davies and Page Turner and Peggy will go free."

"Helen, you're more romantic than Melanie. You really do believe in happy endings," Sarah said.

Helen went back to her cash register. The clock hands continued to crawl. At three p.m., the letter carrier brought in the store mail. She handed the big stack to Helen and said, "There's a package for you."

Helen never got mail. But the package definitely had her name on it. It looked like a shoebox wrapped in brown paper. There was no return address. Helen did not like this. Dr. Rich could be sending her something, or Gabriel. Neither one would give her a pleasant present. She shook the box. It sounded harmless. She held it up to her ear. No ticking.

Here goes, she thought. She pulled off the brown paper, then lifted the lid.

What she saw inside made her gag.

It was a dead parrot.

Chapter 28

Helen gathered her courage and looked again. The green feathers were too bright. That color was not found in nature.

It wasn't a dead parrot. It was a Styrofoam bird covered with dyed green feathers. Helen could breathe again. Pete was OK. She saw she'd been clutching the counter for support. Gayle was standing next to her, looking worried.

"What's wrong, Helen?" she said. "Are you sick again?"

"Someone sent me this weird thing," Helen said.

Gayle looked in the box. "Is that a dead bird? No, it's a fake. But it looks dead. That's horrible. There's a note in the box. It looks weird, too."

The letters were cut out of magazines and newspapers and pasted to plain white paper. The note said, *If Peggy wishes to gaze upon her darling bird again, you must stop your sleuthing. Cease or her beloved pet will feel the cold gaze of mortality.*

"'Cold gaze of mortality'?" Gayle said. "What does that mean?"

"Someone's going to kill Pete the parrot," Helen said.

"Should I call the cops? What sicko wrote that?"

"I have a good idea. I've got to go home. Someone may hurt Pete."

"Go on. I'll cover for you," Gayle said, but Helen was already running out of the store. If her investigating led to Pete's death, she'd never forgive herself. Peggy would never forgive her, either. Peggy might give up if anything happened to Pete.

Helen couldn't bear the thought. She came to a street corner and was held up by the world's longest red light. Twice, she tried to dash across. Twice, cars nearly ran her down. Angry drivers honked at her. One man leaned out the window and yelled, "Are you trying to get killed, lady?"

I'm trying to stop a death, she thought. She willed herself to take deep breaths until the light finally changed.

Pete will be OK, she told herself. He's with Margery. She's tough and smart.

She's seventy-six years old. What chance did an old woman have if a killer surprised her? Helen redoubled her running efforts. She tripped on an uneven sidewalk and fell forward, landing on both hands. Her palms were scraped, but nothing felt broken. She wasted no more time looking for potential damage. Helen ran.

She could see the turquoise Coronado sign on the ice-cream-white building. She could hear the rattling air conditioners. Best of all, she heard a parrot squawk. She hoped it was Pete and not one of the wild birds in the palm trees.

Helen knocked on Margery's door.

Silence.

"Margery! Margery, are you home?" She hammered her fists until the jalousie glass rattled and her knuckles were raw.

"I'm coming, I'm coming. Hold your horses." Never had bad-tempered words sounded so good. Her landlady opened the door. She'd clearly been asleep. One side of her hair was flattened, her red lipstick was smeared, and there were sheet wrinkles in her skin.

"Where's Pete?" Helen said.

"Asleep, too, for a change. That's how I finally got some shut-eye."

"Are you sure?"

"Of course. His cage is right over—"

But his cage wasn't there. Only the stand and a scattered pile of seed remained. "Where'd he go?" Margery said, bewildered. "How the heck did someone get into my place and steal that parrot?"

Helen looked at the door lock. "Lock picks. You have a Tandy DE345 lock. The killer picked it and took Pete. It's Melanie. She killed Page Turner. She kidnapped Pete to make me stop looking for her. She says she'll kill him. She has a cat. A big mean Siamese. He'll tear Pete to pieces, if she doesn't."

"Oh, Lord, if anything happens to Pete, Peggy will kill both of us," Margery said, then looked at Helen. "I didn't mean that."

"I know," Helen said.

"Do you know where this Melanie lives?"

"No, but I know how to find her. Where's your phone book?"

Helen called the Mr. Goodtooth Clinic. "Melanie has left for the day," the receptionist said.

Melanie took the afternoon off for a little birdnapping, Helen thought.

"Do you have her home phone? This is Page Turners bookstore. We're trying to get in touch with her."

"Page Turners! I know she's been wanting a book signing at your store. She'll be so disappointed she missed your call. Melanie left early to go to a wedding at the Tree of Life Baptist church. You need her home phone? She may still be at home getting dressed. I'm sure she wouldn't mind if you called."

"Could I have her address also?" Helen said. "We want to send her our author-information packet."

The receptionist obligingly gave out Melanie's address and phone number.

"I'll drive you there," Margery said. She had miraculously put herself back together during that short phone call.

They made it in ten minutes, with Margery breaking the speed limit. Melanie lived in a spectacularly ugly 1970s apartment complex. Helen expected the *Saturday Night Fever* John Travolta to come dancing out the door.

"That's her building—two-twelve," Margery said. "She's in apartment A on the first floor."

Even from the parking lot, Helen could hear outraged squawking and cat yowls.

"Pete!" Helen said. "Pete's in trouble. Those aren't his usual squawks."

Margery rang the doorbell and yelled, "Melanie, it's your aunt Purdy. Are you home?"

"Aunt who?"

"That's in case the neighbors are watching," Margery said. "Nobody's home. Can you pick a lock?"

"No, but I can break a window." Helen grabbed a big rock out of the planter and smashed one of the slitlike windows beside the front door. Two more sweeps removed most of the glass shards. She squeezed her hand in and unlocked the dead bolt. She got a long scratch on her arm, but it didn't bleed much.

"I'm coming in with you," Margery said.

"I need you to stand guard out here," Helen said. "Yell if she comes back."

Helen followed the cat yowls and parrot squawks to Pete. His cage was in the guest room on a dresser spread with newspaper. The room was a riot of cabbage-rose wallpaper, cat hair, and bird feathers.

Pete sat unharmed in his cage, his eyes glittering with rage. A scowling Siamese cowered under the bed. Fear puffed its fur to twice its size. The cat hissed at Helen and started toward her, but Pete squawked again and the animal backed under the bed. Helen grabbed the cage, shut the door on the cat, and ran out of the room.

She could hear Margery talking as she approached the door. "I'm sorry that bird was making such a racket," she said. "Melanie called and asked us to take it away."

Really, Margery was the most incredible liar, Helen thought as she opened the door. Her landlady was standing in front of the broken window to hide as much damage as possible, and talking to a woman with gray permed hair and thick glasses. Helen hoped she couldn't see the shattered glass.

"There you are, dear," Margery said. "That bird's racket has been disturbing the whole complex, Brenda says. My niece will take care of the bird while I'm at the wedding. By the way, Brenda, can you direct me to the Tree of Life Baptist church from here? I'm a little flustered."

Margery forgot she was wearing purple shorts, hardly proper attire for a church wedding. Brenda didn't seem to notice. You got used to bizarre costumes in South Florida.

The woman gave Margery directions to the church, three blocks away. As they climbed back in the car, Helen said, "Take Pete home. I'm going to that wedding to make sure Melanie doesn't get away. Call Detective Gil Gilbert and let him know what's going on. I don't know if a birdnapping is enough to get his interest, but tell him about the lock picking and the smothering scene in her book. Oh, and don't forget the Cinderella shoes."

"I'll call him as soon as I get home," Margery said. "Then I'm calling a locksmith."

At the church, Helen was glad she was wearing her bookstore clothes. She could pass as a wedding guest, if she picked the feathers out of her hair and took off her Page Turners name tag.

She looked around the church and saw no sign of Melanie. But she did see a choice spot in the back row on the groom's side, between a huge man and a woman with a hat the size of a truck tire. Helen figured she could hide between the two and observe the other guests. The man must have come straight from work. He was wearing a security-guard uniform and looked like a minivan in a tie.

Helen squeezed in between the hat and the minivan and looked for Melanie. She didn't see her. Helen was getting nervous. Did she have the right wedding? Did Melanie decide to bolt? No, she wouldn't leave her cat.

When the processional music started, she finally saw Melanie. She was a bridesmaid. Her dress would have sent Scarlett O'Hara into a jealous fit. It was powder-blue chiffon, with a hoop skirt that stretched from pew to shining pew. Ruffles cascaded down her front and dripped off the sleeves. Her flowing blond hair was topped with an enormous picture hat. Dyed-to-match ankle-strap heels peeped out from under the swaying skirt. Her bouquet was big as a shrub. Melanie looked sublimely happy. For her, this was romance with a capital R. She did not notice Helen as she floated down the aisle in her blue chiffon dream.

Four more blond bridesmaids followed, skirts swaying like lamp shades in a hurricane.

The brunette bride came out in a simple white satin princess gown, her skirt about half the size of her bridesmaids' dresses. Clever woman, Helen thought. She looked impossibly skinny and sophisticated in that sea of chiffon.

The groom and his men were up there somewhere, overwhelmed by yards of fabric.

Baptist weddings were conducted at breakneck speed

compared to the Catholic ceremonies Helen knew. Within fifteen minutes, the minister was introducing the new Mr. and Mrs. Farley Ostrander to the congregation. Helen clapped dutifully along with everyone else.

The bride and groom left arm in arm. Then Melanie wobbled back down the aisle on the arm of a groomsman. Helen edged closer to the hulking security guard, hoping to go unnoticed.

But Melanie saw Helen as she came down the aisle. Her face mirrored her panic. Melanie tossed her bouquet into the nearest pew and tried to cut through the pews on the bride's side. Her huge skirt wouldn't fit. She picked it up and held out it at an angle, exposing sheer-to-the-waist panty hose and unromantic white underwear. The church was speechless with shock as Melanie ran through the door at the end of the aisle.

Helen followed, stomping on the feet of a woman in a coral silk suit. Someone screamed. The other bridesmaids and groomsmen halted in the aisle.

"Stop that woman. She's ruining my wedding," shouted the bride, and the wedding party took off after Helen. A welter of skirts tried to squeeze after her. Helen heard the snap of a hoop and an "Ouch!" The other bridesmaids followed Melanie's lead and tilted their skirts either forward or backward, displaying garments rarely seen in church.

Helen went through the door and then locked it. She could hear Melanie clattering down the steps. She followed and locked the door at the bottom of the steps, too. Now she was in a church reception area. At least, Helen thought that's what it was. This wedding was very different from the lavish Catholic affairs she was used to.

The Baptist wedding reception had cake and punch and a pretty flower centerpiece. The punch was pale pink with something fizzy. An ice ring of strawberries floated in the massive cut-glass bowl. It was a classy little reception.

There were real china cups for the coffee. The caterers were setting out some nifty canapes on a silver tray. Helen's stomach growled as she passed the miniquesadillas. The sesame chicken skewers looked good, too.

Helen could hear the wedding party. It had broken through the first door and was pounding on the second. The hulking groomsmen would have it open soon. Helen looked for another way out, but didn't see one. She did see Melanie. Her hoop skirt was back in its proper place. Melanie was swaying with rage, and moving swiftly for someone in ankle-strap heels. She threw her picture hat on the floor, grabbed the ornamental cake knife, and went after Helen.

Slash. Slash. Ribbons and lilies of the valley ripped through the air, and left a long cut in Helen's shirt. Helen had no idea those cake knives were so sharp.

Melanie was doubly dangerous. The ruffles didn't hinder her furious thrusts and parries. Together with the wide hoop skirt, they served as protection. She would be hard to stop.

"You've ruined my life," Melanie sobbed. "All I ever wanted was to write, and you've humiliated me."

"It wasn't me. It was Page Turner," Helen said.

"Don't say that vile name!" Melanie said. She lunged at Helen with the cake knife, and Helen dodged a nearly lethal swipe at her heart. She heard a ripping sound. There was another deep cut in her shirt.

Helen looked for a weapon to defend herself from the wild knife thrusts. She saw only coffee spoons, china cups and saucers. Helen picked up a coffee cup and hurled it at Melanie. It shattered.

"Hey!" yelled a caterer, but the woman backed away when she saw Melanie's slashing knife.

"Call nine-one-one," Helen shouted, and threw another cup. That one bounced harmlessly off the lurching skirt. Chiffon was better than Kevlar. Helen reached for more ammunition from the coffee bar. The coffee urn wasn't out yet, or she would have unleashed gallons of hot coffee. Instead, she grabbed a fistful of delicate china saucers. Two went wide of their mark. One bounced off Melanie's arm. A cup hit a wad of ruffles and slid harmlessly away. Helen was desperate. Melanie and her knife were moving in for the kill.

Helen ducked behind the wedding cake for protection, but Melanie kept coming with the knife. She was a terrifying sight. Her blond hair looked like it had been electrified. Her ruffles whipped back and forth. Her skirt swung crazily. She was the bridesmaid from hell.

"I'll kill you," she screamed. "I'll kill you like I killed him."

Helen knew the three-tiered cake would be no protection against Melanie's jabbing, stabbing knife. That knife was designed to cut cake into little pieces.

Helen had only one choice.

She picked up the wedding cake and heaved it at Melanie. The mad bridesmaid went down in a welter of white icing and chocolate layer cake. The top layer was cheesecake, which was really slick. Melanie's skirt belled out modestly around her, covering a lot of splattered cake. Melanie tried to get up, but her foot tangled in the hoop. She slipped in the butter-cream frosting, twisting her ankle, and slid back down in the squashed cake.

"My ankle," Melanie cried.

"My cake," the bride cried, bursting into the room. "You ruined my cake."

She picked up the huge bowl of sticky pink punch and hurled it at Helen.

Chapter 29

"Halt!" said Detective Gil Gilbert. "Drop it! Right now."

The bride had already emptied the cut-glass punch bowl on Helen. Now she was preparing to smash her head with the heavy bowl. Helen was too punch-drunk to move.

"You'll kill her if you hit her with that," Detective Gilbert warned.

"I want to kill her," the bride said, raising the bowl over her head. "She ruined my wedding."

"You'll lose your deposit on the bowl," he said.

At that, a portly tuxedoed man stepped forward and took the bowl from the bride. "This has cost us enough already." Helen assumed he was the father of the bride.

Melanie sat quietly on the floor, the ruined wedding cake mostly hidden by her huge skirt. The knife had been confiscated by Detective Tom Levinson, who showed up with Gilbert for some reason Helen never figured out. He was reading Melanie her rights and was preparing to take her in quietly for questioning. But Melanie, who lived in her own romance novel, refused to go without a scene.

"I'll tell you everything, but I want the world to know

what I suffered," she said. "Otherwise, I'll call a lawyer now and never say another word."

Helen thought the print-on-demand author looked remarkably pretty. Her gown had only a smear or two of cake icing on it. Her blond hair tumbled down her back. Her bosom was a seething blue sea of ruffles.

No amount of persuasion would convince Melanie to change her mind. She was determined to have her audience.

"My own guilty conscience made me ruin Beth and Farley's wedding," Melanie said, when everyone stopped talking and she was once more the center of attention. Helen noticed the wedding photographer was taping her statement. She wondered if the police would confiscate the video.

"The burden has been too great to bear. When I saw her"—she pointed dramatically to Helen—"sitting next to a man in uniform, I thought the police had come to arrest me."

"It was just Uncle Chuck," the bride said. "He's a security guard at Wal-Mart."

Melanie grabbed the attention back from the bride. "My life was ruined by an evil man. He seduced me with empty promises. He defiled my love. He even videotaped it. A kindhearted saleswoman tried to show me the error of my ways, but I wouldn't listen. Instead, I ran to Page in his office and sought succor. Page Turner was intoxicated. He said vile things. Things I can hardly bear to repeat."

But she managed. It was juicy stuff. Even Helen, shivering from a bath of cold, sticky punch, was spellbound.

"Page laughed at me. He said, 'Yeah, I screwed you, but not as bad as your publisher. Your book might as well be printed on toilet paper, for all it's worth.'

"He did indeed have a secret recording of our lovemaking. The scoundrel invited me to watch it. 'Then maybe you'll stick to what you know how to do—and it isn't writing.'"

A charming blush stained Melanie's cheeks and she tossed her golden hair. Every man in the place stared at her, and Helen was sure they weren't thinking literary thoughts. That was quite an endorsement from the late stud, Page.

"His mocking laughter followed me out of the room. My soul was seared with words no woman should ever hear. But I held my head high. Then I heard that little man say, 'There goes another fool.' My shame was complete. Everyone knew. I was ruined."

Brad's four little words brought down the mighty Page Turner, Helen thought. If he'd kept his mouth shut, Melanie might have gone back to her job, and Page would still be alive. But then, if she and Gayle hadn't tried to open Melanie's eyes, maybe none of this would have happened. Helen shivered, cold to the heart at the thought of her own role.

After her humiliation in the bookstore, Melanie's thoughts turned to murder.

"I vowed revenge on the tyrannical Turner. He insulted me and my precious book. I sat in the parking lot for hours, brooding on my ravishment. I must have revenge. The kind saleswoman told me Page had befouled another woman, a Peggy Freeton. I couldn't believe he could be so cruel twice. She said, 'If you don't believe me, ask Helen. She lives in her apartment complex.'

"That night, when she got off work"—Melanie pointed at Helen again—"I followed her home. I saw the distinctive yellow mouse car of the Truly Nolen termite people. I knew what that meant. A termite tenting. It was a simple matter to get Peggy's apartment number from the mailboxes and steal her termite information notice.

"Then I began my plan. I would avenge all womanhood. It was the best plot I've ever done," Melanie said proudly.

She knew about tenting. Her own building, like most older buildings in South Florida, had been tented. She'd had the lectures about the dangers of Vikane and the necessity of SCBA gear.

"I researched SCBA systems on the Net, and found a used one at greatly reduced prices. I had it overnighted."

Melanie knew Page liked kinky sex, although she didn't say it that way. "I had his cell phone number and I called him that Friday to arrange a rendezvous. I told him to bring the video. I promised to add another interesting episode.

"When I picked him up at the bookstore, Page was already sodden with drink. I brought more of his favorite tipple." Melanie modestly forbore to mention it was Bawls and vodka. "Soon he was staggering drunk. He had his arms around me, but it was not an embrace of love. The Coronado apartments were deserted. Everyone had moved out. I put on my latex gloves. I'm afraid they gave Page Turner some very wrong ideas about my plans for the night. It was a matter of minutes for me to pick the lock, even with Page's filthy paws all over me. I'm quite accomplished with the picks.

"Page staggered into the apartment and fell on the bed. I tied him up with scarves. Handcuffs would have left marks. I'm afraid he was anticipating something quite different. He fell asleep before I finished. He was snoring. It was as if an angel guided me to the pillows on the bed."

Helen thought that line sounded familiar. She also thought an angel had nothing to do with it.

"I put the pillow over his face and pressed down. His snores stopped. Soon, so did his struggles. I felt I'd struck a blow for women everywhere.

"I rolled the body off the bed and into the closet with the

sliding doors. It was only two feet away. I hid him behind some long bridesmaid dresses. No one could see him.

"I remembered to take Page's briefcase. Inside were two videos, both labeled. One was mine. The other was Peggy's. I dropped the briefcase and the videos in a nearby canal. The first part of my plan was complete."

The wedding party and the caterers looked like wax figures. No one said a word while Melanie told her bizarre tale. The bride and groom were holding each other, as if protecting themselves from the bridesmaid from hell.

"Once the Coronado was tented, I came back late Saturday night and donned my SCBA gear. Then I took the clamps off one corner of the tent and slipped in. It was hot, dark, and spooky inside. I picked the locks again on Peggy's apartment and went inside.

"I slid the body back on the bed. That was the hard part, but I wanted everyone to know he was a philanderer. I heaved the head and shoulders up, using his belt as a sling. Then I dragged the legs onto the bed."

"No way. A little thing like you moved a big guy like that?" a groomsman said.

"Never underestimate the power of a woman scorned," Melanie said.

Or her upper-body strength when she's worked out at the gym, Helen thought.

"I wasn't completely successful. I wanted Page found on his back, but when I tried to turn him over, he kept wrinkling the spread and it didn't look nice. Also, he smelled yucky. So I left him facedown.

"Then I went to the kitchen for a butcher knife. I wrapped it in a towel to preserve the prints, held it below the handle part, and stabbed him in the back. That felt so good, I wanted to keep doing it, but I was afraid I'd mess up her prints."

Melanie vacuumed the drag marks off the rug. "Then I

deposited the SCBA gear in a canal, along with the scarves. I knew the butcher knife might implicate Peggy, but I was sure she would never be convicted. Good always wins out."

Helen snorted. The wedding party glared at her.

"After that, I began to heal. I realized Page Turner was wrong. I was a good writer. I had created the perfect locked-room mystery. My big mistake was to kidnap that parrot. I thought it would make her"—Melanie pointed at Helen for the third time—"stop investigating. Instead, everything unraveled. Perhaps I had a subconscious desire to get caught. I'm not a bad person."

She looked winsome in blue chiffon and white icing. Helen almost believed her, until Melanie tried to justify killing Mr. Davies. "He was so old and lonely, I was doing him a favor. It was a blessing, really. What was he—eighty-three? Who would miss him?"

I do, Helen thought. The store was not the same without his gentle presence.

When Melanie finished her tale, she waited as if for applause. Instead, there was only the snap of handcuffs. Melanie looked surprised. Maybe she expected to talk her way to freedom. Two uniforms took her away. "I'll be auctioning the movie rights," she said as they led her out.

Detectives Gilbert and Levinson took statements from the wedding party.

Someone slipped out to Publix and came back with a white sheet cake that said *Happy Wedding* on it in white icing. Helen thought she could see the word "Birthday" faintly in the frosting. The caterers swept up the broken china. The church janitor cleaned up the squashed cake and spilled punch. Another bowl of punch appeared, without the strawberry ice ring.

The wedding reception was about to start, minus one bridesmaid.

*   *   *

There was another party, this one for Peggy. She was out of jail and fully exonerated. Margery celebrated her home-coming—and Pete's departure from her place—with a bar-becue by the Coronado pool. Peggy looked thin and worn, and Pete's feathers were still ruffled. But they were to-gether at last. Helen knew both would recover.

"Awwwk!" said Pete, but it was a contented screech. He was once more sitting on Peggy's shoulder. She was in her chaise longue by the pool. Peggy gave Pete an asparagus spear. He held it in one foot and gnawed on it.

Helen wondered if Pete knew that Peggy had gotten a big bouquet of flowers from one of the cops she met during her stay at the jail. He wasn't at the party, but they had a date next week.

This was a gala affair, far more cheerful than the beach party. Margery contributed T-bone steaks. Helen brought champagne. Sarah made crab cakes with a luscious sauce. Peggy made a salad, although she had to borrow Margery's butcher knife. Madame Muffy brought another chocolate cake. Cal the Canadian showed up with two tomatoes, un-sliced. They looked a little shriveled, and Helen wondered if they'd attended the first party.

Even Madame Muffy toasted Peggy's freedom with champagne. She announced she was leaving the Coronado and moving to Miami.

"Please let me read your palms," Madame Muffy said to the partygoers. "It will be my good-bye present."

"Er, no thanks," Peggy said.

"I'm too old to have a future," Margery said.

"I'm too superstitious," Cal said.

"I'm game," Sarah said.

"Me, too," Helen said.

Sarah held out her hand and Muffy contemplated it. "I see health and success for you," Muffy said. "You have a Martha Stewart aura."

"Muffy tells that to all the girls," Helen said. "She said I had one, too."

Sarah giggled. Muffy glared at her.

"What about my love life?" Sarah said.

"You are content as you are," Muffy said. "You do not need a man to complete you."

"You got that right," Sarah said. "Your turn, Helen."

Helen suddenly wished that she wasn't doing this. When she was growing up in St. Louis, the nuns said it was dangerous to seek knowledge of the future. Lord knows Muffy's predictions had caused Peggy enough grief.

"Do I see a handsome detective in your future?" Margery said. "That Gil Gilbert seemed awfully interested in you. You gotta love a man who shows up in the nick of time. The bride was about to bean you with that cut-glass bowl."

"It would have put me out of my misery," Helen said. "She'd already drowned me with pink punch."

"I don't understand why that wedding bash didn't wind up on TV," Cal said. "Somebody had to have a video camera. They could have sold the tape to the networks."

"There were several video cameras," Helen said. "But the bride and groom's families promised to sue anyone who gave a tape to TV."

Helen had been afraid the wild wedding would wind up on the news and her ex, Rob, would find her. But she was lucky. There was no publicity. The police were happy to take credit for solving Page Turner's murder. Helen escaped the limelight.

"Don't change the subject, Helen," Margery said. "What about Detective Gilbert?"

"Gil Gilbert is married and an honorable man. He wouldn't think of cheating on his wife. And I don't do married men."

At least, not when I know they're married, she thought.

"Besides, my luck with men has not been too good lately. I'm not in the market till I get my head on straight."

Sarah applauded. Helen presented her palm. Madame Muffy's grasp was firm and strangely warm. Her brown eyes grew intense. "What do you want to know?" she said.

"Might as well make Margery happy. What's my romantic future?"

Madame Muffy studied Helen's palm for a long moment, then said, "I see a man for you. A man worth waiting for. He is free, but he's let himself be caged for noble reasons. He is loyal and true, brave and colorful. And he's right here in your own backyard."

"Awwwk!" the little green parrot said.

"You can't have him," Peggy said. "Pete's my main man."

Epilogue

Page Turners bookstore closed two weeks after the Going Out of Business Sale sign went up. Most of the stock sold. The remainder was too tattered to return to the publishers.

On the last day, all the staff was gone except for Gayle and Helen. The store was empty and echoey. Helen thought there was nothing sadder than a dead bookstore. She and Gayle were in the stockroom, amid torn author posters, empty display racks, and stacks of flattened cardboard boxes.

"That's about it, except the junk in this corner," Gayle said. She carried a stack of flattened boxes to the Dumpster out back.

Helen started sweeping the floor. "What happened to the other booksellers?" she asked.

"Albert got a job with the new chain bookstore on Federal Highway. If he stays six months, he'll get health insurance. You won't be able to pry Albert out of that place. Brad's working there, too. In the magazines."

"Good," Helen said. "He'll be with his beloved J.Lo. What about Matt?"

Gayle threw a pile of blank order forms in the trash can. "The guy with the great dreadlocks? Matt was smart. We already knew that, since he had the good sense to walk out of here when his check bounced. He got a scholarship to law school. He wants to be a civil-rights lawyer."

"And young Denny?"

"Wait till you hear that one. He went to a karaoke night at a club in Pompano a couple of weeks ago and did his Sting imitation. He's working there now. His eighties oldies act is drawing huge crowds. The kid's an overnight success. A South Beach club is talking with his new agent about a gig down there."

"Just think, we saw it free when he sang to a floor mop," Helen said wistfully.

"If he really gets famous, I'll go down in history as the moron who made him scrub the counter he danced on."

Helen laughed. "You were just doing your job. Will you be working at another bookstore?"

"No. Astrid and I are moving to Key West," Gayle said, flattening and stacking more shipping boxes.

"What will you do there?"

"You don't have to do anything in Key West," Gayle said. "You just have to be."

"What will you be?"

"Happy," Gayle said, and she looked as happy as anyone could in deep black. "What about you?"

"I start Monday as a telemarketer," Helen said, leaning on her broom. "I'll call you at dinnertime one night."

"And I'll hang up on you," Gayle said. She stopped folding boxes and looked at Helen. "Telemarketing is an awful job. Are you really going to do it?"

"The money's good and I'm tough," Helen said. She kicked an empty box to move it out of her way, but it didn't budge. "Ouch. My toe. I think I broke my toe. This box is full."

Gayle opened it up. "It's a case of Burt Plank paperbacks. I'm not paying to send that old lecher's books back. Will you do me a favor and strip the case?"

Burt Plank. At the mention of his name, Helen felt his fat hand crawling up her leg like a spider.

"My pleasure," she said.

Madame Muffy, the preppy psychic, moved out of apartment 2C shortly after Page Turners closed. She would not be living in a mansion with a Turner family fortune. DNA tests proved conclusively that Madame Muffy was not the daughter of Page Turner III.

She promised to keep in touch, but like most people who made that promise, she didn't. Helen had not thought about her in months. She and Margery were eating popcorn and watching an old movie on late-night TV when they saw an ad for Madame Miranda. The psychic looked exotic with her jangling beads, flapping fringe, and dangling earrings.

"Call Madame Miranda now. Know your future today," she said, earrings swaying hypnotically. "I can feel your aura through the phone. I will find what's blocking your road to future happiness. And order my new book, *Madame Miranda's Past Look at Your Future*. For only twenty-nine ninety-five, you can have my book and a special reading. Operators are standing by. Call now for—"

"Holy shit," Margery said, and nearly swallowed her cigarette. "It's Madame Muffy. She took my advice and ditched the preppy getup and stupid name. Now she can afford TV ads."

"Her prediction was right," Helen said. "She just interpreted it wrong. The spirit voices told her she would come into a lot of money. She heard the words 'book' and 'nine hundred.' Muffy thought she would get a share of the nine-hundred-million-dollar fortune from the Turner bookstore family. Instead, she got a nine hundred number and wrote her own book."

*   *   *

Melanie Devereaux DuShayne wept prettily during her double murder trial. She said she was driven to kill Page Turner "to ease her soul-searing shame."

The prosecution argued that the deceased was a respected literary figure killed by a cold, premeditated murderer. The judge allowed police testimony about the videos, although they could not be shown in court. Page Turner looked like pond scum. If Melanie had not killed him, the jury would have.

Unfortunately, there was also Mr. Davies' death. The jury, whose average age was seventy-three, did not take kindly to someone who snuffed out an elderly man like an old dog, no matter how blue her eyes and blond her hair. The judge was no spring chicken, either, although the scrawny old plucker rather looked like one. He agreed with their recommendation.

Melanie was sentenced to life in prison without possibility of parole for the murders of Page Turner III and Zebediah Davies. She was a model prisoner and developed a prison dental education program.

Her POD book, *Love and Murder—Forever: A Mysterious Romance or Romantic Mystery,* sold briskly, thanks to the trial publicity.

Helen, Peggy, and Pete were out by the pool one morning some time after the trial, reading the paper. Helen noticed a hickey on Peggy's neck, on the other side from where Pete sat. She was still dating the cop.

Peggy had yet another scheme to win the lottery. "Next week is a full moon. Nobody knows why, but double numbers are more likely to win during a full moon."

"You mean like twenty-two, forty-four, sixty-six?" Helen said.

"Exactly. Some think the double numbers affect the balance of the balls, and, combined with the gravitational pull of the moon, it's enough to tip them into the winning slots."

Helen figured this was more moonshine, but she was glad to see Peggy back at her old pastime. She was trying to find the news story about the newest Lotto winner for Peggy when she said, "Hey, here's an article about Melanie."

She read the headline: *Killer Deal for Convicted Murderer.*

"Melanie's getting a million bucks for writing three mysterious romances or romantic mysteries," Helen said. "A New York publisher has picked her up. Critics compare her potential to Danielle Steel's."

"I don't believe it," Peggy said. "I lose weeks of my life, not to mention my bed and my butcher knife, and she gets a million bucks. I thought you couldn't profit from your crimes."

"Awwwk," Pete said.

"Took the words out of my mouth," Peggy said.

"She's writing fiction," Helen said. "That doesn't count. Maybe you could send her a bill for your time. It says here her new novels are very pro-police."

"I guess she is pro-police. The cops locked up the wrong person. If you hadn't started investigating, I'd be sitting on death row."

"Not with Colby for a lawyer," Helen said. "Here's a quote from her editor. She says, 'Melanie is the perfect writer. She has no distractions. I only wish the rest of them were locked up.' "

Helen felt her guilt over her role in Melanie's murders melt away as she read the story of her new contract.

"I think Melanie got what she wanted," Helen said, "a successful writing career, lots of attention, plenty of romance, but no dastardly men."

"If only the prison uniforms had ruffles, she'd be in heaven," Peggy said.

Don't miss the Dead-End Job series from national bestseller

ELAINE VIETS

Shop till You Drop
Murder Between the Covers
Dying to Call You
Just Murdered
Murder Unleashed
Murder with Reservations
Clubbed to Death
Killer Cuts

"Wickedly funny." —*Miami Herald*

"Clever." —Marilyn Stasio,
The New York Times Book Review

**Available wherever books are sold or at
penguin.com**

LOOK FOR THE BOOKS BY
ELAINE VIETS
in the Josie Marcus,
Mystery Shopper series

Dying in Style
Josie Marcus's report about Danessa Celedine's exclusive store is less than stellar, and it may cost the fashion diva fifty million dollars. But her financial future becomes moot when she's found strangled with one of her own snake-skin belts—and Josie is accused of the crime.

High Heels Are Murder
Soon after being hired to mystery-shop a shoe store, Josie finds herself immersed in St. Louis's seedy underbelly. Caught up in a web of crime, Josie hopes that she won't end up murdered in Manolos...

Accessory to Murder
Someone has killed a hot young designer of Italian silk scarves, and the police suspect the husband of Josie's best friend. Josie tries to find some clues—because now there's a lot more than a scarf at stake, even if it's to die for...

Murder with All the Trimmings
Josie Marcus is assigned to anonymously rate year-round Christmas shops—easy enough, she thinks, until she learns that shoppers at one store are finding a deadly ingredient in their holiday cake. Josie must get to the bottom of it all before someone else becomes a Christmas spirit.

The Fashion Hound Murders
Josie Marcus has been hired to check out a pet store's involvement with puppy mills. When the employee who clued her into the mills' existence shows up dead, Josie realizes that sinking her teeth into this case could mean getting bitten back...

Available wherever books are sold or at penguin.com

Penguin Group (USA) Online

What will you be reading tomorrow?

Tom Clancy, Patricia Cornwell, W.E.B. Griffin,
Nora Roberts, William Gibson, Robin Cook,
Brian Jacques, Catherine Coulter, Stephen King,
Dean Koontz, Ken Follett, Clive Cussler,
Eric Jerome Dickey, John Sandford,
Terry McMillan, Sue Monk Kidd, Amy Tan,
J. R. Ward, Laurell K. Hamilton,
Charlaine Harris, Christine Feehan...

You'll find them all at
penguin.com

*Read excerpts and newsletters,
find tour schedules and reading group guides,
and enter contests.*

Subscribe to Penguin Group (USA) newsletters
and get an exclusive inside look
at exciting new titles and the authors you love
long before everyone else does.

PENGUIN GROUP (USA)
us.penguingroup.com

Acknowledgments

Page Turners and its staff are purely imaginary. No such bookstore ever existed. But I worked at the Barnes & Noble in Hollywood, Florida, for a year to learn the business. I want to thank manager Pam Marshall and her staff for their help and kindness.

Thanks also to Joanne Sinchuk at south Florida's largest independent mystery bookstore, Murder on the Beach in Delray Beach, for her book-world expertise. And to bookseller John Spera for his support.

All writers thank their spouse, their agent, and their editor. But I could not write this book without my beloved husband, Don Crinklaw, my pitbull agent, David Hendin, and my enthusiastic editor, Genny Ostertag. Thanks also to the New American Library copy editors and production staff, who were so careful.

So many people helped with this book. I hope I didn't leave anyone out.

Thanks to my loyal friends Valerie Cannata, Colby Cox, Diane Earhart, Jinny Gender, Karen Grace, Kay Gordy, Debbie Henson, Marilyn Koehr, and Janet Smith for their advice and encouragement.

Ed Seelig at Silver Strings Music told me what a Clapton fan would have in his home.

Mark at Safetyman SCBA and Safety Equipment gave me SCBA information.

Terri Magri advised me about dreads.

Thanks to Bob Brown at Truly Nolen's Hollywood, Florida, office. Bob drives one of those funny yellow mouse cars. I nearly drove him crazy asking questions. Thanks also to Truly Nolen's Darryl Graves, fumigator and man of infinite patience, who let me follow him around while he tented a building. Leon A. Johnson, roof man, performs amazing feats of strength on Florida rooftops, and Brandon A. McFarley clamps the sides of tented buildings.

Thanks to Detective RC White, Fort Lauderdale Police Department (retired), who answered countless questions on police interrogations and procedures. Captain Kim Spadaro, commander of the Broward County Main Jail Facility, and Deputy Deanne Paul gave me a tour of the Broward County Jail. Thanks also to author and police officer Robin Burcell, who wrote *Deadly Legacy.* Any procedure mistakes are mine, not theirs.

Jerry Sanford, author of *Miami Heat* and federal prosecutor for the northern district of Florida, answered many complicated legal questions.

Thanks to public relations expert Jack Klobnak, and to my bookseller friend, Carole Wantz, who could sell iceboxes in the Arctic Circle. Special thanks to Anne Watts and Sarah Watts-Casinger, who are owned by Thumbs the cat.